PENGUIN BOOKS

GETTING AWAY WITH MURDER

Benny Cooperman first arrived on the scene in 1980 with *The Suicide Murders*. That first case was followed by seven others including *Murder Sees the Light*, which won the 1984 Arthur Ellis Award. Benny has also been brought to television in two successful CBC dramas starring Saul Rubinek.

Cooperman is the creation of Howard Engel, who was born in Toronto, raised in St Catharines, and worked as a journalist and broadcaster in Nicosia, London and Paris. For many years he was a distinguished CBC producer. A founding member of the Crime Writers Association of Canada, Mr Engel is also the winner of the 1990 Harbourfront Festival Prize for Canadian writers.

D1250429

By the same author

Benny Cooperman Series

The Suicide Murders
The Ransom Game
Murder on Location
Murder Sees the Light
A City Called July
A Victim Must Be Found
Dead and Buried
There Was an Old Woman

Mike Ward Series

Murder in Montparnasse

Getting Away with Murder

Howard Engel

Penguin Books

A Benny Cooperman Mystery

PENGUIN BOOKS
Published by the Penguin Group
Penguin Books Canada Ltd, 10 Alcorn Avenue, Toronto, Ontario,
Canada M4V 3B2
Penguin Books Ltd, 27 Wrights Lane, London W8 5TZ, England
Penguin Books USA Inc., 375 Hudson Street, New York,
New York 10014, U.S.A.
Penguin Books Australia Ltd, Ringwood, Victoria, Australia
Penguin Books (NZ) Ltd, 182-190 Wairau Road, Auckland 10,
New Zealand

Penguin Books Ltd, Registered Offices: Harmondsworth, Middlesex,
England

First published in Viking by Penguin Books Canada Limited, 1995
Published in Penguin Books, 1996
10 9 8 7 6 5 4 3 2 1

*Publisher's note: This book is a work of fiction. Names, characters, places
and incidents either are the product of the author's imagination or are used
fictitiously, and any resemblance to actual persons living or dead, events or
locales is entirely coincidental.*

Manufactured in Canada.

Canadian Cataloguing in Publication Data

Engel, Howard, 1931-
   Getting away with murder

ISBN 0-14-024574-X

I. Title.

PS8559.N49G4 1996   C813'.54   C95-930004-X
PR9199.3.E54G4 1996

For my son Jacob Harry Engel
and his grandparents
Arthur and Doris Hamilton
and
Lolly and the late Jack Engel

Prologue

The trees were leafless, holding black fingers against the sky. Stubborn and sullen, the snow was receding from the front yards on Henrietta Street. The white wood siding of the old houses along the eastern side were bathed in late afternoon sunlight. It wasn't a warm light; there was little warmth in it at all. Still, the tall man with white hair brought out a red metal box of tools and a mechanic's castered board for working flat on his back. He placed the tools beside his ten-year-old Buick before returning to the garage. There was almost too much equipment for a little job like changing his winter oil. If he waited a week or two, the weather would be gentler. He wheeled out a hydraulic jack and proceeded to position it under the car. After hoisting it above the driveway, he stretched himself out on the creeper board and rolled himself beneath the car. From time to time an arm appeared to reach for a wrench or a greasy rag. The man was humming to himself so he didn't hear the footsteps in the driveway.

The car looked as though it had been washed every other day since it left the showroom. There were no rusty patches on the fenders or doors where highway salt eats freely of cars in the Canadian winter. His tools looked well cared for. The jack, for instance, was in mint condition, the sort rarely seen away from a professional service garage. There was a handle, the up-and-down working of which raised the car incrementally above the driveway. There was also a valve, the turning of which lowered the car again so that its weight rested on its four regularly rotated tires.

The song that he was humming was an old army song, something off-colour, and only half-remembered. The tune changed pitch as he stretched to reach for an oily rag, which he pulled out of sight. The leg that was visible was mottled with marks of age. The flesh looked grey above a navy blue sock.

The footsteps stopped by the jack. The humming stopped.

"Who's that?" the man under the car asked, seeing feet standing in the drive. That is all that was said. A hand turned the valve and the car settled. The weight of the Buick returned to the driveway. Footsteps retreated. There was no one nearby to hear the scream.

Getting Away with Murder

Chapter One

"Get up!"

There was a swimmer somewhere out in the lake. I could see a flashing line of rope playing out. It was a life-preserver thrown from a boat. I felt myself sinking. I was the swimmer. I was in trouble. The water was sucking me down.

"Come on, you bastard! Get up!"

"Show a leg, Cooperman!"

"Let me get him going, Phil. I know how to do it."

My dream evaporated. The lake and the rope vanished just as I could begin to feel the tug of the line getting taut, shaking bright beads of water out of the rope. I was awake now, although my eyes were still closed. I felt a hand on my shoulder shaking me. I tried to locate where the various parts of me were lying: hand, head, feet, groin. I could feel hot, peppermint breath on my face.

"Get out of bed! You heard me, damn it!"

I struck out with all my strength, aiming at the smell and the heat of his face. I connected. I felt the pain in my wrist and fingers. At the same time, I opened my eyes. I'd knocked one of them to the foot of my bed. But there were two others. I knew it was all over then. Even as the man with the Lifesaver breath, the one called Phil, was rubbing his chin, I could feel the futility of resistance. I

1

pulled my legs from under the covers and touched the carpet with my feet.

"Good!" said the man with his back to the door. "Now put your clothes on. You're coming with us."

The man I'd punched was still sitting on the end of my bed rubbing his chin. What did I expect? I'd only hit him a moment ago, yet it felt like three or four minutes since I first felt his hand on my shoulder. Where was the life-saver with the rope attached? Was I translating his breath into my dream? I'd have to figure that out one day when I grew to be a very old private investigator watching my grandchildren scamper in front of the fireplace.

I reached for my pants on the chair where I'd left them the night before. They seemed to belong to another age: "before." This was "after." How carelessly I'd left my clothes heaped in the order I'd taken them off. With my audience of three looking on, my clothes looked like artifacts in a museum, like the flints and baskets and stone axes in the diorama of Neanderthal life in Toronto's big museum. I got dressed, trying the while to get my mind off the irrelevant. But the only things I could think of were the irrelevant. I'd been expecting the tired old Late-Late Show of my life spinning back before my eyes, but all I could think of was dirty underwear and overdue library books. Obviously, I had to try harder.

First, there was the dream. Something about a struggling swimmer. What had that to do with anything? Not much. I'd been quietly canoeing up at Dittrick Lake. Then it had gone sour as I was shaken back to consciousness. I could let that go. It was a beginning.

I tried to go over in my mind who I had crossed lately. I wasn't working on a big case, just a couple of small-claims cases and a trail of credit-card flimsies that were leading me farther and farther away from ever seeing any more business from where my client was living. I couldn't see my friend Mendlesham resorting to violence over the fee I was trying to collect from his law firm. Mendlesham was the least violent of lawyers, and my claim on his books from last year wasn't the biggest headache in his medicine cabinet. I couldn't see any heavy muscle coming from any other direction either. I tried to reopen in my mind a few old cases with loose ends hanging out of the files. I still couldn't come up with anything that would get a trio of hoodlums out of bed before dawn and loid the two locks that should have protected me from the likes of them.

I walked into the bathroom. Two of the hoods didn't move; Phil, the one on the bed, glanced over at the others. "Leave it open," said the man with his back against the door to the apartment. He was the boss of the three. Older, calmer, he exerted authority. He'd read my mind as I thought of closing the bathroom door. I left it open. The candour between us was perfect, if a little one-sided.

How do you escape into a tube of toothpaste? That's what I wanted to know as I examined my face in the mirror. Seeing nothing better to do, I brushed my teeth. When I reached for my razor, a voice in the doorway said: "Leave it!" I turned on the tap and gave my face a rub with a cold, wet washcloth.

There was a fire escape just outside the large bathroom window. If it had been summer, the window might have been open to let in the hope of a breeze, but this was March, the weather outside clinging to February. I knew that the window was jammed with paper and locked. The face of Phil, with a red mark on his chin, appeared in the mirror. "You can quit stalling. We gotta get this show on the road!"

I was rushed down the stairs, herded by the flanks of my keepers to a car that was puffing a warm exhaust trail up into the frosty air. The man behind the wheel didn't bother to look at us as I was thrust into the back seat between two of the men, while the head man climbed in front with the driver.

The local radio station was sending unwanted bright chat into the early dawn. There was steam on the windows from the driver's breath. He turned on the wipers, which arced across the windshield, doing, of course, no good at all. This was the kind of person I was dealing with. I waved goodbye to sweet reason and settled back into the seat to take stock.

I was still breathing. That was in my favour. If they had wanted to kill me, they could have done it in my room where I might not have been discovered until the neighbours started complaining. They could be in Las Vegas by the time the cops opened a file on me.

Then I thought of Anna. She could have found me. I was glad that these hoods were saving me that at least. Even freshly slaughtered, I didn't want Anna to first-foot it into my late presence. Anna was the person I most hated leaving behind. She—

I had to cut myself off. This was no time to become sentimental. If I was being taken for an old-fashioned ride, I had to keep my head clear. Thoughts of Anna might keep me from hitting upon what had to be done. "Cooperman," I said to myself, "get me out of here!" As though my inner life had been betrayed by the outer. As though part of me was lugging the rest of my anatomy to the nearest ditch.

"Turn that radio off," said the man beside the driver.

"What? That's Dusty Rhodes."

"You heard me! Turn the damned thing off!"

"Okay, Mickey, okay!" The sound disappeared. There was no comment from the back seat.

Mickey was the tallest of the trio, wearing a well-cut brown leather coat over a white Irish sweater. In his fur hat, he almost looked like a Horseman on leave from his Regina training ground. Under the hat I could see neatly shaved greying sideburns and the attentions of an early-morning razor. He had all the high seriousness of a heavy without a suggestion that he split all of his infinitives.

The driver wore a black leather cap. There were acne scars on the back of his neck. He was wearing a dark green parka. The man to my right was Phil, the one with the sore jaw and peppermint breath. He was stocky, with short arms and legs. Would have made a good fur-trade paddler two hundred years ago. No room for excess legs in the canoes of the Hudson's Bay Company. Anna had told me that. Always running back to Anna. Get back to your man. It had been a lucky punch. I had to admit that. But it had been launched with my eyes closed. The other senses had come into their own. I'd been lucky that a bedsheet or blanket hadn't impeded my aim. I turned my head; he didn't seem to be in lasting pain.

"Sorry I hit you," I said, trying out a gambit without being too clear where it might lead.

"Shut up!" said the man on the other side, punctuating his words with his elbow in my ribs. "We got a long drive ahead of us. The less noise in the car, the better."

"Where are we headed?" I asked with feigned innocence. Sharp pains hit ribs on both sides at the same moment. Nobody said anything. I settled on noting the year and make of the car. It was something to do. It wouldn't have much *post mortem* value, but it showed me that I was being professional right up to the end.

The guy on my left was weedy in a silver-studded black leather jacket. His head was shaved to the scalp and he wore an earring in one ear. A dark blue tattoo of a scimitar on his wrist made his skin appear unnaturally white. He was chewing gum. I was guessing that it was gum.

It wasn't as long a drive as the skinhead promised. Maybe it seemed shorter because of his advertisement. Maybe the situation was making me edit out the irrelevancies. Things like time were the first to go. This was tragedy pure and simple roughed in with a black brush.

Anyhow, the motor died after a time and the bodies on each side of me shifted. Were we in a quiet corner of a hardwood bush? I could picture a patch of skinny saplings stretching up towards the grey sky. I had seen this scene in the movies a dozen times. As good a place for it as any, I thought and shrugged. There were four of them. Would the driver come out to watch? Or would he stay in the car, already planning to cop a plea: "But, Your Honour, I was in the car! I was behind the wheel! I didn't see nothing!"

Once out of the car, the frosty bush vanished. I took a deep breath. I wasn't standing on the margin of a wood-lot with snow still lingering under the trees. I wasn't going to be buried under a snowdrift with last year's blackened leaves covering my remains. Not now anyway.

The car was parked behind a dark house that seemed to rise out of the chilly mist that clung to the ground. I could hear the frost cracking wood far away. Closer I could see the rooftops of other houses. Everywhere I looked, my imagined rural details were replaced by an urban reality: telephone poles, curbs, asphalt, fire hydrants. "At least gunshots are out!" I thought. Other nasty ways to go came into my head, as I was prodded towards a back door.

A light was shining through an open doorway half-blocked by a female figure standing between us and the light. "You were gone long enough," she said to no one in particular. I was grateful for the light and for this feminine presence. They both seemed to stand between me and a sudden change of state. "He's in a hell of a temper, Mick," she said. "He wants this over and done with."

I swallowed hard. Again I was pushed forward. "I'm going. I'm going!" I said.

Chapter Two

"**C**ome in! Come in, Mr Cooperman! Come in!" The voice was gruff, impatient and elderly. It came from somewhere behind the woman in the doorway, who quickly moved to one side. I heard a whispered instruction from the figure that was silhouetted against the light, and the woman retreated back through a hallway out of sight.

"Mickey, get his coat!" the man ordered, and Mickey and the other three of my conductors all reached at once to remove my outer clothing. Once divested, I followed the figure in front of me as he moved through a high narrow hallway, made a turn, passed a glimpse of a kitchen, and entered a large, high-ceilinged, well-appointed room. I was grateful that I was no longer being prodded from behind. In fact, the sinister shapes had almost all been eclipsed by the warmth of the house, the radiance of oil paintings on the walls and the heavy deep red draperies covering the front windows. The only scary things in the room were little brown statuettes mounted on stands or on small tables; primitive terracotta figurines: votive idols, fetish figures? Who knows? In the indirect electric light and the changing glow of the fire, they looked evil.

"Come in!" he repeated. The voice was gruff, as I said,

but there was now an attempt to sound amiable about it, like a cobra trying to sound like an English butler in the movies. I moved forward into the room, while I tried to take in my host and our surroundings all at once. When he finally faced me, the light from a green glass lampshade gave me a distorted first glimpse. I was looking at a bald-headed little man with a large mouth and almost Tartar eyes. They were smiling as he moved about the room trying to find the right chair for his early-morning visitor. He was tanned to the jutting tops of his ears, dressed formally for this early hour, with a white shirt and a knotted tie pushed so tight it made me wince. His blazer was blue and sported a crest woven in gold thread on the breast pocket. A mounted terracotta mask of a scowling monster stood next to a gold pen and marble ink stand. I pass on these impressions as they occurred to me, in no particular order and with the room itself competing with the man for my attention.

"Sit down," the man said in a friendly way, although I felt the invisible hands of his minions pushing me down by the shoulders into an arrow-backed chair not far from the big partners desk in the middle of the room. He extended a hand with two rings flashing gold. There was an abundance of black hair extending from his starched shirt-cuffs to his fingers. I'd seen his watch in a Tiffany's ad in the Toronto paper. He retreated behind the desk when I rejected his greeting and sat down.

"My name is Abram Wise, Mr Cooperman. You may have heard of me...."

The voice went on, the mouth continued to move, but I could only hear the name "Abram Wise" booming back and forth between the hemispheres of my brain. I would have been less overwhelmed if he'd said "I am Count Dracula," or "I am Al Capone." Heard of him? Is there anybody in this country who hasn't heard of Abe Wise? Even *Time* magazine called him the biggest crook in North America who's never been in prison. I blinked and tuned in again to what he was saying.

"...I won't apologize for the manner of this meeting. There's no excuse for it that you would accept. So, let's forget about it." I looked him in the eye trying to withhold any promise of absolution in my expression. No sense throwing away the few weapons in my possession. For a moment he seemed to be having trouble finding a place to put the hand I had not taken in mine. He was having a new experience and he wasn't liking it.

"Mr Cooperman, let me assure you right off the bat that you are in no danger here. I can guess that you've been imagining all sorts of things." If that was his idea of how to break the ice, he should try being awakened in the pre-dawn by a bunch of murderous-looking hoods sometime. I make him a gift of it. He was now staring at the assorted rings on his tufted fingers. He was still feeling rejected. "My men do as they are told. They don't ask questions. My methods may be crude, but they get results, which is what I'm really interested in."

There was a muffled knock at the door. It was the woman I'd glimpsed on my way in. "We'll have some tea, Victoria. You'll have some tea with me, Mr Cooperman?" It almost sounded like an invitation. And when he added: "since you're here," I could no longer keep a straight face without blowing my nose. I nodded assent and heard the door close behind me. Wise sat back, as though the woman's departure signalled the beginning of a new chapter in our relationship. He was playing at building an alliance between us against a hostile world behind my chair. He even attempted a smile. It sat awkwardly on his mouth, but became his eyes well enough.

"Mr Cooperman, I've heard a lot about you. I know about the pictures you located for Arthur Tallon's Contemporary Gallery. I remember about that Larry Geller business a few years ago, and your part in the murder in the sauna investigation—"

"Why not cut out the flattery, Mr Wise, and come to the point."

"I've got a job for you."

"I have office hours, Mr Wise. Most people do business with me without scaring me to death beforehand."

"Yes, I understand. But there was a certain urgency in this case."

"Everybody's case is urgent. There are no other kinds."

"Are your other clients about to be murdered?" he asked, and I could feel my back coming away from the chair. He could see that he had finally succeeded in impressing me.

"What makes you think that your life is in danger?" Wise got up from his chair and walked slowly towards the door. He opened it and closed it without saying anything.

"The mechanic at my garage," he said, at last, certain of my attention, "reported to me that the drive belt to the power-steering pump of the Volvo had been cut almost through. Somebody who knows I like to drive in excess of the speed limit did it. I went down and saw the car myself. I could see it was cut; it wasn't wear or any other normal problem." He let go of the doorknob and walked towards the window behind his desk, where he found a cord hidden behind the curtains. When he pulled it, the curtains parted revealing two twelve-pane windows letting in the first light of day. "You see this?" he asked. I got up and walked around the desk. He was pointing at a small hole in one of the glass panes. It was a medium-calibre bullet-hole. "I was sitting in that chair when the shot was fired. It came that close," he said, holding a hairy knuckle an inch away from his left ear. "That close!" He looked right at me to make sure I hadn't missed the significance of what he had told me. Standing beside the bullet-punctured window, Wise looked very small. Sitting, he looked taller, but this was an illusion too. Our eyes were almost on the same level.

"The bullet landed in the pine hutch across the room," he said. "Maybe you can dig it out with this." He handed me a jewelled paper-knife and closed the curtains once more. The room had a warmer feel to it with the early light locked out. I placed the paper-knife on the desk and returned to my chair.

"Look, Mr Wise, 'I'm sorry for your trouble,' as the Irish say, but I can't see how I can help you. I don't even know that I *want* to help you. I don't much like the way you have of getting a person's attention. With your lifestyle, you must run into this sort of thing all the time. Violence begets violence."

Wise nodded as I talked. The green lamp made his white shirt shine and still maintained his face in shadow. The brass on his desk glinted. "There are a couple of things, Mr Cooperman. One is that I value my life and I don't want to lose it just because I refuse to take the right precautions. The other is that you come highly recommended. I won't take 'no' for an answer. Naturally, you'll be well paid and—"

"I don't give a damn about the—"

"Now you listen to me!" He was leaning over his desk, his face dark and the tendons in his neck tight as bowstrings. "If you like living, you'll shut up and listen when I'm talking! You hear? What kind of a man are you? I tell you that someone's trying to kill me and you want to walk away from me when I'm talking? I won't hear of it!" He subsided into his chair again and lowered his voice. He had made his point. He didn't like interruptions when he was talking.

"Look," he said, showing his open palms under the green light, "I know all about you. I know where your parents live. I know where the Abraham girl lives and I know you don't want them getting hurt. Right? I also know that you value your own life, which, by the way, is hanging by a thread right now. A call from me, and you could join Larry Geller and all those other people who became parts of bridges and highways after midnight. They're building a new piece of the canal over near the Forks Road. You wanna become a lasting part of it? I don't think so. What I'm tellin you is that you haven't any choice. You do your job and you'll go home with a tidy sum of money to put in your mattress. What could be more reasonable?"

"If I take on this case—"

"We're not talking 'ifs' here!"

"Okay. 'When.' When it's over, I'll know too much. How do I know you'll let me go?"

"Mr Cooperman, I'm a businessman, plain and simple; a lot smarter than most of them. I'm just a little impatient, as you may notice, with rules and regulations. I know this about myself. Now, you may not think that the word of someone like me is worth much, but it is. Even in *my* business you gotta build trust. Trust is all I've got! I can't write contracts. I can't make letters of agreement. I'm the board of directors. Everything is an understanding that is never written down. Never a word on paper. That means that trust means more to me, my *word* means more to me than it has to mean to the president of your bank, in your case the Upper Canadian on St Andrew Street. Do you understand? I give you my word that you'll walk away from this when you've done your job. The threats against your family and Anna Abraham will become null and void. You've got my word on that and my word is my bond."

"Mr Wise, that's all very well for you to say now, but what kind of assurance do I have? How much do your men know about your reason for bringing me here? Whoever is trying to kill you can just as easily start by killing me."

Wise shrugged. My life was only worth that to him. For a moment, I thought he was going to say something about making omelettes without breaking eggs. My shell was feeling fragile. But my mind had been made up for me. I thought of Anna. Even if all that talk about his word of honour meant nothing at all, or that on second thought I couldn't be allowed to walk away from Wise with a cheque and a handshake, any way I looked at it, I didn't have a choice.

"When do you want me to get started?"

"Good! That's what I wanted to hear!"

At that moment, Mickey came through the door with an old-fashioned tea trolley on rubber wheels. There was a silver tea service, the first I'd seen for years not covered in Saran Wrap, and china cups and saucers. There was a basket of fresh rolls and cinnamon buns. I found that the conversation had awakened in me a sizeable appetite.

"Why don't you let Mickey do this for you?" I asked, after Mickey had left us alone again. "You don't seem to be understaffed." Wise shook his head as he poured the tea.

"My people all know their jobs. I keep them on because they are good at them. When I want an outside view, Mr Cooperman, I depend on the likes of you. As an outsider, you'll not make foolish assumptions. That's important."

"I suppose I don't have to tell you that I'm a one-man band? I don't have operatives standing by waiting for my orders."

"I know exactly what I'm getting."

"And that doesn't include security. I'm no bodyguard. I don't carry heat. I—"

"I said 'I know what I'm getting,' Mr Cooperman. You find out who's trying to kill me. That's your end. Leave the security to me."

Wise filled his cup and we stopped talking while we took a few sips.

"How are we going to make this work?" I asked, putting my cup down in its saucer noisily. The tea was excellent; a factor I was obliged to take into consideration. Wise looked at me over the rim of his cup.

"I've given it a lot of thought," he said. "I could put you up here and have all your meals sent in to you, but that would tend to put some people on their guard. It would also upset my domestic arrangements. I want to know you're on the job, Cooperman, but I don't want to run into you every time I turn around. Besides, you have too many friends at the Niagara Regional Police. Your temporary disappearance would only cause trouble. Pulling you out of your own life would only serve to create unwanted publicity."

"So, I'm getting a lift back to town after this conversation is over?"

"Did you ever doubt it? But don't for a minute think I'm taking my eyes off you. I'm putting three shifts of my boys on your tail. Just like the cops do. They'll keep me posted about your movements and will get very upset if they see you with a suitcase in your hand. If I were you, I would avoid travel agents for the time being. And, don't forget about Manny and Sophie. Such lovely parents, a son can be proud of! Not that Anna Abraham is someone to be ashamed of. Nobody wants to see them get hurt. That's your department. As long as you are working for me and not trying to disappear, they got nothing to worry about. You understand what I'm saying?"

I nodded, then shrugged. "I can't see how I'm going to help you, Mr Wise." I tried to look as serious and straightforward as I could. "I told you I don't have a band of faithful followers who go out and do my jobs for me. That means that everything I do takes time—"

"You don't have to worry about money. That's taken care of."

"Who's talking money here? Look, Mr Wise, I may be suffering from an inflated reputation. I'm only human. I can't get blood from a stone. I can't always get milk from the fridge. I'm limited. That's what I'm trying to say."

"Go on."

"Apart from your reputation, I don't know anything about your business. How am I going to discover who your associates are? Where am I going to learn who's who in your life? None, or very little, of this is on the public record. You see what I mean? If I'm going to get a line on who's trying to kill you, I'm going to have to get firsthand knowledge of everything you've ever done and everything you're doing right now. Personally, if I were you, I wouldn't want anybody, even me, knowing that much about my life."

"I see the stories I've heard about you aren't exaggerated. I like that."

"Hello? Are you listening? Enough with the congratulations! Let's be frank with each other. I won't butter you up and you do me the same favour. The truth is our only friend, Mr Wise. I don't know who you've been talking to about me, but you're going to see that I'm the wrong man for this job. That's my professional opinion, no hype."

Wise shook his head, as though he wanted to put whatever was in my head out of it. When he spoke, he was reading from a prepared text. "There's a man in Grantham named Rogers. Dave Rogers. His name used to be Rottman, but he's been Rogers now for forty years. We're about the same age. Dave and I went to public school together. We did time at the Collegiate too. Why don't you start with Dave. He can give you all you want to hear about me in the old days. When you've talked to Dave, let me know and we'll take another step from there."

He passed me a slip of paper with Rogers' name, address and telephone number printed out for me. What kind of investigator did he think I was I couldn't find a Dave Rogers in a town the size of Grantham?

"I've got another number for you," he told me, getting up, indicating that it was time to end the conversation. "This is the number for me when you *need* it. I don't want it to leave this room. I value my privacy." He held out another, smaller, piece of paper. I took it from him, glanced at it and put it in my mouth and began to chew. When your head's on the block, you might as well crack wise.

"Okay, now I can get in touch with you," I said. "But I'm going to want to talk to people who've known you more recently. Rogers knows the older stuff. Who should I see about recent history?"

"I'll think about that. You'll probably have to talk to Paulette and Lily. I can't see how you can avoid it. Yes," he said, rubbing his large nose, "Paulette and Lily, if they'll see you, of course. Give me a few hours to talk to them."

"You want to tell me who they are?"

"My wives, Mr Cooperman. My two wives. In tandem, of course. My matrimonial life has been a model of propriety, if you overlook the fact that they both ended in divorce. Paulette and Lily will help you to see Hart and Julie, my children. They wouldn't give you the time of day if I asked them. May I wish you a safe trip home, Mr Cooperman? Mickey will see that you get back safely. And remember, Mickey Armstrong or another of my associates will be near you at all times. I don't want you to forget that. Good-morning."

Chapter Three

I'd awakened for the second time that Monday morning holding to the notion that I'd just escaped from a particularly realistic nightmare. God knows I've had enough of them. Usually they have all sorts of personal dangers in them. This one spread the dangers to Anna and my family with me not being able to do much about it. I tested my dream theory by pulling myself out of bed and looking down to the street through my rain-streaked window. No wonder my bare feet felt cold as I recognized the car from the nightmare. It was parked across the street and although I couldn't see the driver, I was willing to guess that he had old acne scars on the back of his neck.

This time, when I got dressed, I shaved. When the hoods of the early morning thought to discourage my delaying tactics, I thought that they were just being practical: a well-turned-out corpse in a ditch or left in the trunk of an abandoned car doesn't need a fresh shave. As I stood there looking at my chin in the mirror, I was suddenly aware of the luxury of time that had been given to me.

Installed in my favourite booth at the Diana Sweets and with breakfast and yesterday's paper in front of me, I could again believe in the rationality of the world. The coffee was what I needed and the familiar golden surroundings of antique wood bandaged me from the evil that lay in wait for me outside.

Other people had problems too, the paper told me on every page. Good! I needed their troubles to buy back my own. I read an account of a hit-and-run case that had been on the front page for three days. The old man who had been tossed by a car through a plate-glass window had finally died and the police were no closer to finding the bastard who did it. A group of former patients of a psychiatrist named Clough were trying to get his licence since he had, they said, taken regular advantage of them in the sanctity of his consulting room over a period of seven years. The patients had all suppressed the memories of these assignations and had tumbled, if that is the word for it, to the fact that this was sex only when they saw similar cases described on television. I tried to imagine the dialogue as they consulted their diaries: "Twelve-forty-five is out, I'm afraid, but eleven-fifteen is possible if you can fit me in."

I *was* in a bad mood! On the bottom of the first page was an account of the accidental death of a former deputy chief of police and a tribute to him. I looked for the name: Neustadt. I remembered him slightly. The picture of the serious frowning face of a man in uniform was so old it was no help to me at all. I must ask Savas and Staziak about him. But I had no patience to read the details of how, where or when he had died.

My second cup of coffee lifted my spirits. So did an ad for McKenzie Stewart's new book. I was a great fan of his detective, Dud Dickens. *Haste to the Gallows* was a good title. I'd pick up a copy as soon as I could. Elsewhere in the paper, I read a few captions, headings, the odd fragment, but I couldn't focus on any more of the stories. I found myself staring at the obituaries—so much for the effects of good coffee—letting the names, dates and pieces of lives that had ended fill my head: Suddenly at Grantham General...in his 57th year...after a brave struggle...survived by...fondly remembered by...resting at...donations in lieu of flowers...followed by cremation..."

Back in my office, I punched in Dave Rogers's number. I missed the trio of bald mannequins, leftovers from my father's ladies' ready-to-wear store, that I had finally cleared away to the basement. For years they had supervised my activities, covered indifferently with unbleached factory cotton in all the unnecessary places. Whenever I had a half-hour to kill, I rarely thought of all the stored junk that had accumulated in my office. Why didn't I give in to the family curse and go into the *shmate* business? I had the window dummies for a start, my clients' chairs were tubular items from an art deco renovation that my father ordered in the 1940s. There might even be some stock in the basement, where my brother, Sam, and I used to play while waiting for my father to close for the night. The phone kept ringing at the other end.

"Yeah?" I was surprised to hear a human voice. It took me a moment to return from my memories.

"Dave Rogers?"

"Yeah. Who wants him?"

"My name's Cooperman. I want to talk to you."

"What makes you think I wanna talk to you, Mr Cooperman?"

"Abram Wise thinks you will." That had him. He couldn't wise-ass me any more. Still, there was a pause.

"Where are you now?"

"Corner of St Andrew and James. My office is on the

second floor of—"

"Meet me at the Chinese restaurant on your left as you come off the high-level bridge. You know the place? Twelve-thirty and don't bring any friends."

"There's an eager beaver from Wise's operations hugging my shadow. I can't do much about him." Again there was a pause at his end. Finally:

"Well, if he's one of Abe's boys, he won't give me any heartburn more than I've got already. Twelve-thirty," he repeated and was gone. I nodded to the instrument in my hand and replaced it.

My watch told me that I had three hours to kill before I had to keep the appointment. I rummaged in a drawer for an old address book that I thought might help me fill the time. The names in it belonged to people who were either dead, moved or vanished into the unknown. Who's going to throw away a thing like that? Under the "Bs" I found what I was looking for and punched the long-distance number into the phone, trying to imagine the voice I was going to hear at the other end.

"Hello?"

"Ella?"

"Yes, this is Ella Beames."

"It's me," I said. "Benny."

"Benny Cooperman! Well, as I live and breathe! I hope you don't mean to pay me a visit. I've got the painters in and—"

"I'm calling from Grantham, Ella. I'm not pushing the tourist season. I'm nowhere near Massachusetts. Don't worry."

"Well, Benny, you gave me quite a turn. I haven't heard a word from home since I got a card from the girls at the library. They think my birthday's in March and it's not really until November. But they've always sent the card in March. I don't remember how it started. *You're* the one with the March birthday. I hope you had a good one. How are you, Benny?"

Ella Beames had retired from the Grantham Public Library at the mandatory age and had left the Special Collections Department in very capable hands. But they lacked, with all the good will in the world, Ella's many years of experience. For a minute we talked about the weather here and in Newburyport, where she had moved on her retirement. Then we talked about local people, mutual friends and public characters. She was surprised to hear that Kogan, a one-time panhandler along St Andrew Street, was now my landlord.

"Kogan was always a caution, Benny. And bright too. He got that from his mother, who was a Dodd. You remember the Dodds? They kept the leather goods down the street from your father's store." I let the conversation ramble; Abram Wise was paying expenses. It was good to hear Ella ramble; she put her heart in it. She said more in a minute than most people do in half an hour and the better part of it was worth remembering. When she finished talking about the Kemps' fish market on Queen Street, she brought herself up short.

"Benny, you didn't call all this way to hear an old woman's twaddle. What's behind this?"

"You never kept a file on crime families at the library, did you?"

"Of course not! Not the local ones anyway. We kept all of the big, international stuff in the morgue downstairs. But you're talking about local crime families, am I right?"

"As usual. I'm trying to find out about Abram Wise. I know he's a bad egg, but I'm still vague about where his illegal earnings come from. I'm having lunch with an old school friend of his, Dave Rogers, but I don't want to go as ignorant as I am now."

"Well, if I were you, I'd avoid the issue and get on a slow boat to China. The pair of them were nothing but trouble if my memory hasn't gone potty."

"I wish I had that option, but I haven't."

"So you called me to find out where I've hidden all of the dirt I couldn't put on file?"

"I took a guess, Ella. I suspected that you squirrelled away what you know under an innocent label, where nobody but you could find it."

"Well, after that crazy Ultimate Church bunch stole our files on Norbert Patten, I've had to use my head. There is a master file marked CHISHOLM, GORDON, Benny. You remember the Chisholm family, don't you? Well, there never was a Gordon Chisholm that I ever heard of, so I made him up to put all of the key data in there. You can look up the names you want to trace and find the fictitious names I've hidden them under. I meant to find a better system before I retired, but I never got around to it."

I tried to remember Ella's face. I could see freckled eyelids and velvet cheeks. I was surprised to find so much of her in my memory. Her voice carried her face, her humour and even the scent of pale roses to my office from a town north of Boston somewhere. Ella has a way of evaporating the miles.

The new face behind the desk that had been Ella's for as long as I'd owned a library card smiled as I came in. Neither of us knew the other's name, but we knew one another the way you do in small towns. We nodded and exchanged a few words before she let me loose with the range of file drawers.

I opened the one showing CATH—CHURCH in the slot in front. CHISHOLM, GORDON was right in its

proper place: after Elizabeth and Fred and before Harold.
I lifted the file from the drawer and found a table near
the corner of the room. After moving a few heavy atlases
out of the way, I opened the file.

The air in the room was, as I had remembered it,
smoke-free and artificial, as though it had been made up
from a recipe in a laboratory where such things as dust,
acid and other computer-eating atoms had never penetrated. Breathing it, besides me and Ella's successor, was
a photographer named Stefan Something, who was a bit
of a town character. Stefan was a regular presence at civic
and cultural functions, where his camera bag got him
past the registration table. The locals knew that he never
represented a paper or magazine. His camera was usually assumed to be empty, so that only visiting digni-
taries were impressed at the quickness of the exposures
he made as he worked his way to the luncheon side-
board or, on special occasions, the bar. Stefan was seated
at a broad wooden table just in front of the main index
terminals, busy reading up on the history of Grantham's
first families. I was glad that he hadn't noticed me. The
last time we talked, he was convinced that he wanted to
go into the detective business.

The master list was a sheet of foolscap divided into
two columns. In the first were the names of the local
entrepreneurs who had run afoul of the law or were at
least believed to have done so whether or not they had
ever been brought to book. As a demonstration of the
assumption of innocence it lacked something. I noticed
the name of a big corporation lawyer named Henry
Markland. Markland took up a career of making licence
plates when he ran out of banks to finance a scheme or
project that, as far as I was able to discover, only existed
in his imagination. He was to be found in a file marked

O'REILLY, NATHAN, a pretty bogus combination if you ask me. There were other names I'd seen in print before. I was glad to see a scattering of Anglo-Saxon ones mixed in with the consonant-happy ethnic names. The right-hand column was almost free of surnames which had arrived on recent boats and planes. It was as though Ella, even in making up names to hide the guilty, didn't want to tarnish people with names that had already had a bad enough run of it.

WISE, ABRAM, was there towards the bottom of the page. To find him, I was directed to look up CLELAND, JOHN. The name whispered something in my ear, but I couldn't catch it. It didn't seem to belong to a local family, crooked or straight. (Later Frank Bushmill, my neighbour, told me that it belonged to the author of *Fanny Hill*, a very famous naughty, once-banned novel. I wonder if Ella would have blushed if she knew I had penetrated her little game?)

I ran my eyes down the paper to see if there was any mention of Dave Rogers or Rottman. I couldn't find it. So, at least Rogers wasn't the superstar Wise was. He sounded tough on the phone, but I shouldn't confuse that with illegal activities.

Wise was bad enough for both of them. I found this out easily enough once I'd replaced the master list and pulled the file on CLELAND, JOHN. Wise was born in 1933, which put him in his seventh decade. He had been walking the thin line between business and crime since the late 1950s, when he may or may not have been behind a ring that supplied the still unnamed flower children with the weed that dreams are made of. A few of his friends did time for this, but he escaped because the local police were unable to find a link between the cannabis grown, packed and stored in a barn out Pelham

Road with the owner of the property, an absentee land-lord whose tenant could not be traced. In the 1970s he became interested in pre-Columbian art and made regular visits to South and Central America. Although searched at all the best airports, he still managed to stay free of the law. When a big drug bust occurred in Toronto and Wise's name was mentioned, no charges were laid and the newspaper was advised by its legal staff to print an apology, which it did. After that, Wise managed to stay out of print until the eighties, when his great interest in pre-Columbian art extended to South-east Asia, Hong Kong and Afghanistan, from where he told one investigative reporter "all the best samples may be found."

From drug-dealing, Abe—I started calling him Abe to myself as we got better acquainted—began to take an interest in the plight of political refugees and stateless persons. This was followed by a passion for shipping and small airlines. He was once called "the wetback's best friend" by a Toronto magazine that not surprisingly changed its address for every issue. Local authorities thought that they had finally caught up to him when a ship loaded with "refugees" struck an abutment of the Peace Bridge near Buffalo and nearly sank with all aboard. The survivors told the police through an interpreter that they were just out for a cruise and hadn't brought any papers with them since they had no intention of landing on the other side of the border. They denied knowing Abe Wise or any of his associates. A week later they were still sticking to their story. Abe knew how to pick his refugees.

Two years ago, a new pattern began to show up. Abe began collecting artifacts from native Canadian reserves along the St Lawrence River. He also gathered arrowheads, beadwork and baskets from the reservations along the New York shore of the river. Quite incidentally, the increased trade in illegal cigarettes began about that time. Abram's interest in the art and history of the original Americans took him to Poland, Romania and the former Soviet Union. Only a couple of sharp reporters specializing in organized crime ventured to link Abram Wise and the sudden appearance in both Canada and the United States of cigarettes that originally had been shipped tax-free to Poland, Romania and the former Soviet Union.

This phase didn't last long and, unlike some, Abe was well out of it before the cigarette game went out in a sudden puff of smoke. Smuggling bonded booze across the border was a ready-made substitute. It used the same boats and trucks he had bought for moving cigarettes.

You couldn't help admiring his cleverness: never an arrest, never more than unfounded accusations. Whenever the police or press became bolder than usual, they had to backtrack and issue an apology. The nearest thing to a bust came in the mid-eighties, when a ship that could be traced to a company he could be connected with was found to have one of its winches stuffed with heroin. It was a multi-million-dollar haul, but only those found on board did any time because of it. I noted their names. Abram explained that he only owned a piece of the company that owned the ship; he didn't know what cargoes any of his ships carried. I rather liked the idea of hiding things in the core of a winch under hundreds of feet of steel cable. It spoke of a fertile mind, one I was learning to know and respect.

I decided that there was a limit to the amount of information I could absorb at a sitting. Now that I knew where the file was kept, I could relax a little. Not as much as I thought I might, because when I looked up from the file I saw Mickey Armstrong leafing through the pages of an 1875 atlas of Grantham. Sitting next to Stefan, the photographer who never exposed any film, he looked up long enough to see if I had any plans for lunch. Mickey had the air of being cut out for better things than shadowing the likes of me. He looked like a soldier whose wartime experience was all in administration. I had to watch him, but I couldn't give him the slip. I needed his regular reports to Wise to keep me alive. When I returned the file to its drawer, Mickey closed up the atlas so that it blew paper off the librarian's desk. By then I had put my coat on and was pretending not to see the photographer grinning at me.

Chapter Four

"**M**y father was in junk, Mr Cooperman. I'm in steel and my kids, Jerry and Bernie, are in the fabrication business. It's all the same: same yard, same office, same books, same people working there. Just the names get changed, like there are innocent parties to be protected."

Dave Rogers was fat. That's the only word for him. He had jowls like a hound and his belly kept the rest of him a foot and a half away from the table we were sharing. I suspected that under all that jelly there were the remains of youthful muscles gone to grass, muscles that used to be able to shift loads of steel about the yard.

"The old man started with rags, bones and bottles like every other junk collector in the 1920s. Then he moved to lead pipe and copper wire and other metals. By the time I came along it was scrap metal not junk. Now Jerry is doing special jobs with I-beams and H-beams for bridge companies. He's got a few government highway contracts. In a couple of years the boys'll be right up there with the big guys like Bolduc. Me? I'm semi-retired. I take things easy: I go to the track, travel, spend the winters in Arizona. Just got back. I don't go to Florida no more. That's too violent down there. It scares the piss out of me, some of the things I've seen."

Judging by the nests of broken capillaries on his nose and cheeks, I thought Dave Rogers had better start looking after himself right here in Ontario, never mind Florida. High blood pressure was shouting at me from the moment I saw him biting into an egg roll. Still, he wore an ancient windbreaker with markings of some long-dead hockey team. My impression that he had been fit once was reinforced by that, even though it had been years since that open zipper fastened any higher than his crotch. A pink-and-blue necktie was displayed over his mid-section like an oversized tongue that had abandoned itself to lunacy. At the upper end, the loosened knot tried to define the impossible: Dave Rogers's neck.

"When I first met Abe, we were both in school. Grade Four! We learned all about Columbus together. It made a big impression on Abe. It didn't show at the time, but later on, he became quite an authority on statues and pots that come from down in Central and South America. Abe can tell you whether a pot was Inca or Aztec or Mayan as fast as I can tell a chopstick from a fork." Dave shook his head, smiling while he chewed. With his jowls in movement, it was quite a sight. "Abe was always smart," he said, touching a large knuckle to his forehead twice. "He always took his cover serious. You know what I mean? He didn't fool around. He *said* he was an expert on pre-Columbian art, so he became one. Nothing fake about his expertise; nothing fake about his collection either."

"What moved him into a life of crime?" I asked. "Was it the Depression?"

"It was the fifties. We were born before the war, but we grew up in the forties and fifties. They were boom years and there weren't too many restrictions on free enterprise. Even in the scrap business, we had to use a little

muscle once in a while. My old man kept two sets of
books. Hell, everybody kept two sets. Abe used to work
in my old man's yard once in a while just to keep me
company. He watched the way the business was organized. He didn't break his back loading trucks when he
could help it. He was knocking off burglaries before he
was buying shaving cream. I went with him one time. I
didn't believe the stories he was telling about the stuff
that was stashed away in those old homes up on Welland
Avenue. He said he did places off Ontario Street and
over on Mortgage Hill too. But I went into one house
with him."

"What did you get?"

"Scared shitless! That's what I got. Breaking and entering is too real for my system. I didn't like it that one time
and it's lasted me ever since. Abe was different. He
didn't have any nerves in those days. He walked into a
house and went through all the drawers like it was his
own place and he was looking for his lost car keys. He
found a box of jewellery that time. It was a tortoise-shell
box. Ain't that funny? I can still see it! There were some
valuable pieces. Abe could tell the good stuff from the
fake, which he didn't bother with."

"You never went back with him?"

"Not me! Anyway, he soon stopped doing break-ins.
The cops were getting more squad cars back then. There
were more cops around and they kept a good lookout.
That was in the days when they still rattled doorknobs
along St Andrew Street to see if anybody'd knocked off a
store. That's a long time ago, Mr Cooperman."

"I thought you said Abe was fearless? What was he
afraid of?"

"Some old woman got herself killed by a burglar over
on Russell Avenue. The cops kept their eyes open after

that. The paper was crying for law and order. In those days it sounded original. That's when Abe quit doing houses."

"Didn't he do them again when the heat died down?"

"Naw. By then he'd discovered the weed. He called it 'the weed of crime.' You ever listen to the old *Shadow* program? I guess you're too young."

"You're talking about marijuana, right?"

"It became big in the sixties. You couldn't have had the sixties without it. The sixties ran on marijuana. That's no secret. Abe got some retired farmer with a bad memory to rent him a field or two. That's where he really got into gear. He had taken four or five crops off those fields before they busted the farmer. And he didn't say anything. I mean, even if he wanted to snitch, he was too old and senile, he couldn't do much damage. Stopped Abe's operation, that's all. But, by that time, he had other people sticking their necks out for him and he was learning about the import-export business."

"And after that he never looked back. Am I right?"

Dave nodded and took a sip from a can of Coke. Classic, of course. Through the windows of the restaurant, I couldn't see Mickey's car, but I knew better than to think that he had found something more interesting to do. "What's Abe up to these days?"

"What a limey who works for me calls 'the lot.' There ain't anything he isn't into. I'm talkin' girlies, I'm talkin' hard drugs, heroin, cocaine, crack. I'm talkin' aliens, graft, protection, numbers and booze."

"Tell me about the cigarettes."

"That's yesterday's paper. Forget it. But bootlegging, he's into in a big way."

He took another sip from his Coke and another helping of fried rice from the big dish sitting between us.

"You see, Mr Cooperman," he said, using my name for only the third time in half an hour, "Abe knows how to diversify. Mickey Armstrong is his right-hand-man. He coordinates all of the sections. There are some Bay Street lawyers in Toronto who get orders from Abe through Mickey.

"Take drugs for instance. For the last thirty years, Abe's been bringing dope into Canada from the Pearl Islands in the Pacific off Panama. He's got an operation in San Miguel that has to be seen to be believed. While the Horsemen are checkin' out the Medellin cartels, and putting the diplomatic heat on the well-known Colombian exporters, Abe's dealing easy as you please out of Panama!"

"The Pearl Islands belong to Panama?"

"Sure. They own the real estate. But the movers are all Colombian."

I nodded, although I'm not sure I grasped all of the details or implications. I wanted to change the subject before my circuits overloaded.

"Tell me about Abe, himself. Is he a killer?"

"Abe? No! Not a face-to-face killer, except for—Yeah, I guess there have been a few times. He—" He broke off abruptly. "He has other people do for him and then only when there's no other way. Abe likes to see himself as a family man. He treats what's left of his family like they're made from Czech glass. His mother lived well into her eighties. I don't think Abe's got a mean bone in his body. What I want to say is, he gets no kick from kicking ass, you know what I mean? He'd just as soon live and let live. He's got an over-developed business sense. He'll protect his interests when they're threatened. I've seen it happen. When he has to, he'll hit, hard, fast and smart, leaving no loose ends."

"Tell me about his family, Mr Rogers."

"Call me Dave, for crying out loud. I get 'mister' at the bank." I gave him leave to use my given name too. He was picking at his teeth now, with a toothpick he must have brought with him, since I didn't see any on the table. "Family? He's divorced two wives and has a pair of grown kids in their thirties. I don't know which one hates him most. They'll dance at his funeral, if you ask me."

"Good! I think we're beginning to get somewhere."

"In his private life, Abe could never get it right. He was Mr Know-all. You couldn't tell him anything. And look where it's got him. Nothing but a big zero! Now, I'm not usually the one to say 'I told you so,' but Abe and me have been dating girls since we were in our teens. I could never get that guy to listen to me about women or about kids. Now I've got three of the best kids in the world. You couldn't want better. But they could have turned out as rotten and spoiled as Abe's did." At this point, Dave passed me a collection of pocket-weary photographs of his family. I looked, admired and handed them back. He examined the faces in the photographs before returning them to his pocket. "Yeah, they're good kids."

"I'm trying to get a sense of Abe's history, Dave," I said. "Could you go back to the beginning. Who was the first wife?"

"Paulette. Paulette Staples. Paulette was a waitress at the Di on St Andrew Street. She worked at the Crystal and the Columbia too, but she was at the Di when Abe first saw her looking like Myrna Loy in the movies. She was a knockout. I mean she was really, you know, built... She... Anyway, Abe got her up the stump before he knew her last name. That was Hart. He was named after Abe's dead father, the way we do. Hart's always

been a pain in the ass for Abe. He could never do anything right for his old man. He was the kinda kid who
shouldn't have had Abe Wise for a father. He was always
putting his foot wrong, trying to get his old man's attention and then falling on his butt. That was when he gave
a damn, before he started feeling his wild oats. Then he
did what he wanted and left it to Abe to pay his speed-
ing fines and get him out of the lock-up. Hart's got a
bigger record than Abe has."

"They hate one another?"

"Amounts to that. Abe can't see where he went wrong
with the kid and hates him for not being easier to raise. I
think Paulette divorced Abe because he wouldn't let Hart
take a few falls for himself just to see what it feels like.
She moved away to the States for a few years, somewhere
in the Catskills, just so she didn't have to see those two
killing one another. She's back now and still clucking and
cooing over that rotten kid like she never left town."

"And Hart?"

"Oh, he's still in town. He's got an apartment on Lake
Street, near the Armouries."

"What does he do for a living?"

"Are you joking or something? Nothing! That's what
he does. Oh, I guess you could say he bought and sold
antique cars, but that was never a living."

"You said there was a second marriage?"

"Yeah. Lilian Garnofsky. She was a teacher. Abe went
from a pretty face to a pretty mind. Lily saw herself as an
intellectual force in Grantham. She was a joiner, a fund-
raiser, a convenor of conferences. She did all the Jewish
organizations first, then moved on into politics and settled down at last with the arts." Dave's description of
Lily lacked the admiration he had lavished on Paulette. I
wondered why.

"I can tell you like her a whole lot."

"Actually, Lily and I got along just fine. She used to kid me about my cigars and my rough edges, if you know what I mean. I used to kid her about forgetting who made the money she was spending like there was no tomorrow and how it was made. Lily hated that. I'd found her weak spot and she didn't like that one bit!"

I tried some plum sauce on a piece of egg roll and swallowed it. Very tasty. I let my silence cue Dave Rogers for more talk about Lily. "She was always trying to improve Abe too, you know. Oh, yeah! She got him to give money to get the opera off the ground in Toronto. Abe didn't mind launching a show or two, just so long as he didn't have to sit through *Swan Lake* or *Tannhauser*. He hated dressing up like a waiter in a black tie."

"When did they part company?"

"Lily and Abe parted more or less by agreement. Must have been eight—ten years ago now. She let her lawyers get rough with him. When he complained, she used to coo to him over the phone, then tell the lawyers to put on more heat. I was in her house and heard her do it more than once. She was good at it."

"What about the child?"

For a moment, Dave looked lost, then: "Oh, you mean Julie! I couldn't think of who you meant at first. Julie must have been a child once, but I don't remember. She was one of those little girls that becomes a woman at about five or six. I don't think I ever saw her wearing clothes bought off the hook. Everything had to have Paris or New York labels. All Julie's money went on her back. There are no two ways about that. Wait a minute! I'm a liar! She liked fast cars too. Like her brother. Julie had her mother's instincts about spending money and both her parents' indifference about where the money'd

come from. She's no tramp, Julie, at least not a cut-rate
one. Let's see, what else can I tell you? I knew her very
well at one time. Oh, yeah! She has always had terrible
luck with men. She marries 'em and throws 'em away.
Abe pays all the bills. I don't think she knows that she's
sharing this planet with a couple of billion other people.
She only sees the people in the fashion magazines. That's
as real as she gets. I remember seeing her walk into a
funeral—it was her grandmother's, Abe's mother's—
wearing thigh-high boots with a mini-skirt, fur hat and a
Colorado suntan, and coming up the aisle half an hour
late on crutches from a skiing accident in Aspen."

"Do you know why Abe asked you to talk to me?"

Dave thought a minute then tried out an answer.
"When I get a call from Abe Wise to be nice to a friend
of his, I start gushing rose-water, Benny. I can't afford to
act any different. He tells me to open up to you. Do I tell
him he's crazy like I should? No, I tell him I'll look after
you. And that's what I've been trying to do. If you think
I've been shitting you, just tell me where I've been holding back. Go ahead."

"Don't get your socks in a tangle! I'm just asking."

"Abe and I go back a long way. But we've been bend-
ing away from each other right from the start. I don't live
the way he does. I couldn't. I only hear from him when
he needs a favour, or one of his kids has hurt him some
way. Do I ever call him? Don't hold your breath. He's got
a fine-mesh screen around his phone. You can't get near
him without going through all those damned people
working for him."

"I'm just about through. Just a couple more questions."

"Sure. There's always a couple more."

"How well do you know his inner circle?"

"Some I don't know at all. Others, like Mickey Armstrong, have been with Abe for years. Not only is he a good man in the office, Mickey's like secret service. He'd step in front of any bullet aimed at Abe if he could. Maybe some of the others have different ambitions. I don't know, so I can't say. Mickey has a few hustles going for himself on the side. Abe encourages him."

"Would you say that he's surrounded by enemies?"

"Hell, Benny, the man's a smart organizer of criminal activities and he's lived that way for the last thirty years. How's he going to get *Time*'s Man of the Year Award? It isn't going to happen. He may have a lot of people on the payroll, but there aren't any who would break step if Abe got hit by a truck. Abe's in the business of making enemies. What can I tell you?"

"Can you get me phone numbers and addresses of the people we've been talking about?"

"Let me have your office number." I wrote it out while I was trying to think of those important questions I hadn't formed yet. Dave was rubbing his face with a skimpy paper napkin. I got rid of the egg-roll evidence on my face too.

"I want to thank you for—"

"Forget it. It was Abe I was doing the favour for. But he didn't say I had to buy the lunch, Mr Cooperman. I guess you're getting expenses, eh?"

Dave got up and stretched. His coat swept the check off the table, blowing it in a gentle arc to the floor. He made no move to pick it up. I did. At his weight, he had to conserve his energy and save his heart. I watched him fight with his zipper just for old-time's sake and followed him out into the fresh air. It was a degree warmer outside, but there was no hint of the coming spring in the grey, sunless afternoon. It was all pretty depressing.

Chapter Five

"What the fuck's going on?" It was Mickey Armstrong. He had come around behind me as I watched Dave Rogers add his weight to the springs under the front seat of his Cadillac.

"What do you mean?"

"You know damn well what I mean! What kind of deal did you cut with Wise? I don't want some hick snoop walking on my grass, Cooperman! Stay clear! You understand?"

"I hear what you're saying. You don't have to shout. I didn't apply for this job, Mickey; you pulled me out of bed. If you can get me off the hook, I'll owe you. But in the meantime, Wise is giving the orders. He didn't present me with alternatives. It's march or die. And I know he's not bluffing. Hell, you know him better than I do. Can we talk?" He took the car keys from my hand and opened the door on the driver's side.

"Get in!" he said loudly, but softened it by handing me back my keys.

"I don't like this, Cooperman," he said.

Once inside, I leaned over to unlock the door on the passenger's side. Through the window I could see Dave Rogers driving away, without so much as a backward glance. Mickey climbed in and glared at me: "Well?" he

40

said.

"Mickey—do you mind me calling you that?"

"It's my name. What the hell are you going to call me? Michael? Only my grandmother calls me that. Everybody calls me Mickey."

"Look, Mickey, I'm in a situation. I've been hired by your boss."

"You gotta do better than that."

"I want to trust you, Mickey, but I'm still trying to find the boundaries. You know what I mean? Dave Rogers says I can trust you, and I mean to, but not yet. I don't know enough."

"You going to do a course or something?"

"Look, Mickey, we both work for Mr Wise, right? We're going to get to know one another, we'll work towards an understanding. In the meantime, he's got a different deal with each of us."

"I thought you'd say that. Keep going."

Mickey still kept my first impression of him alive. He looked like an RCMP old boy. He was even wearing a Mountie winter hat with great fur flaps tied on top like a deerstalker. But it was more than the hat. There was something in his size, his rock-steadiness that did it. His clean-shaven face added a chapter too. The rest of the book, beyond the vague military feel I got from his carriage and grooming was an air of competence in a crisis. True, at the moment he was trying to frighten me into telling more than I was ready to tell. His manner to me spoke of loyalty to Wise. He was hurt that Wise had sent for me instead of trusting the matter to him and the boys. Seeing that this hadn't happened, he wondered about the status of himself and his crew of early risers. Obviously, Mickey was a man to stay on the right side of.

"I've said just about all I can say, Mickey, until I've

heard and seen more. What else can I tell you for nothing? Whatever I'm doing has nothing to do with you or your men. You can forget that angle. I'm not an efficiency expert about to tell you how to do your job better. I'm a private investigator. I'm trying to find out one piece of information and then I'm through. If Wise ever lets anybody say he's through, that is. If you've been giving him full weights, you've got nothing to fear from me. Even if you've been nicking him a little, creaming off the top, that's none of my business unless it comes between me and finding out what I'm being paid for. I want to learn one thing and one thing only. But to get there, I'm going to have to ask a lot of questions. As you see," I said, inclining my head in the direction of the Chinese restaurant, "I've already started."

"You think I'm going to answer your questions?" He said this with almost a sneer. He was pretty sure of himself.

"When the time comes, Mickey, yes, I do. I'll ask Mr Wise to have a word with you. I think that'll do wonders, don't you? We'll talk down the road a few days. You pick the time. I think you're going to be a big help to me, Mickey. A big help when the time comes."

"I been reading up on you."

"Yeah? Where?"

"He got me to do a rundown on all the PIs in the area. I even checked out a couple of guys in Niagara Falls and Buffalo. Mr Wise was impressed by the job you did when that old lady starved to death last year."

"I didn't make a dime on that case. Don't remind me. A few more like that and I'll have to start searching titles for a living again. I've got a cousin always after me to go to work for him. He's a lawyer."

"That would be Melvyn Cooper, right?" I grinned at

his knowing my cousin's name.

"You should go into my business, Mickey. You're good at it."

"Now you're buttering me up. You want to rub my belly, Cooperman?"

"Hey!"

"Let's get this straight. I work for Wise and whatever he says goes. But that doesn't mean I gotta like it. As a matter of fact I don't like this whole thing beginning with you. So don't mess with me!"

"I hear you. You get top marks for putting on a gaudy show, but it doesn't change anything. I'm still going to have some questions for you and you better have some answers for me. You understand?" I tried to give my best imitation of my friend Chris Savas's tone when he was running out of patience with me, when the balance of the things that I'd told him and the things I was withholding was still tipping in my favour. Savas was almost always angry at me in a professional way, but we remained friends apart from that. Why couldn't Mickey see things that way?

"Thanks for the high-school pep talk," Mickey said, opening the car door and stepping out into the chilly weather. I got out my door too, just to see if there was life after high school. For a moment he stared at me over the roof of the Olds, as though he was questioning my right to breathe the air in West Grantham.

"I was born a couple of blocks from here," I told him at last, when he made no move towards his own car.

"Yeah? I opened my eyes on Dexter Street. You know where that is?"

"We could crawl there from here on our hands and knees if we had to." He didn't quite grin, but I could see the battle to suppress it in his face.

"Can you tell me who it was who met us at the door this morning?"

"Where?"

"At Wise's place. Good-looking woman. He called her Victoria. Does she live with Wise?"

"That was my wife, Mr Cooperman." I could see I'd lost yards again just when I thought there was a chance of a first down. "We live in the house with Mr Wise. Is there a problem?"

"Uh, no. I see. Does he have a female companion of any kind?"

"Who the hell...!"

"Cool it, Mickey, I'm just doing my job."

"Well, I'm not the *World Almanac*. Answer your own damned questions."

"You can at least put names to our companions on the drive. Come on! I'm asking small potatoes." He returned my look but said nothing, as though he really didn't know how to answer questions. At the same time, I could see he found my persistence funny.

"Never mind, Mickey. I'll ask your boss. You'll be hearing from him about cooperation. Cooperation with Cooperman is a big theme with him these days."

"I haven't heard a stop order on last night yet. Until I do you can call them Moe, Larry and Curly for all I care."

"I couldn't have put it better myself. And does Mickey get the odd custard pie in the face?"

"Mickey learned a long time ago you never feel sorry for things you don't say."

"Well, we all learn to eat our words, Mickey. See you around."

From where I stood, I watched him cross the street and get into his car. He didn't look back either. If he had, he would have seen me staring in a concentrated way at the bare, thick twigs and branches of the chestnut tree silhouetted against the horizon where Henrietta Street ran downhill away from me and my growling stomach. What does my stomach know from egg rolls? I got back in the car and drove across the high-level bridge.

On my way back to the office, I tried to think of a practical way to yell "help!" Mickey was in my rear-view mirror, of course. Where else would he be? The panic I felt was not for the moment, but for down the road. How long was I going to be able to stand the face of Mickey or one of his boys being reflected in my soup. They could give me a lot of aggravation if I wasn't careful. This was also no time to think of using my off-and-on contacts with the local cop shop. I could bring them into it later, if there was one.

My answering service told me that a Mr Dave Oddjers had called and I wrote down the phone numbers and the names that my egg-roll-eating friend had promised. I started with Paulette. The first Mrs Wise seemed safest, next to Rogers the best contact I'd been given. I dialled the number and waited.

"Yes?" The voice sounded as if it was coming up from thirty fathoms.

"Paulette Wise?" I asked.

"Who is this? I've no use for the name Wise. I've been Staples again for I don't know how long. Who is this?"

"My name's Cooperman. I'm a private investigator here in Grantham. I'd like to talk to you."

"If this is about the Triumph, that's all been cleared up. The bank agreed not to press charges. Have you talked to Mr MacLeod?"

"I'm sorry, Mrs Wi—Staples, this has nothing to do with that."

"Hart told me that it was all tidied up. If it's not the

Triumph, what is it, Mr Cooper?"

"Cooperman," I corrected. "I'd like to talk to you."

"What is this all about? Are you giving hints, or do you want me to guess?" She was sounding more like what I imagined was her usual self, although I had no way of knowing for sure.

"Sorry. I didn't mean to make a mystery out of it: I want to talk to you about your ex-husband, Abram Wise."

"Ha! You've got a lot of nerve! I wouldn't talk to the Mounties and I wouldn't talk to the local police. Why on earth should I talk to you?"

"I can't make you talk to me."

"You're damned right! I bet you don't even have any paper."

"Right, again. No warrants, no subpoenas. Not even a note from the teacher. I wish I had something to catch your attention, but I haven't. The only thing I know for sure is that somebody is trying to kill your ex-husband."

"Why didn't I think of that?" She laughed at her joke and I tried to go along with it. I wasn't handling this at all well and I had a feeling that it was going to get worse. I held on to the pause that followed for as long as I could. "Are you still there, Mr Cooperman?"

"I'm here, but it isn't doing me any good, is it?"

"You give up too easy. What do I get out of this? And where are you coming from?"

"Mr Wise hired me. I never met him until a few hours ago, when he sent some people to get me out of bed. He—"

"Well, at least I know you aren't shitting me. That's Abe all over. He'd never think of writing you a letter or calling you on the phone. So, he's put you on the payroll. Good for you. Now, what's my end?"

"What can I tell you, Mrs—"

"Call me Paulette, for Christ's sake! What does your mother call you?"

"Benny. I don't have any money to give away, Paulette, not money that you'd call money. But I might be able to look into that Triumph business on the side. I know a few people in town. I can't promise anything."

"Hart's not a bundle of joy to me these days, Benny. He's more damned trouble than he's worth. But, he's mine. What am I going to do? I can't let them send him to jail!"

"I'll see what I can do. When can I see you?"

"Give me an hour to put my face on. You know where I live?"

"I've only got your telephone number. I heard that you used to live over the river in the States. When did you move back here?"

"Six months ago. I still don't know what you're after, Mr Cooperman. I came back because after a lot of moving around, this is where I want to be. Besides, I'm getting to be of an age when it's good to know where your doctor is when you want him and whether or not he can get you a hospital bed if you need one."

"Are you in bad health, Paulette?"

"You've met Abe, haven't you? Well, Abe has been bad for my nerves for forty years. And I was older than him when we met. I'm not getting any younger, Mr Cooperman. But of course, you don't mean to pry, do you?"

"I'm in a prying business, Paulette." She laughed at that then gave me an address on Duke Street, not far from Montecello Park. I could walk there from my office in five minutes, if I didn't run into too many people. I glanced at the clock. Why was it two hours earlier than I thought it should be? I should try to schedule a nap into my calendar for today.

I picked up the telephone again and did the same number I'd just done on Paulette with Wise's second wife, Lily. She was more polite and cultured in her conversation, but she turned me down flat. She did it so well that it took me a moment to realize it. Lily had dealt with a lot of Fuller Brush people in her day. I had to hand it to her.

Chapter Six

It was a big house with a catalpa tree on one side of the porch and a ginkgo tree on the other. There were no leaves on the trees to give me clues, but the long black pods on the one and a few brown fan-shaped leaves at the base of the other helped me make my diagnosis. I climbed up the broad front steps to the large, fan-lighted door. There was an old-fashioned doorbell with a hand-crank. I gave it a turn and heard a wheezy ring for my trouble.

I could see a figure moving from the front of the house towards me through the curtains that covered the glass panel in the front door. In the last century, when this house was built, nothing was as safe as houses. Glass in a door was as good as steel. Privacy was universally respected, except by professional and amateur burglars, which was to be expected. In general, a man's home was his castle and a closed door was as good as a locked and bolted one.

"Are you Benny?" Paulette Staples asked as she opened the door. I nodded and she moved back so I could enter the hall. "Come in out of the cold," she said. "I don't know when this winter's going to give up. Here, let me take those." I shed my coat and hat and she hung them on the porcelain-tipped hooks of an ancient hall stand. I could imagine the original owner looking in the mirror, making last-minute alterations to his headgear before braving the cobblestone streets of the 1890s. As a matter of fact, I don't think they were cobblestone: in Grantham they went from dirt to cement without any in-between stages.

Paulette led the way to the back of the house, where the old kitchen had been turned into a sitting-room. She had reserved, as I guessed, the front room for her sleeping arrangements. "I've got tenants upstairs," she told me. I wasn't sure whether that was a warning or just information. It was all grist to the mill; I simply filed it in an open and unlabelled dossier in my head. She indicated a comfortable wicker chair for me to sit on. I removed from it a cushion with a few months of accumulated cat hair and sat down.

Paulette Staples appeared to be a middle-aged woman with good skin and a look of having been around. Her clothes suggested that she wasn't gadding about much any more. She was wearing a pant-suit with a flowered blouse. Her eyes were sharp and busy taking in the stranger. "Would you like a drink?" she asked, with an air of confidentiality and devilment.

"Why not?" I said. Why should I tell her that I hardly ever took a drink during the day. I didn't have to make her a present of my whole life. She went to a cupboard, which hid a fair collection of bottles and asked, without turning: "Scotch?"

"Rye with ginger ale if you have it."

"I thought you were a drinker," she said, busying herself making comforting sounds with ice and glass. When she turned, she held two old-fashioned glasses and delivered one of them to me. Her eyes were a grey I hadn't seen for some time. I could tell that she had been a great beauty in her day. Dave Rogers had said that she reminded him of Myrna Loy, the late and lamented Hollywood beauty queen. I wondered how many people would remember Myrna Loy's side-glances that spoke volumes in the language of sex and humour.

"I don't have to tell you that Abe isn't my favourite character, do I?" She lit a cigarette, which seemed completely in character. She knew how to talk and time what she said with her smoking. It was an art and it was disappearing from the face of the earth. "I first met him when I worked at Diana Sweets."

"I just came from there," I said, trying to help break the ice with a fib.

"I was waiting on tables in those days and Abe was a young kid on the make. I knew what he wanted, but in those days that was what everybody wanted. I had this look or something. It wasn't anything to do with me. I just had it and Abe wanted some." She took a long sip of her drink, then set it down on a glass-topped coffee-table.

"When did you meet him? What was he like then?"

"I'm not good at dates, but this must have been in the fifties sometime. Say 1950 or '51. He wasn't twenty yet and I wasn't much older. You knew I was older than Abe? Did he tell you?"

"I haven't had a lot of conversation with him. I only met him this morning."

"Ha! Yeah, you were telling me! Abe's up with the birds. He doesn't sleep more than four hours a night. Used to drive me crazy! Nobody but Abe is on the phone before five in the morning. He used to call me all hours of the night. He'll probably call me after you leave. Does he have Mickey Armstrong following your every move?"

"That's right."

"I knew it. He always has a Mickey to do his legwork

for him. In my day his name was...I forget. Billington! Christopher Billington! How do you like that for a tame thug?"

"So you met at the Di?" I hoped that she wouldn't mind me attempting to stage-manage the interview.

"Yeah. I forget exactly the circumstances. He was always a good tipper and kept on teasing me about things. He was very glib and made with the fancy talk. I thought he was a salesman at first, but he was so young. I mean where did he get all that bright chatter from and him still in high school?"

"Did he try to take you out?"

"Sure. He was always trying to get me alone. But, in those days, 'alone' was the hardest thing for me to be. That's why it doesn't stick in my mind in particular."

"Did you know where his money was coming from?"

"Oh, sure! He never made any bones about that. He was proud of himself. Me, I didn't give a damn, but I thought that he was going to get put away if he didn't watch his mouth better."

"Was that the way he always was?"

"At first. But, you know, he changed. From being a bit of a show-off, he became the opposite. After a while, I couldn't get him to tell me anything."

"Was that because he was getting into drugs?"

"Maybe, but I don't think so. By then I was going out with him. No, he stopped talking to me all at once. I mean he still talked. He could talk my head off. But he didn't talk about the jobs he was doing any more. You know he was breaking into houses in those days?"

"You knew his friend Dave Rogers?"

"Oh, sure, Dave. His name wasn't Rogers in those days. Yeah, he and Abe went everywhere together. Then Abe started seeing me and Dave got a girl of his own..."

You know how it is."

"What did you like about him?"

"Oh, I always went for the tough guys. Gangster types. I liked living the danger at second hand. I still get a kick out of it. I still know a few of the bad boys from Miami. They call me when they're in town. I guess they liked the way I could keep buttoned up. I never told tales. That's why it makes me nervous talking about this stuff with you."

"Can you think of anyone who would want to kill Abe Wise, Paulette?"

"Ever since you called, I can't think of anything else. You know, there are a lot of bad characters who pick up the hates wherever they go. Abe was never like that. What I liked about Abe was that he loved a good time. He didn't pretend that I talked him into it the way some of the boys do. He loved being seen with me and showing me off. He got a bigger kick out of it than I did, to tell you the truth. I liked his jokes and the tough guys he always surrounded himself with. Have you ever heard of Frankie Carbo? He used to fix fights in New York and all over…"

She was moving away from the area of my interest again. I knew that Frankie Carbo wasn't a current crime figure, although I couldn't remember where or how he'd met his fate.

"What about somebody wanting to kill him, Paulette? I'm not talking about the old days, but about right now."

"Benny, I don't see him any more. Not for the last ten years. If it wasn't for the phone… But people don't change. I'm sure he still rubs people the wrong way. He has a vile temper. But he tries to keep his business as fair and square as a crooked businessman can. He never went out of his way to buy trouble. Even when he drank, he was a happy drunk, big tipper. Still..."

"Still?" I coached, hoping for a breakthrough.

"Still, Abe was what he was. He did what he had to do. And he did it fast, and as tidy as he could. Like the pro he was. None of the Mafia-style dramatics. That wasn't his way."

I heard a noise in the hall followed by the sound of the door being slammed. Before we could both readjust, a redheaded young man with a wedge-shaped face strode into the room. His face was bright with anger.

"Hart! I wasn't expecting—"

"Shut up, Mother! Just what do you think is going on? What are you doing to me? Can't you leave me alone for ten minutes?"

"Darling, what are you talking about?"

"Him, for a start."

"Darling, I told you on the phone about Mr Cooperman. Mr Cooperman, this is—"

"The last thing I need is a private eye prying into my life! Get rid of him!" I returned my outstretched hand to my glass.

"Hart, he's here as my guest."

"*Get rid of him!* I want him out of this house!"

"Darling, be reasonable!" I got to my feet. The last thing I needed was a fight with this madman.

"Maybe some other time," I said to Paulette. When I turned, Hart was standing blocking my way. "Excuse me," I said and repeated it in the same reasonable tone. Hart remained fixed like a post. Paulette's face had gone quite white as she felt the conflicting roles of hostess and mother. Hart still hadn't moved when I looked back at him, so I sat down again, which seemed to confuse him.

"*I want you out of here!*" he said, not quite facing me. "You have no business mixing in our lives!"

"Maybe you'll clear a path to the door. I can't walk through you." Hart sputtered, then moved over to his mother's side, as though completing an alliance that had only been hinted at. I got to my feet again.

"Mr Cooperman, I hope you'll understand," Paulette said, her eyes pleading with me louder than her words.

"Mr Cooperman will keep out of my business, if he knows what's good for him." He was gambling on the unlikely possibility that I would knock him down with his mother in the room. I had already decided not to lay hands on him, even mine, unless he touched me first. I collected my hat and coat and left the tender scene to unroll without me.

The dark green Triumph was parked in front of the house. I walked around the sports car twice, taking in as much as I could before marching away up Queen Street, looking for maple buds in the trees overhead. I couldn't see any. In the bookstore across from the *Beacon* I went hunting for mysteries at the back of the store. There were a few favourites in paperback, which attracted me. I may have been a little rougher than usual as I pulled them off their shelves and flipped through the pages. I was getting rid of the feelings I carried away from Duke Street with me. Then I saw McKenzie Stewart's new book, the one I had been reading about. Five copies of *Haste to the Gallows* were displayed face front. They took up a whole shelf. Very impressive for McStu, I thought. Still, it was in hardcover. I paused in my resolve to buy it, flipping through the pages looking for a flaw. But McStu was a friend, the only local author I knew, although I heard there was one at Cranmer College. I hated buying hardcover books, but since I might run into McStu at any time on St Andrew Street, I softened and carried the book to the cash.

"You know that this one's non-fiction, don't you, Benny?"

"What? Sorry, Sue, my mind was unplugged." Susan Torres who ran the bookstore usually looked out for me. She put me on to Walter Mosley, John Dunning and William McIlvanney.

"This newest title by McStu isn't a novel, Benny."

"You mean Dud Dickens isn't in it?" My enthusiasm had developed a slow leak.

"It's about a *real* case, Benny. I know you'll like it because it's a local story."

"Great!" I said, "Great!" damning McStu under my breath and passing my plastic to Sue. I wouldn't even let her put the book into a bag for me. I slipped it into a pocket and returned to Duke Street feeling as though McStu had played an expensive joke on me. The Triumph sports car that had been parked in front of Paulette's front door was gone. I should have given it a kick when I had the chance. I rang the bell a second time.

Paulette looked relieved when she saw me standing on her threshold. "I'll bet you could use a drink," she said. "I know I could." She backed out of my way and we returned to the back room. Paulette poured shots of Scotch without asking my preference or forgetting what I had in my glass when Hart walked in. I sat where I'd been sitting, looking forward to the Scotch.

"I hear that Hart hates his father. Is there anything in that?"

"If there is, you won't hear it from me. I try to be as loyal as I can. Hart sometimes tests my patience, as you've just seen. You mustn't let that little drama sour you on the boy. I try to be fair to both the kids, both Hart and Julie."

"Julie? I don't understand. Isn't Julie Lily's problem?"

"Not when Abe gets on the telephone after midnight. God, I've been intimate with all of her problems from diaper rash to the present. Abe spares me nothing. In our divorce settlement, Abe got the phone and he plays it like, like a—a—"

"Virtuoso?"

"Yeah, like that," she said, smiling at me with her eyes over her drink. "God knows, I tried to get Abe to show a little common sense in dealing with them. They always got their own way. Abe saw to that. As a result, they got a pretty distorted picture of what the world was like when Abe wasn't there to put in some money or some muscle."

I waited. I didn't want to fill the pause with another question until I got a good answer to the last one. She went on: "It's not Abe they hate, you know. It's what he's done to them. They couldn't tell you about it in so many words, but that's what it is. He's spoiled them from having ordinary decent lives. Bad enough having a criminal as a father! But having a father who's as bull-headed as Abe is a combination that's hard to beat. That's another thing: Abe hates losing. That goes for bets and for people. That's why I went to live in Hunter."

"Where?"

"Hunter. It's in New York. You know the Catskills?"

"Oh. I think my parents stayed at a hotel in the Catskills. But as you were saying?"

"I'm a sentimental old woman, Mr Cooperman, and you can discount everything I've said, but I know that in spite of everything he has done to hurt them, in spite of everything they've done to hurt him, he loves his kids. I know it."

"But they can't stand him. I get the picture." Paulette didn't respond except by making a face. I thought I'd better move on. "Paulette, I've tried to get Lily to talk to me. She won't play. Do you think you could help me? I know that it's asking a lot."

"Not as much as you think, Benny. Lily and I came to an understanding a long time ago. Remember we've got a lot in common. Oh, we've had a great deal to laugh at over the years about that crazy, crooked bastard we were both married to. I hear what you're saying and I'll see what I can do. I can't be fairer than that, can I?"

I had run out of questions. I knew I could talk to her all day and hear all sorts of interesting stuff about her colourful life, but it wouldn't get me anywhere except maybe by accident. To finish up, I asked her about Hart's difficulties about the Triumph that she had mentioned on the phone. She gave me the details and I scribbled a few names on a piece of paper.

Paulette poured another drink for herself and tried to refill my glass, but I covered it with my hand. The last thing I needed on this long day was to be high on top of everything else. I thanked Paulette for her help and paved the way for a return visit when I was deeper into the investigation. She put down her glass long enough to see me out of the house. I could tell that she wasn't getting all of the company she could accommodate, but it was a busy day. I said goodbye at the front door, and she let me shake her hand, which was the only part of her that looked like it had seen more years than Abe Wise himself had.

Chapter Seven

In the Diana Sweets, between sips of coffee, I took the book out of my pocket. It looked like a novel, it was the right size for a novel, but it did say "true" on the back and on the front as well, when you really took a second look. *Haste to the Gallows* was a catchy title. I tried to get some idea of the contents from the back cover. A woman named Mary Tatarski was the subject of McStu's non-fiction sabbatical. I'd seen the name somewhere recently. Yes, it was the case that Duncan Harvey, a local architect, was perennially trying to get revived. In the centre of the book was a block of black-and-white pictures: a pretty young face in a high-school year-book, a soldier in uniform, a confused-looking middle-aged woman with a kerchief covering her dark hair. There were others, but I was growing curious about the text. I started reading the first chapter and lost myself in it for some time until I felt that I was being observed. It was an uncomfortable feeling. I put the book away. Looking around the restaurant, I saw nothing unusual: lawyers were joking over coffee, storekeepers were unwinding after a bad half-hour with the bank manager. I thought I saw a shadow pass across the window. For a moment, I had a sense of relief when I saw that it was only Phil, one of Abe Wise's hoods. Then I had to laugh. How quickly we adapt to any situation.

I drove through the double line of fast-food outlets and service stations to my parents' town house off Ontario Street. It was the first house in the row and my father's car was not parked in front. He must have been showing off his gin rummy prowess at the club. I could picture him, still smelling of talcum and a little pink from the sauna. I let myself in and found my mother watching television.

"Manny? Is that you?" Her eyes must have been temporarily blinded from looking at the screen.

"It's only me," I said, taking off my coat and hanging it over one of the dining-room chairs. "What's up?" I asked.

"Up? What should be up at this time of day? I've got potatoes to peel, that's what's up. It's a woman's lot, Benny. But first I'll watch the end of this program. I hope you're not thinking of staying to dinner. I only have two steaks, one for your father and one for me. You should let me know when you're in need of a home-cooked meal."

"As a matter of fact, Ma, Anna is cooking for me tonight at the apartment."

"Anna. Good! A girl that young needs all the practice she can get."

"By the time she gets her second set of teeth, she'll be able to boil an egg."

"She's still living with her father. I hear he has a French cook. Tell me you never eat snails, Benny."

"Ma, it's a big house and Anna has her own apartment in the back. And as for the snails, I've only seen the dining-room twice. Both times the table was covered with drawings from her father's collection."

"Why don't you make us both a cup of tea?" I did that

and when I returned to the orange living-room, Ma's program was over and the set turned off. I put the tray down on a coffee-table.

"Be careful of my Chinese ginger pots, Benny. I love them better than my life." Ma wasn't exaggerating. Once, when Sam and I were still in pyjamas with feet in them, Grantham was hit by a small earthquake. Instead of carrying her two children out of the house, Ma took the ginger pots away from danger wrapped in a blanket. Sam says the blanket came from one of our cribs, but I think that that's big-city cynicism showing.

"Ma, I've been thinking that it's been a long time since you and Pa have had a holiday. Why don't the two of you take off?"

"What have you been smoking, Benny? Just like that, we should go away! Why? Do you need the house? What are you thinking about?"

"I just thought that you could use a change of scene, that's all. Is it a crime to wish you out of this cold weather? It's been a long winter and you didn't get away at all."

"Except for the two weeks in Miami Beach."

"Yeah."

"And the week at Myrtle Beach."

"I forgot about Myrtle Beach. Okay, you don't *need* a vacation. I was just thinking that Pa looked a little frail when I saw him last week."

"Frail? Manny frail? Why shouldn't he be frail? He's seventy years old, Benny. A lot of people his age have been dead for ten years."

"That's why I suggested that you both get away. Treat yourselves to a second honeymoon."

"Are you coming up with the airline tickets?"

"I wish I could afford to send you on a trip around the

world: London, Paris, Rome!"

"And as for a second honeymoon, the less you and Sam know about that part of our lives, the better I like it."

"Don't you just want to get out of Grantham when the winter won't stop? It's supposed to be spring, but where are the buds on the trees? Where are the crocuses?"

"How do you manage to boil a kettle and make cold tea, Benny?" I could see I wasn't going to move my mother beyond the reach of Abe Wise's influence. I could hope to do better when my father arrived. If he came down against the proposition, Ma would begin to see some virtue in it. I didn't lose heart and I wasn't surprised. I just had to make the attempt, that's all. The price of a little peace of mind was cheap. It only took the effort. Half an hour later, when my father came in and draped his coat on another of the dining-room chairs, I put the idea of a southern holiday to him. He cocked his head as though I was going insane before his very eyes and said that he would think it over.

"What's to think over, Manny? Money doesn't grow on trees in Ontario."

"I wouldn't mind Palm Beach," Pa said.

"You can't get another day's wear out of that white suit, Manny. Forget it. Besides, it'll be spring in no time. I love a Canadian spring. It's over so fast. You blink and it's gone."

"Why don't you fly down to Arizona? They do a great spring in Arizona," I said, selling the idea with as much conviction as I could muster.

"Paul Weinberg found a scorpion in his garage in Arizona. Are you trying to send us to our deaths?" The conversation drifted from the Arizona murder plot to other things.

"Boy, did I get a shock at the club this afternoon," Pa said. It was his way of announcing the death of one of their contemporaries.

"Manny, I don't want to hear about it!" Ma always tried to postpone the news. Maybe she thought she could breathe a moment of life into the dear departed by keeping at bay the specifics of who exactly had died.

"And he was only retired a few years."

"I don't want to know!"

"A better hand at poker you couldn't wish for."

"Are you talking about Dave Kaplanski?"

"I thought you didn't want to know."

"I don't want to know if you'll shut up about it. If you won't shut up, then I've got a right to guess. Is it Louie Stein? He played poker. And I think he just came back from Florida. I thought that such a tan was criminal. Now he's dead. That's the way the world goes."

"Sophie, what are you talking about? Lou Stein's face told you every card in his hand. A poker player? Lou Stein couldn't understand Snakes and Ladders! I'm talking about the old deputy police chief, Ed Neustadt, not Lou Stein. Lou's been in his grave for six—seven months already."

And so it went. I tried my best to save their lives in Palm Beach or Flagstaff, but to no avail. I looked at my watch, kissed them both and left them to their steaks. I was beginning to feel hungry, so I pointed the Olds in the direction of home.

Chapter Eight

"**B**enny! Which way did you go?" I was sitting in my apartment at the all-purpose table with Anna Abraham staring across at me. With the certain knowledge that Phil, the hood, or one of his pals was keeping at least half an eye on my windows, I was not brilliant company.

"Huh?"

"I couldn't have said it better myself. Benny, what's the matter with you tonight? You sulked through dinner and haven't been listening for at least the last twenty minutes. Are you telling me that you could do with less of my company? I can take a kick in the pants as well as the next girl."

"I'm sorry, Anna. I know I'm being lousy company."

"An understatement if I ever heard one!"

"I said I was sorry." I stared at the wine stain on the tablecloth. I'd poured salt over it to prevent it becoming permanent, but I wasn't sure it wasn't just an old wives' tale. The wreckage of two approaches to eating grilled salmon lay before us: Anna's tidy clean plate; my chopped-up remains, partly hidden under the mashed potatoes.

Anna had come early, letting herself in with her own key, and had a good dinner on the stove when I returned from playing travel agent at my parents'. I was delighted to see her, of course, but I knew that I had put her in danger by just knowing her. I wanted to tell her, but I was afraid of the consequences. I was sure that she would stick by me. In fact, her loyalty was the problem. The last thing in the world I needed at the moment was damn-the-torpedoes loyalty. What I needed was every-day indifference, the sort of long-standing arrangement that might allow for Anna to not see me for a couple of weeks. The last thing I wanted was to have Anna know more about Abe Wise than was good for her. I had already quizzed her during dinner about her responsibil-ities at the university. She couldn't take any time off and that was that. What would have happened to her, I won-dered, if she had been with me when Mickey and the Three Stooges paid their call?

"Do you remember what I was saying?"

"You were talking about... No, I don't remember. You caught me fair and square."

"Well, you're honest, at least." She was looking at me. I knew it, but I couldn't return her gaze. I wasn't sure what I might not say once I was caught staring into Anna's salamandrine eyes.

"Let's start again. Okay? I'll try harder. I'm not the rat fink you think I am. I'm just careworn from a bad day at the office."

"Office. You haven't been in your office for hours. I tried calling you there umpteen times. You're not going to tell me what this is all about, are you?"

"This is something you don't want to get involved in."

"Benny, you're always saying that the only way to pro-tect yourself from the consequence of having guilty knowledge is to pass it around. Secrets get people killed. You say it all the time! Well, why not take your own advice? What's going on in your life that I should know about? Are you tracking down a serial killer? Are the fuzz about to bust you for non-payment of your many secret operatives spread out across the nation, around the world?"

"Very funny!"

"Maybe it isn't business at all. Let me think about that. The blonde hasn't arrived to displace me, has she?" Anna has always been kidding me about my falling for a blonde bombshell with no brain and a full bra. I know it is just a joke, but she brings it out whenever she's feeling peculiar about our arrangements. We have been seriously not living together off and on for nearly three years. I could go on like this forever, but Anna and Anna's father would like some resolution to the informality. My own parents are noisily silent on the subject. I get looks across the table when Anna's name is mentioned. I catch exchanged glances and sense the undercurrent in the room. I once was kicked under the table when Pa got close to the subject of rabbis and invitations. I didn't know how to pass along the warning from Ma, but my father got the idea from my cry of pain.

"The blonde is in the closet under my laundry," I said. Anna looked over at the closet door then back at me.

"She's very quiet."

"She's well brought up. Breeding does it every time."

"Is that a reproach to my father's new money?" she said, brushing a lock of hair back where it belonged.

"You know I'm indifferent to your old man's millions. It's your body I'm mad about."

"What about the blonde under the laundry? Doesn't she have a body? Maybe she can't pull herself away from your smalls."

"Don't knock it until you've tried it. Dirty shorts are a

very big kick. Maybe not my kick, but a kick nevertheless. Come over here."

"Aren't you saving yourself for her?" I answered the question by getting up and walking around the table. The next half-hour has no place in the report about Abe Wise's call on my professional services. Although I hadn't answered Anna's questions, I had forgotten that she had asked them. Maybe she had too. It was a long time before I thought of Abe Wise or of his minions stationed across the street.

The light was gone when I rolled over. The candles had guttered out in silence while I caught thirty winks in Anna's warm arms.

"She isn't making much noise in there," Anna said at length.

"I thought you were asleep."

"I was, but I was feeling sorry for the woman with your smalls."

"I told you; she likes it in there."

"Until I'm gone and then she jumps out to behave in the most abandoned manner."

"You've been looking in my window."

"I've been reading your mind. Why don't you give the poor dear a break while I sit in a hot tub. I'll only give you ten minutes. I call that generous, I do," Anna said, wrapping the top sheet around her. She made no move to abandon me.

"Why not make it a shower? There's room for two."

"I'm talking about cleanliness and all you can think of is more sex. No wonder you keep the blonde in there. If she wasn't a figment of your warped imagination, I'd call the cops on you. And there are a few women's groups that should be informed too. I think you should be seeing somebody about this. If Freud were alive..." Anna delayed her tub for several minutes with a dissertation on my mind and what the world of psychiatry was missing. I thought again about making things more permanent with Anna. There was a natural male reluctance in me. Anna had pointed it out a few times. She said I was addicted to having the blonde in the closet. As a figure of speech for my wild bachelor years, the blonde was carrying a lot of dark meaning, most of it Anna's. But who am I to interfere with her illusions about me? I decided that this was a bad time to talk about the blonde coming out of the closet and leaving town. Abram Wise and his boys had a lot to answer for. Was I just turning to Wise as an excuse for continuing in the old established, make-it-up-as-we-go-along ways, or was I really worried about Wise and what he might do to Anna? I was worried.

"Before you head for the bathtub, Anna, will you scratch my back?" Anna moved around and pulled herself up on the pillows. She caught me in a straight look.

"Can't get her to do it, eh?" she said. "It figures. Roll over."

Chapter Nine

I called the Upper Canadian Bank and got nowhere trying to talk to the Bill MacLeod who was dealing with Hart Wise's antique-car problems. By pretending that I knew more than I did, I fooled him into letting slip a few names, and details new to me. Crumbs from head table, really; but that's what my job is: picking up crumbs and trying to get them to say something.

I telephoned the secret number that Wise had given me, partly to show him that I was on the job and also to show him that I was penetrating beneath the skin of his family life. Maybe he would have second thoughts about our early-morning meeting. Maybe he'd tell me to go to hell. I was hoping he would, as a matter of fact. I was getting tired of running into Mickey Armstrong every time I looked up from my coffee cup.

"Who the hell gave you this number?" he shouted at me. Good, I thought, now I'll be cut loose and returned to civilian life.

"You did, Mr Wise. Yesterday morning. This is Benny. Benny Cooperman. Remember in the very early morning?"

"All right. All right! What's your problem? This better be good."

"What can you tell me about Hart and his antique

Triumph?"

"Are you telling me that Hart's behind this plot to kill me? I don't believe it!"

"I'm not saying anything of the kind. I'm just trying to find my way in a family I'd scarcely heard of when I went to bed last night. Are you having second thoughts?"

"No, damn it! I've got too much riding on this. You want to know about Hart's car?"

"The antique Triumph—"

"The TR2. I know the machine. It's the 1954 model. A peach of a car. Reminds me of the Morgan I once wanted and couldn't afford. What do you want to know about it?"

"I want to know how the car became a headache. The bank won't tell me anything. They are bothering Paulette about it. How has it soured things between you and your son?"

"Hart fell in love with the car and bought it from a dealer without checking on his bank balance. He wrote a bad cheque. The dealer went to his lawyer, the lawyer saw that this was a chance to involve me, so he served a writ on Hart. I have friends in this town, Mr Cooperman. That's how I found out about it. Knowledge is my armour. Of course Hart was furious. He didn't want me to know anything about the business. He wanted to handle it himself. It was a stupid mistake, but the lawyer's trying to make a federal case of it. They're getting at me through Hart, but the boy thinks I'm interfering in his life again. As a father, I can't do anything right. I tried to give him the money to cover the overdraft, but that only made things worse. He won't make himself admit that he's being used as a pawn to get at me."

"Are you and Hart on speaking terms?" He thought a

moment before answering.

"I try to remain on cordial terms with both my children."

"But that's easier said than done."

"Some day, Mr Cooperman, you'll have children."

"These children—not mine, but yours—are well into their thirties, Mr Wise. They have left home, have formed attachments, I suppose, and even bounce the occasional cheque. Maybe it's time you stopped treating them like children?"

"I hired you as an investigator, Cooperman, not a sob-sister! When I want your advice about matters other than my life and death, I'll send Mickey around to tell you. In the meantime, stick to your damned job!"

"Speaking of Mickey, I want to talk to him. I'm not having an easy time getting his ear."

"I'm beginning to wonder whether your services weren't over-sold, Mr Cooperman. But, I'll have a word with Mickey. I trust him as I trust few others. He's a good man, and more enterprising than most. Is that all?"

"Tell me about your will. Who gets your money?"

"My visible assets and as many of the invisible ones that survive probate go to Hart and Julie in equal shares. In the event of the death of either, the remaining child inherits everything. There are some fairly sizeable gifts to institutions, charities and people close to me, but the bulk of it goes to Hart and Julie. Is there anything else you need?"

"I can't think of anything. Oh, yes, Lily won't talk to me."

"I hear what you're saying. I'll look after it. I can't promise anything with Lily. Never could. If there's nothing else, I've got to go. It's a busy day and there's a funeral I have to attend."

"Would that be the one for the former deputy police chief? I wouldn't have guessed that you were all that close."

"We weren't, my friend. But having an unsavoury reputation has this peculiar advantage. When I turn up at Neustadt's funeral, everybody will think he was a bigger son of a bitch than he was, which is going some."

"I guess you crossed swords more than once?"

"Once was enough! Now, I don't have time to banter with you, Cooperman. Goodbye!" I got my ear away from the phone just in time to save my eardrum from rough use. I was glad that I wasn't in daily contact with Abe Wise. I don't think I could take it.

I knew when I bought it that I should have spent some time seriously looking at McKenzie Stewart's new book. As the only living author of my acquaintance within a hundred miles or even a thousand, he was bound to run into me sooner or later. Sooner, if I hadn't read his book. That's the way the laws of probability work around here. I was right. He was coming out of Christopher's Smoke Shop with a couple of foreign newspapers under his arm and a fresh pouch of pipe tobacco, which he was tearing open with complete absorption.

"Ah, Benny!" he said, putting a big brown hand on my shoulder. "How are things in the world of crime?"

"McStu!" I said. "I just bought your new book this morning," I lied. McStu, when he wasn't writing crime novels, was teaching English or Creative Writing at Secord University up on the Escarpment. He also travelled a lot lecturing on black writers.

"Thank God somebody bought it!" he said emphatically. "It might as well be you. I told them that *nobody's* going to buy that book, Benny. *Nobody*."

"But it's a local story, isn't it?"

"Well, we'll sell a few around Grantham. But Grantham isn't the world. My US publisher wasn't interested. My English publisher said he'd skip this one. So all I've got to look to are Canadian sales. What did you think of it?"

"I...I've just started it," I said, stammering. "The beginning is great!" I said as enthusiastically as I could.

"Yeah, I got all that stuff about the execution from the hangman himself, an old gaffer named McCarthy, who lives in Grimsby. And three guards who are still around told me things."

"You really think she was innocent?"

"Hell, Benny, all I can say I said in that damned book. What it boils down to is the fact that I don't think the Crown made its case. There wasn't complete disclosure of the police evidence to the defence or to the Crown. Oh, it was a miscarriage of justice all right. No two ways about that. That Neustadt fellow, the old cop who died this week, kept his witnesses writing statements until they said what he wanted them to say. The defence never saw the early versions. Duncan's still trying to get the case reopened, you know?"

"Duncan Harvey, the architect. Yeah. What does he get out of this?" Today I was suspicious of everybody.

"Duncan's the last of the good guys, Benny. A genuine concerned citizen. Last of a dying breed. He writes letters to the editor and even sits through City Council meetings. Amazing man. There's a crown on high waiting for Dunc. He's been trying to do something about the Tatarski case for years."

"I can't see what good it will do. They can't give the woman her life back, can they?"

"But, you see, Benny, they can remember what happened to Mary Tatarski the next time they think they have an open-and-shut case. Nothing in life is simple. Making mistakes is what we do best."

"You got time for a coffee, McStu?"

"Lay on, Macduff!"

Less than five minutes later we were seated facing one another in the middle section of the Diana Sweets with the hope of coffee moving in our direction.

"How did you get involved doing a book that didn't have Dud Dickens in it?" I asked.

"Dud was getting on my nerves. I wanted to change the rules just for one book before I went back to him. I needed a sabbatical. Then Dunc offered to let me see what he had in his files. By the way, Benny, I'm almost finished a new Dud for your Christmas stocking. Don't worry."

"I wish I could talk to you intelligently about the Tatarski book, McStu, but I just bought it."

"When you've finished reading the book, we'll tear it apart together, okay?"

"What kind of reviews is it getting?"

"Toronto papers liked it. Local reviewer complained I got street names wrong. There was a letter in *The Globe* accusing me of being the latest bleeding heart to burst into bloom in southern Ontario. There were letters in the *Beacon* too. Interestingly enough, one of them was from Ed Neustadt, the cop who did the original investigation."

"Interesting."

"Speaking of cops, have you seen those two sergeants of yours lately? I need to talk to one of them about a technical point in my new book."

"Savas is on holiday. I think he's gone back to Cyprus for a few weeks. But Staziak is still around."

"Good! I'll give him a call." Coffee had by now arrived and soon McStu was telling me about the latest Hamilton harbour scandal and how he was using a thinly veiled version of it in his novel in the works. I took a long shot and asked:

"Is Abe Wise involved in that?"

"Name one dirty deal within this hemisphere that Abe Wise doesn't have a thumb in, and I'll eat the rest of his digits."

"How close is he to the action this time?"

"He has made a lot of people angry, Benny. That, I admit, is unusual for the old smoothy. Shee-it, he could get himself killed. You see it's not just money running on this, it's reputations. And people will go farther to protect their names than they will for a dirty buck."

"I'll remember that. How does he get away with it, McStu?"

"Wise has a legitimate business running parallel to all of his crooked ones. Keeps the cops guessing. For some reason the local cops have never bothered him much. He must buy a lot of tickets to their annual ball. I don't know."

"How is Cath?" McStu's new wife, Catherine Bracken, read the evening news on the local TV station. I'd been hired a few months ago to keep an eye on her. It was the best job I ever had.

"We're expecting a baby, Benny. I guess it's okay to tell you. You're practically family."

"Congratulations to both of you! When's the big day?"

"Cath is going to work right up to the middle of June and then take time off to get ready."

"That's wonderful! Give her my love."

"I will. I will," he said and we drank our coffees silently for a few minutes, trying to think of something to say that wouldn't be an anticlimax after news like that. Neither of us could, so we continued to drink in silence.

A few minutes after McStu pulled himself away with the lame excuse that he had students to meet up at Secord, I walked back down James Street to the library and spent twenty minutes reading up on the Letters to the Editor going back to the weeks following the appearance of the first reviews of McStu's Mary Tatarski book. I wasn't surprised to find the one signed Deputy Chief of Police Edwin Neustadt, Niagara Regional Police (retired) so easily.

> Sirs,
> I am astonished that your paper has given room for a review of *Haste to the Gallows* by McKenzie Stewart. I was intimately involved with the original investigation of this case and find that all attempts to lift it into the realms of the exotic or sensational are ridiculous. It only serves to titillate morbid unhealthy appetites. It was a very ordinary case. There was nothing at all remarkable about any of the people concerned. Yet the present author is trying to make us believe that the woman involved was executed without a thorough investigation or fair trial. I object to this view in the strongest terms. Mary Tatarski was a headstrong, abandoned creature, who would have killed anyone who stood in the way of her wilfulness. The best thing that can be said in her favour, which the defence had ample opportunity to say at the trial, is that Anastasia Tatarski was an old-fashioned woman, who objected to having her daughter away from the house until all hours, leaving her infant child in her care. If this is ignorance and backwardness, I think we could do with more of it more than forty years after that poor woman's violent and premature death. Killing her

mother may have been the crime for which Mary Tatarski suffered, but it must, in all fairness, be remembered that her father, Joseph Tatarski, a veteran just back from the reconquest of Europe, was also murdered under that same roof. It is incredible that weak-kneed sentimentalists have nothing better to do than try to create martyrs from such twisted human rubbish...

I came away from the library with half a wish to have known more about this moralizing deputy chief of police. I guess it was at that moment that I decided to take the time, a couple of hours later in the afternoon, to go to Neustadt's funeral. Unless he had been kidding, Wise would be there. It would be a good opportunity to observe the intensity of Wise's feelings about the dead man. It would be a further insight into Wise. God knows I needed all the insights that I could get.

Chapter Ten

I hadn't been back in my office long when the phone rang. It was Wise's second wife, Lily, although I didn't catch on right away.

"You're doing some work for my husband?"

"Who is this? I work for a lot of husbands in my line, lady. Are you going to help me out with a name or do you want me to recite a list of my active files."

"A comedian! I always said Abe can pick them! Look, Mr Comedian, I'm Lilian Wise. Does that mean anything to you?"

"Sure it does, Mrs Wise. What can I do for you?"

"Still making jokes! I'll save my laugh for later. I heard that it's *you* who wants to talk to *me*."

"That's right, Mrs Wise. When can I see you?"

"You're getting expenses, so I'll let you buy me lunch."

"Great! Where shall I meet you?"

"There's a little place I like on Wellington. Just a little north of Church Street. I forget the name."

"I know the place. What time?" She told me to meet her at twelve-thirty and to make the reservation. It took me a while to remember the name of the place, but I located the phone number and made the reservation. That left me an hour and a half before our meeting. To kill the time, I called the car dealer who was holding

Hart Wise's bad cheque.

"Yeah?"

"Is this Gordon Sawchuck?"

"Shaw. I do business under the name of Shaw. Who the hell is this?" I told him and he agreed to see me after lunch. My social calendar was quickly filling up. I should get a gold medal from Wise for attention to duty, or at least be allowed to go on living.

To fill the rest of the time before lunch, I returned to Diana Sweets where I tried to make a list of what I knew about the assembled threats against the life of my client. I chewed on my pencil for a long ten minutes. Frustrated, I turned to the crossword in yesterday's *Beacon* and the better part of the time flew by like a breeze.

I'd left myself time for a bookstore browse on my way to the restaurant. I was looking for fiction about far-away places. But this idea was frustrated too.

"Okay, Mr Cooperman. What do you want to know?" Mickey was standing in the doorway of a store next to Diana Sweets. He grabbed my arm as I walked by him and held on to it like I might try running across the street into the one-way traffic.

"Oh, it's you, Mickey. You had me worried for a minute."

"You were right the first time. I want to talk to you." He pulled me into Helliwell Lane and hustled me through the brick canyon to where it opened up into a nest of trendy cafés and restaurants. From there it was a short push on my arm until I was forced to his car, parked illegally at the intersection with Brogan Street. "This will do fine," he said, opening the door and shovelling me into the passenger side. He walked around to his side and got in too.

"Is this a new conversation or a continuation of the

last one, Mickey?"

"You better stop this horse-shit, Cooperman. I've got a short fuse where you're concerned. Leave the funny lines to the talk shows."

"That seems to be the consensus. This morning, anyway."

He lit a cigarette with a pocket lighter and breathed the smoke in my face. He thought it might annoy me, but it was the best thing that had happened to me so far today.

"Okay," I said, popping a Halls into my mouth, just to keep me sane, "where do we go from here?"

"You're the one with the mouth. Ask your questions." Wise had obviously had a quiet word with Mickey and he was sticking me with his resentment. I guess it's natural. I tried to think of some questions related to the investigation. It was harder than I thought.

"Mickey, where did you come into the picture?"

"I met Mr Wise through some people he used to deal with in the States. I used to live in Buffalo, but I have relatives on both sides of the river. Part of my schooling was at a half-baked military school on the Chippawa Creek. They used to clobber us if you couldn't bounce a dime on your new-made beds. A few of the kids and I started moving stuff across the Niagara River in a boat for this guy."

"Above the falls?" I asked. He nodded. "That takes guts," I said. "Lije Swift operates a speak down in St David's. He used to run a fast boat during Prohibition."

"Thanks for the lesson in local history. Ain't it colourful? Do you have questions to ask me or what?"

"So that means you've been with him for how long? Five years? Ten?"

"He bought me from the guy I was talking about eight years back. At first I just mixed in and helped out. There was another man doing what I do now."

"What happened to him?"

"You don't want to know."

"So, when he left, you were slotted in?" He nodded again without elaboration. "There's somebody, Mickey, who's trying to kill your boss. It's my job to find out who. He's already tried a few times, but he's only come close. Your boss is a very careful man. He looks under his bed at night and I suspect he lets you open up his mail."

"So that's the score," he said, running a finger along the edge of his chin. "Why couldn't we handle it inside? What do we need a peeper for?"

"Take that up with Wise. I tried asking him and got nowhere. My guess is that he wants a clean sweep of his whole life: business, private, past, present and future. You can't do a clean job with an old broom." I regretted the "old broom" as soon as it was out. Mickey winced, but kept his hands where they were.

"So that's why you want to know about Cook? The guy before me. He met with an accident while on holiday abroad."

"Panama?"

"Hey! Not bad. Yeah, those crazy hammerheads. But I still say I could have done a better job from inside with what I know about the operation."

"I'm not making rules, Mickey, Wise is. I'm just trying to stay alive. This wasn't my idea, remember?"

"So, somebody's got Wise down for the chop." His finger and thumb were working on the cleft at the point of his chin.

"Does that surprise you?" I asked. "Wise's business tends to rub a lot of people the wrong way. He must be on a few hit lists." I was trying out an idea on him to see what his reaction might be.

Mickey Armstrong thought for a minute, his knuckles now were exploring the back of his right ear. "The cops want him, sure. Feds, provincials, locals. The Americans want him too. But I don't think they want him dead. He's no angel, but he doesn't pull the heads off dogs and cats either. He's living where they can see him. He's smart, but he ain't stealing the widow's mite yet. They know that. They know he plays by the rules. And his games are all covered by legit operations, like his import-export business."

"What about his business partners and competitors?"

"Everybody likes him. He doesn't screw around with them. He leaves the heavy jobs to his key men. They take the heat if there's a problem. They are hard guys and they get paid for solving problems without a fuss. Wise delivers on what he says he's going to do. He keeps his word and he's proud of it. There's no bullshit with Wise. What you see is what you get."

"I thought you said they hate his guts?"

"Mr Wise is a hard businessman. He cuts no slack. You have to know what you're doing to do business with him. But, given that, he keeps his word."

"What about Hamilton harbour? Are the people there mad at him?"

"Shit! They're just trying to cover their asses, that's all. Wise gets no joy from embarrassing anybody. He doesn't go for the blackmail lark. The Hamilton heavies have already fallen into place. There's no sweat in Hamilton. Everybody's on side."

"That brings us to his family. From what I hear, there's not much love lost. I've talked to his first wife."

"Paulette? I sometimes think she's the best of the bunch. Sure, she hates his guts until there's somebody else coming against him. Then she's a mother hen and the Texas Rangers rolled into one. I guess you saw that, if you talked to her?"

"She tries to protect their kid, Hart. From what I hear he could do with fewer people looking out for him."

"He'll never take a fall on his own as long as either one of his parents is alive. The sun shines right out of his ass. Hart is the biggest bastard I ever met, and every time he screws up Wise buys his way out. So Hart goes on messing his bed. Bigger messes. Bigger beds."

"He could buy a fleet of sports cars with the money coming to him in Wise's will."

"He could buy a big chunk of the factories in England and Italy where they make them too. So what?"

"Is Hart our man? He needs the money."

Mickey squeezed the butt of his cigarette and popped it out the window. "All I know is that I never let that one get behind me."

"Thanks. And the girl?"

"Julie's a lot of fun until you cross her. Wise is too cool a dude to forget that. She knows how to use a gun. Did you know that? She shoots with the experts."

"So far there's only one shot, and it missed. If she's such a hot shot with a gun, that tends to put her in the clear."

"Maybe she was trying to warn him, or give him a scare?"

"Could be. But whoever put that shot across his desk knew what he was doing. The slug landed in the hutch in the room where we first talked." Mickey whistled and made a face. It didn't mean anything in particular, just that he was processing the information. I expected a "Please wait" sign to flash across his forehead.

"Cooperman, I can't figure you out. You said you wanted to ask me a few questions, but you've said more than I have. Why are you being so free and easy with the information? How do you know I'm not the bad guy? Maybe I've got reasons of my own for putting Wise away for good."

"I've thought of that, Mickey. It wouldn't be the first time that a big hood was removed to make way for new blood. I guess I'm taking a chance on you. Have to start somewhere. You and Paulette seem to be firm ground. But that's instinct talking, not my head. If my head worked better than the itch I get at the back of my knees, I might be in some safer line of work. Why don't you do me a favour and have another cigarette?"

Mickey grinned a genuine grin and reached into his pocket. When the cigarette was going, he gave me a welcome puff in the face. "Tell me, who is there besides Dave Rogers that Wise trusts?"

"Well, there's me. Only he just gives me the gist of things. The only time I ever had a real heart-to-heart with him was the time I found out there was somebody on the other side of the door he didn't want to talk to in a hurry. He tells some tall tales, you know. I sometimes think that he makes up a lot of what he says. Imagine that! Him! Abe Wise!"

"Give me a for-instance."

"Like the time he told me that he once got away with murder. I don't mean recently in a business way, but a face-to-face sort of thing. He usually boasts that he's never harmed a fly. That's why he's survived in the rackets so long. But he told me he killed and got away clear. Another time he said that he had won a sports-car rally when he was in his twenties. Hell, when he was in his twenties, he couldn't afford to belong to the clubs that run those rallies. I know that because another time he told me how hard up he was when he was just getting started. Used to make his money with a hammer and chisel working the better-off neighbourhoods for hidden jewellery and cash. I checked out some of those neighbourhoods. Hell, if they looked good to him, he was starting below the bottom. He doesn't look like a burglar today, does he?"

"I think you like the guy, Mickey."

"He treats me okay. I got no complaints. He's always behaved decent to Victoria and me. Never made a fuss when she came to live with me in the house after we got married. I think he's a little soft on the two of us."

"You can't say the same about his feelings for that cop who died this week."

"Neustadt? He hated that crooked cop. If Wise was ever moved to kill anybody, it would have been that son of a bitch!"

"Why him more than the next cop?"

"Something between the two of them. He never told me. You better ask him next time you come up to the house."

"I'll remember that. One more thing: what's behind Wise's office? I couldn't see in the dark."

"Just the garage. It's a big one. Fits six cars."

"Thanks, Mickey. You've been a big help." I couldn't stop myself shrugging after I said this. "But, you understand, it's too early to know for sure. If you want to help keep Abe Wise alive, beef up your security at the house. Break up his routines, rearrange his schedules at the last moment."

"I know my job, Mr Cooperman!"

I caught the last gasp of smoke in my hungry lungs and opened the door. On parting, we each nodded politely, like we were passing in the street and weren't sure of the other's name.

Chapter Eleven

The restaurant Wellington Court was literally just around the corner from where I'd talked to Paulette Staples, Wise's first wife. His second wasn't waiting for me when I asked for my table inside this converted house a chilly block away from the business centre of town. To my right, as I sat facing the door, were a series of bright watercolours of doorways and window sills in some sunny Mediterranean setting. The bar, not far from the door, looked, at first glance, like it never served anything stronger than a Shirley Temple, but a closer examination showed that it stocked all the standard items, with a few locally brewed beers thrown in.

When she came in, I could see that she had spotted me right away. She started over to my table, but was sidetracked by a shout from a woman in a blue outfit with enough salad in a bowl in front of her to keep her and her best friends fed for a month. The woman introduced Lily to the woman with her. They laughed together. They laughed again and then Lily continued towards me. Lily Wise was a small woman who looked like she might boast that she still weighed what she had when she was twenty-five. She now looked fifty, was lean and well taken care of. I could picture her doing aerobics in a black leotard, while an off-stage voice counted off the stretches. She wore glasses with thick lenses and pale blue frames. Her hair looked like it had been cropped short by someone who knew what he was doing. There were strands of white mixed in with the prevailing black. I could picture her on committees, working with people, managing things.

"Mr Cooperman?" she asked as I started getting up. When I was on my feet she added: "Don't get up," and I relaxed back into my chair again. She sloughed a mink coat which she draped over the back of her chair like it was off the rack. Some people are sensitive about wearing furs nowadays; apparently not Lily Wise. She rubbed her glasses with tissue and a waiter brought her a red drink. "They know me here," she explained. "That's why they indulge my passion for Campari. Are you having something?"

"I just got here myself, Mrs Wise."

"You better call me Lily or Lilian. I'm not all that fond of my married name."

"That's what Paulette said."

"One of the things we agree about." I invited Lily to use my given name too, but she looked like she had a bitter almond in her mouth when I told her what it was. "Actually, Paulette and I agree about a lot of things." I decided to try out the drink she was sipping. When it came, I enjoyed its astringent tartness, like the drink was sucking my cheeks from the inside. We both ordered our lunch: Lily, a quiche with a salad and I, a fancy pasta with vegetables. As long as Wise was picking up the tab, I thought I could experiment. It proved to be pretty good, a better choice than Lily's. At least I ate mine, she just played with hers as though eating wasn't something she approved of. While we were eating, she told me about her years of teaching before she met Wise. She grew up in Toronto and had that Toronto certainty about her.

"Well, Mr Cooperman. Time to put away the table chat and get down to business. What do you want to know?"

"How much did Paulette tell you?"

"Somebody's trying to kill Abe and you're trying to stop it."

"Good. Do you have any candidates?"

"There was a time when I had reason enough, but I've mellowed with the years. I don't know who he's in bed with these days. She might be worth talking to. Intimacy breeds the killer instinct, I find."

"As far as I know, he's not with anybody. I mean, there's a woman in the house, but she's married to Mickey Armstrong."

"That would be Victoria. I've heard a lot about Victoria. From what I've heard, she's not the compliant type. Nor is Mickey. No, I think you can rule her out as Abe's bedroom companion at least. She may have a reason for killing him, but I doubt if the reason would be sexual. Are there just the three of them living there?"

"I'm not sure. There are some low types who flex their muscles from time to time."

"The boys live in the house next door. Abe owns two of the houses on Dorset Crescent."

"I didn't know that. Thanks. Does your daughter get along with him, Lily?"

"Julie has to be polled on that question fairly frequently, Mr Cooperman. Sometimes she thinks that he is her own Teddy bear daddy, and at other times, she could gladly cut his throat."

"Nobody's tried using a knife yet. That's a mark in her favour, although I hear she's pretty good with a gun. What does Julie do for a living, Lily?"

"Nothing," she said, taking out her irritation at me or the question on a piece of lettuce. "Julie is between marriages just now. Her current boyfriend is a mover and shaker in the fashion industry. Have you heard of *Mode Magazine*?"

"I haven't, but that doesn't mean anything. I'll ask my father. He was in ladies' ready-to-wear for over thirty years."

"What a joy for you! But, Mr Cooperman, we are not talking about the same thing. Monsieur Didier Santerre has never spent an afternoon on Spadina Avenue in Toronto, which is where, I'm guessing I admit, your father learned the *shmate* business. I mean no offence, Mr Cooperman, it's just that there are worlds of difference between Spadina Avenue and the Champs Elysées."

"I begin to see," I said. "But why don't you start calling me Benny? I'll feel better."

"My late brother was a Benny, Mr Cooperman. It's not a name I like to use."

"Try Ben or Benjamin. Anything you like. I feel peculiar calling you Lily while you're still calling me mister."

"Yes, I know a family where they call the cleaning woman Mrs Tarnapol and she calls them Harry and Bernice. What odd times we live in, Mr C."

"That's a little better. We were talking of high fashion."

"You know, of course, that Julie's best friend is Morna McGuire? You've heard of her at least?"

"That's not a name I know."

"You should be ashamed of yourself. Morna McGuire just happens to be the world's most famous, and highest-paid, model. She's a world-famous celebrity. She also happens to come from right here in Grantham."

"Good for her and bully for us. What does this have to do with Julie's relationship with her old man?"

"Julie would never introduce her friends to Abe! She's deeply ashamed of her father, Mr C. She doesn't use the name Wise—"

"But I understand she spends his money."

"No need to be offensive! She has a right to use Abe's wealth. She is his only daughter."

"We keep coming back to that. Does she spend any time here in town or is she off on the Champs Elysées?"

"She has an apartment on the Île St Louis, but she still has a house here in Grantham. As a matter of fact, Morna and Didier spend time here as well. Morna's family lives here and Morna's still a relatively simple, unspoiled girl."

"Not the sort who would try to shorten Abe Wise's days, I'll bet. What does this Santerre guy have to do with the magazine and the model?"

"I can't imagine anyone so insulated, Mr C. You really are a phenomenon."

"Yeah, I hear that all the time. A magazine costs a pretty penny to put on the stands. Is it in good shape?"

"Advertisers are trampling one another trying to buy space. Didier is the publisher and founder. He is an important man of our times. Morna has been his protégée since she was fourteen."

"Protégée. I like the sound of that. So, neither one of them is interested in any of Abe Wise's big bucks?"

"Hardly, Mr C."

"And what is Julie's attraction for Santerre and Morna McGuire? Is she a designer or something?"

"Julie has a flair for creating interest. People watch her. The columnists notice where she goes, what she does and, of course, what she wears."

"I begin to understand, Lily. Do you think Hart would kill his father?" I said, trying a new direction.

"He might want to," she said, without changing her expression, "but frankly I doubt if he has the guts."

"Can you think of an enemy, from the present or the past who might want to see him dead?" She thought for a moment, while I finished off the last strand of linguine or fettuccine or whatever it was lying there alone on my plate.

"He's led such a strange life. It's hard to imagine where to start looking for enemies. But, apart from the general hurly-burly of a life in criminal circles, and a lot of people who would figuratively like to wring his neck, I can't think of a solitary name. Nothing stands out."

"Thank you for helping out, Lily."

"I only hope I haven't muddied the waters."

"Oh, one thing: what do you know about a policeman named Neustadt?"

"He's the one who just died, isn't he? That was a strange sort of accident. Like falling up a flight of stairs. Abe used to talk about him. He thought that he wasn't straight. There was something not quite right, crooked, maybe, about him. I've heard others say it too. I think he went a little off his head, didn't he? I know that Abe hated his guts, that's all. Abe used to brood about Ed Neustadt. I suppose it was mutual. Those things often are. I think he was funny about women."

"How do you mean, 'funny'?"

"I met him a few times at different functions when he was deputy chief or acting chief. A woman senses these things."

"If Neustadt wasn't already dead, I'd say I'd found the man trying to kill your ex-husband."

"Maybe you have, Mr C. Have you thought of that? When did he die? If Abe discovered that Neustadt was trying to kill him, he'd put out a contract on him pretty quick. Maybe you aren't the only one working on this case. Maybe Abe's already taken care of it."

"But why would he hire me?"

"Why as a cover, of course. Don't you ever read mystery stories?"

Chapter Twelve

Brighton Motors occupied the space where the old county jail used to stand on the east side of Niagara Street. I could still remember the forbidding grey building with dead ivy clinging to the high walls. Now the property was a used-car lot specializing in British and foreign cars. There was a showroom in front with an antique red MG in the window and a garage with a dusty black Jaguar on the hoist. Beyond was a lot-full of dodgy investments in metal and rubber with prices marked on the windshields in large digits. I walked past three idle salesmen on my way to the office. They were staring out the showroom windows watching the wind blow paper garbage into snowbanks sheltering in the shadows.

Shaw was sitting behind a desk that was even messier than mine was in the middle of a case. He was a bull-necked, squat man with short-cropped red hair, kept that way to try to hide the fact that his hair was rapidly making way for a better view of the top of his head. The shirt he was wearing was on its second day, and the knot in his orange-and-black striped tie was staying as far away from the open collar as it could. I was happy to have the cluttered desk sitting between us.

"So *you're* Cooperman. I've been hearing about you."

"Nothing actionable, I hope?"

"You changed the balance in the legal social register in this fair city. Putting Julian Newby away like that. The local fan hasn't been hit with anything like that since that big toxic-waste trucking scandal. Hell! You were involved in that too!"

"We try to be useful. What is going on between you and Abe Wise's son, Hart?"

"Ah! The old boy speaks through you, eh? I was wondering in what form he'd appear." Shaw swivelled around in his chair so that he could really look me over. Before this I'd been given an oblique survey while his main attention was turned to the venetian blinds.

"That's a fair assumption, based on what you know, Mr Shaw, but not necessarily correct. I may have my own reasons for wanting to know about this. And Hart has a mother too, you know."

"What kind of silly smokescreen are you trying to spread, Cooperman? You're working for the old man. Let's not play games. Sit down and maybe we can see how we can both make a dollar." I sat down in the worn customer's chair with the stuffing just beginning to show from under the arms and waited. I was hoping that he would make the first pitch. Instead, he began rearranging an assortment of ballpoint pens in a shiny black distributor cap.

"The kid comes in here and gives me some bad paper, Cooperman," he said when he had thought about it for a second or two. "That makes me mad. Anybody else and it's an offence. But for him, it's like rolling over in bed. He doesn't even notice. It's like he's trying to tell me that he lives by a whole different set of rules from me and you. How would you react to that?"

"It's pretty hard to prove intent to defraud, Mr Shaw.

Haven't you ever bounced a cheque by mistake?"

"Mistake? What are you talking about?"

"We both know that, Shaw. The question is, what are you going to do about it?"

"I've already done it. Right away I called up Whitey York. There's nobody like Whitey for making a sweet settlement. It's in his court now, if you'll pardon the pun. I'll just sit back and wait."

"Aren't you taking a risk? Suppose Wise is involved. Or, suppose he makes it his business whether the kid likes it or not. They say kneecaps take a long time to heal. Are you up to this, Mr Shaw?"

"Is that your message from Wise? I'm surprised at you, Cooperman. I thought you played it right down the middle."

"Like you, Mr Shaw?" Shaw grunted and fiddled with some of the paper on his desk. It wasn't very convincing. "Who is Whitey York? I've heard the name, but I can't place it."

"I thought you kept up with these things? When Rupe McLay left Wilson, Carleton, Meyers and Devlin, Whitey York took over his office. He doesn't drink as much as Rupe used to, and he chases more ambulances. Whitey's a go-getter and still in his twenties."

"God help us! Look, Mr Shaw, this is from the horse's mouth. Abe Wise is not on good terms with his son. Not only isn't he interested in Hart's bad paper, he's not even interested in breaking your kneecaps. What Hart does is Hart's business. If the kid can't cover his bad paper, how do you expect him to pay your costs on top of the price of the car? I think you are holding a stone with the last ounce of blood squeezed out of it."

"I hear what you're saying, Cooperman, but I also see where you're coming from. Wise's paying your way, not

Hart."

"You think Abe Wise hires PIs to settle his small claims? Get smart. Get a little smart."

"Sure, I know he has a lot of muscle. But what am I supposed to do with a rubber cheque?"

"Give it to me," I said, holding out my hand.

"Whitey's got it."

"Great!" This was information, a fact if it held up, a scarce item in my trade. "What was the amount, if you don't mind sharing it with a complete stranger?"

"We're talking in the neighbourhood of forty-five grand, Mr Cooperman. What with wear and tear on my nerves and costs."

"Wilson, Carleton still on King across from the market?" He nodded and I put my hat back on. I looked through his back window, while I was buttoning my coat: more used sports cars than you'd see at a summer rally.

"There's still bodies buried out there."

"What?"

"Bodies. You know. This used to be the jail. They moved some of them, the recent ones, but they couldn't find them all."

"You mean bodies of prisoners who died in custody?"

"Those that the county wouldn't bury. There were the two that were hanged buried back there. That old jail was right out of Dickens. *Great Expectations* and *Oliver Twist*. It was built back in the 1860s with walls twenty-five, thirty inches thick." Shaw held his hands apart to show the distance, just in case I was slow with numbers and spacial relationships. "But six people escaped, you know. Not a bad record for the century or so it stood here." He was looking out the window with me and, for the moment at least, not seeing his fleet of aging canvas tops and rusting chromium.

The sign in front of Wilson, Carleton, Meyers and Devlin hadn't formally added Whitey York to the establishment, but upstairs outside the new burgundy-painted front door they did own up to having an R.B. York as a junior partner in the firm. I could see where it had been added to the space vacated by Rupe McLay.

I gave my name to the receptionist and waited for her to check my name against her list of appointments. When she brought to my attention the fact that I was appointmentless, I suggested that she walk my name through Whitey York's door to see if that helped. It must have, because I hadn't advanced very far in *Maclean's* magazine before a tall, youthful man with a shock of the fairest hair I'd ever seen outside a baby carriage was stooping over my reading. "Mr Cooperman? This is a great pleasure! I just got a call from our mutual friend telling me that you might be paying a call. Will you come into my office?" I followed him and he led the way to the very place I'd had a long heart-to-heart with McLay three months ago. McLay's decor was gone, of course. All those touches that advertised failure had vanished. A paint job and the best of new designer office equipment had been substituted. "Would you like a coffee?" he asked. I shook my head before discovering that I would very much like one. I must try to get closer to my innermost feelings.

The formalities out of the way, York sat behind his desk with a steeple where his fingers should be. I told him that I was representing Paulette Staples, the mother of Hart Wise, in the matter of the bad cheque. I told him that the money and reasonable costs would be paid if the bad joke stopped here and now. I was going out on a limb, but I couldn't see any saw marks. "There is no way that you are going to involve Abe Wise," I said. "Your harassment of the boy is becoming a serious hazard to his health. We are considering action."

"Boy? That kid is thirty-five if he's a day! And if his health can't take a boilerplate form letter, then—"

"There has been harassment on the phone as well."

"Harassment? You're out of your mind!"

"We want this business settled, Mr York, today."

"I'll have to discuss this with my client, of course, Mr Cooperman."

"You just got off the phone with your client, or have you forgotten?"

"We don't want to be rushed into a hasty decision, Mr Cooperman."

"I thought that you were all in a tizzy about getting your rightful money? Have I been misinformed?"

"Ah, not at all. I'm still trying to assess our damages, but we are glad to see that reason and good sense are prevailing. Far too much time is wasted on unnecessary legal work."

"I couldn't agree more. Would you be able to send an invoice to my office by the end of the day?"

"We'll certainly be in touch."

"By the way, where is the car now?"

"Car? Oh, you mean the car! Hart Wise has that, I *think*. Better ask Shaw."

"I'll do that. Thanks, Mr York. Good to do business with you."

We shook hands, and in another minute, I'd climbed down the stairs and was walking through the open-air farmers' market. I suppose I should have made my way south on James Street to my office, but I wandered around the market stalls for a few minutes enjoying a glimpse of sausages and hams, cheeses, and early hot-house vegetables instead. It made thinking easier. I was wondering whether I had been wasting my time with Shaw and York. Was it their pressure on Hart that threatened to turn him into a parricide? I doubted it, but at least it was action, something accomplished.

Hart had been driving the Triumph when I saw him at his mother's. There was no doubt about who had possession of the car. But Whitey York had been vague about it. As I guessed, neither Shaw nor York gave a damn about the car; it was Hart they were after. They needed him as a stick to get at his father. I had a sudden image of boys poking at a wasps' nest. I began to feel pleased with my progress. I only hoped that Abe Wise had a sense of humour about expenses.

Chapter Thirteen

All of the local mandarins were there with their darkest suits and warmest coats on to wish a final farewell to Edwin Ernest Neustadt, late of this parish. They stood on the graves of other men and women to press as close to the open grave as possible. From my pitch at the rear, I could recognize many familiar faces wearing their most solemn expressions looking across the plastic green grass that had been thrown over the disturbed earth. I'm sure that I would have known most of the faces belonging to the backs in front of me as well. The Niagara Regional Police was well represented. The police band played a slow march and the casket was lifted from a gun carriage by six strapping officers in their parade uniforms. Pete Staziak was standing near a tall monument that pointed skyward, with his expression blending into the uniformly sombre vista. A eulogy was read by a high-ranking Salvation Army officer, an old friend of the deceased. Neustadt had, he told us, in ample quantity all of the manly qualities. His word was his bond; his virtues beyond enumeration. His time with the police force had seen many important changes, of which Edwin Neustadt had been a part. He was seen as one of the architects of the Regional Police which succeeded the earlier, more primitive Grantham Police

Force. Neustadt's elderly widow stood steadfast at the grave-side, supported by a married daughter and her husband. A hymn was sung, or at least attempted, while the police band tried to lead, then to follow, the singing. We heard the ashes-to-ashes section of the burial service. Again the words hit me as though they were directed at me personally. The coffin was lowered into the ground and the widow shook the hand of the Salvation Army eulogist. After that, everything began to break up.

I had spotted Abram Wise standing beside Mickey and his wife a few rows in front of me. It was Victoria I saw first. Her dark hair was covered by a kerchief. Wise was almost hidden by the people standing between us. Mickey's attention to his boss's other business gave me a sense of relief. I felt almost free, and postponed a look over my shoulder to see who was in charge of keeping me in sight.

I stood my ground as the company dispersed. The bandsmen marched off smartly as did the uniformed police. But Staziak was still talking to a brother plain-clothes officer across the open grave from me. He was rubbing his hands in the frosty air. Wisps of vapour told me which of them was talking even when I couldn't see their faces. Staziak stomped his feet and plunged his hands into his overcoat pockets.

An old survivor of the police force was being helped away by a middle-aged man in a windbreaker. "Did I have a coat?" he asked, not noticing the one he was wearing. Even in civilian clothes, you could see that he'd worn a uniform for decades. He kept looking back over his shoulder. "Wasn't there a woman with us when we came?" The man in the windbreaker moved him slowly away from the grave.

Wise too wasn't in a rush to leave the grave-side. He

was examining the faces of those who had come to assist, as the French say, at the funeral. He seemed to be amused when he discovered people staring at him. When his eyes reached mine, he stopped. "What are you doing here, my friend?" he asked when he had closed the distance.

"You are my business, Mr Wise." I nodded a greeting to both Mickey and his wife. Mickey smiled back. "You told me that you were coming to the funeral. I was interested to discover why."

"Did you find that out?"

"Not yet, but I may get lucky. Too bad Chief Neustadt can't tell me."

"A lot of grief died with Neustadt, I'll tell you, Mr Cooperman. A lot of grief and evil! How are you coming along since we talked?"

"I think that I've eliminated the threat of embarrassment over that antique car. It will cost you, but I didn't think that was a consideration. Your name won't come into it."

"My retarded son's business is no concern of yours, Cooperman. I'll deal with Shaw and York in my own way. I suppose you want to be thanked for your efforts, eh? But don't forget why I hired you. You lose me and you won't see a penny, I can assure you."

"Thanks for the testimonial, Mr Wise. I could get fat and rich on an endorsement like that."

"Save your wit for your work, Cooperman. Good-afternoon." He pulled at Mickey's arm and the three of them moved through the thinning crowd back to a car parked somewhere on the narrow lane that twisted its way through the cemetery.

"You never know what you'll find at a funeral!" I knew it was Pete without turning. He must have doubled around behind me, because I was still looking at the spot on the other side of the open plot where he had been standing.

"Hello, Pete. This is a bad day for the force. My deepest sympathy, Pete."

"Thanks, Benny. Nice crowd?"

"I guess it's a major loss, eh?"

"Old Ed had been retired from actively contributing to our efforts for some years, Benny. But this is the send-off he would have wanted: parade uniforms, muffled drums, slow march, all of that stuff. Ed liked the drill. Me, I don't much care for the soldiery, all that military stuff. It leaves me cold."

"All funerals do that. What took the late chief off to his reward, Pete? Some kind of accident, wasn't it?"

"Deputy chief, Benny. He never made it to the top. He was acting chief for a year; that was enough."

"That colonel from the Sally Ann gave him a first-rate send-off."

"He's a major, Benny, not a colonel."

"I guess he was well-liked, eh, Pete?"

"He had a few fans, Benny."

"Not enough to get him confirmed chief though?"

"Damned good thing too."

"You must have liked him a whole lot to spill this much affection in the shadow of his cortège, Pete. What's the story?"

"They tried to get rid of him years ago, but he wouldn't go. He held us back for years. He was an old-fashioned cop, Benny. He couldn't make the changes into modern times."

"I thought he led the way to reform."

"Eulogies, Benny. They take a tolerant view of the facts."

"So he was another casualty to progress?"

"He couldn't be budged until his sixty-fifth birthday. The Niagara Regional Police has been making great strides since he retired. We're almost caught up to Toronto."

"What took him in the end? What sort of accident?"

"Didn't you see it in the paper? If you didn't read it and you didn't know him personally, Benny, what brings you here this frosty afternoon? You working?"

"Maybe I'm interested in becoming a part of local history, Pete. Look at all of those tombstones. How many of them have Staziak or Cooperman written on them?" Behind Pete I could see Victoria Armstrong helping Wise into a limo. Mickey was standing on the driver's side looking at me.

"That's 'cause we come from good hardy stock, Benny. We don't fade away. We've got staying power. Hey! Are you trying to put me off? I asked if you were working, damn it!"

"I am. And it could get me into a lot of trouble if I was seen talking to the fuzz, Pete. Will you be at home tonight? I'll call you."

"Are you pulling my leg or is this for real? Yeah, I'll be at home minding my tropical fish."

"I'll be talking to you." Without looking in his direction, I moved off in the direction I'd seen the others go. The old policeman with his keeper was feeling all of his pockets as though he had lost his car keys or glasses, while the man in the windbreaker waited to help him into the front seat. My car was somewhere along the lane too, parked on the margin of brownish grass by the back wall. Looking up, I could see the dark branches of the maple and beech trees were putting on signs of the season to come. I put that down to the southerly slope of the cemetery away from the lake. Twigs were fattening and buds were looking shiny. Through the windshield, as I drove along the curved cemetery lanes to the street, I could see that it was starting to snow.

That night I called Pete from a phone booth in the lobby of the library. I had the idea that my own phone might not be safe. I was paranoid, I'm sure, but I thought that it wouldn't hurt to play it safe. Pete was home. I inquired after Shelley, his wife, and his kid, who always beat me at chess, and finally his damned fish to get his full attention. Then: "Okay, Pete, tell me about Ed Neustadt. It may help me in something I'm working on."

"He was a nut and a son of a bitch and a first-rate fellow officer. Which version are you looking for?"

"Spare me the praise. I got that this afternoon."

"Yeah, Ed and Major Patrick went back a long way. Their families went camping up near Bancroft. Some trailer camp. They used to go to hangings together."

"What? The families?" For a moment I imagined a scene from *The Oxbow Incident*.

"No, Benny, just Major Patrick and Neustadt. The major was the default clergyman. If the prisoner didn't send for the clergy of his choice, they'd send for Major Patrick. They really believed that eye-for-an-eye stuff. Oh, I don't blame the major. He was just doing his job, but Ed Neustadt just liked to be there. He liked to watch and then talk about it afterwards. He made me sick. Oh, the two of them were quite a pair."

"Is that what you mean by his being a nut-case?"

"It's a start. You couldn't penetrate him, Benny. When he had an idea in his head, no amount of evidence to the contrary could make him see reason. Once he had it in mind that you were guilty, he'd not rest until you were put away."

"Are you saying that he was a conscientious officer dedicated to his work, Pete?"

"You know goddamned well I'm not! He was Captain Bligh on Church Street, Benny. There was no sense of fairness or mercy in the man. No sense of when enough's enough. He was a bully, that's what he was, a bully and a sadist. I'm not saying that I'm glad he's dead, but, hell, I'm sure glad he isn't in charge of the day room any longer. Ask Chris when he gets back from Cyprus. Oh, he made my life hell for years. Everybody'll tell you that. No, that's not right. They'll all *say* he was the salt of the earth. And that's the memory that's being enshrined. For his widow's sake. For his daughter's."

"Tell me about his accident, Pete. I didn't read the account in the paper."

"He was fixing his car in his front driveway."

"Heart attack?"

"No, Benny. The jack holding the Buick up somehow released while he was trying to take the nut off the oil pan and the car came down on his chest. He was smashed up pretty bad. Must have been fast, though." Neither of us said anything for a minute. We both listened to the rock music that was somehow playing on our line as though from far away.

"What makes a jack come down like that, Pete? Don't you have to ratchet them down bit by bit? Or did it fall over?"

"This was hydraulic, like you see in garages. He went in for all the professional equipment. You should see his garage; looks like a car repair shop."

"That kind of jack doesn't ratchet down a stop at a time?"

"Can do. But mainly you release the valve and the car settles back to the driveway, or whatever."

"Pete, how does an accident like that happen?"

"Damn it, Benny! I'm getting the same ideas you're getting and I don't have any better answer than you do."

"What if somebody had it in for Neustadt?"

"I hear you."

"If you were under your car and I came along and knew my business, there's not a lot you could do about it, is there?"

We were quiet again for a few moments. The rock music had gone and had been replaced by distant voices, high-pitched women's voices, talking rapidly many miles away from Grantham.

"I'm going to look into this thing, Benny. I don't think anybody around here gave it a thought. I'll look at the report and see what has to be done."

"I'll be hearing from you, then?" I asked.

"The hell you will. This is police business. Internal. I won't even tell the Inspector about this until I've got something I can hold in my hand." I asked him about our friend Savas's holiday in Cyprus and speculated on the date of his return. Neither one of us could get very interested in that. Savas in the flesh was a formidable presence, but off at the eastern end of the Mediterranean he wasn't enough to keep the conversation going. So I hung up, just in time to see Phil, the hood I'd socked from my bed yesterday in my pre-dawn kidnapping, busy pretending not to be busy watching me from the coffee stand. He hadn't noticed that the stand was shut up for the night. A good man can never find the cover he needs when he wants it.

Walking home, I thought that the tidiest solution to the problem of Neustadt's death was this: Abe Wise, that long-lived crook, was living at this moment because he hired more than one man to look after his business for him. Ex-wife Lily was right. If Wise's enemy was the retired deputy chief, then someone would have been told to do something about it. It seemed an easy enough task to walk up a driveway, release a valve while asking street directions.

But, if Wise was responsible for Neustadt's death, why would he draw attention to himself by going to the funeral? He told me that his attendance at the funeral was just a device to help blacken Neustadt's name. That was a joke, wasn't it? There was no figuring Wise out. That was the only sure thing I got out of my walk.

Anna was waiting for me when I got in. Big surprise. Twice in one week! Once again, I tried to interest her in taking a short vacation in the middle of term. It wasn't on for a number of reasons. The one I liked best was "because you're not coming." It was an honest attempt, but I didn't get very far trying to argue with her.

Chapter Fourteen

The next morning I hoped that things would look better. The view from my window was not reassuring: more dull, cold weather. But the car across the street had become a steadying sign of continuity. Today was linked to yesterday and the rude awakening of the morning before that by that black Toyota. I recognized that there was a time when I had never heard of Abram Wise. That had become, in my imagination, a golden time, something to be likened to the Garden of Eden.

Anna had left hot, fresh coffee on the counter for me. I showered, shaved and dressed thinking of it. While actually drinking the coffee, I started thinking about Ed Neustadt and his Old Testament sense of justice and fair play. But Pete had suggested more than that. He spoke of a kind of craziness, some sort of sadistic fascination. That was getting me a long way from who was trying to kill Abe Wise, but I couldn't get rid of the notion that it was important.

How could the case of a hard cop, recently dead, have anything to do with my job? If Neustadt had been the threat, then he had been rubbed out. From my point of view as a hireling of Abe Wise, the threat was over and my time as a minion of this arch-crook was about to be terminated. If I was being careful before, now I would have to be doubly careful, because Wise might find it easier to pay me off with a bullet behind the ear rather than with negotiable paper.

With the night-time hours I'd put in yesterday and the day before, I thought I would open the office late on this, the third day of the job. As a matter of fact, I'd decided to finish the pot of coffee and read McStu's book from cover to cover. And that is what I did.

The story began as the Second World War came to an end. Sergeant Joseph Tatarski was demobilized with the called-up men in his regiment at Camp Niagara, a few miles from here. After being away from home for most of the war, Joe returned to his wife, Anastasia, his daughters, Margaret and Mary, and young son Freddy. All went well until Joe surprised a burglar one night in 1946. There was a fight and Joe was hit over the head and killed. The burglar escaped, leaving a sack of silver-plated wedding presents behind. The investigating officer, young Corporal Ed Neustadt, made a routine report to his sergeant.

Five years later, the burglary was, amazingly, repeated with a similar tragic ending. This time Anastasia, Joe Tatarski's widow was beaten to death with a table lamp while the household was apparently sleeping. Once again Ed Neustadt, now a sergeant, was in charge of the investigation. McStu suggests, short of inviting a writ for libel, that Neustadt approached this second murder with what he already knew about the first in mind. Picking his words carefully, McStu paints a picture of a policeman discovering that in the earlier case he'd been played for a sap by young Mary Tatarski. The two burglaries ending in two murders were just too convenient except in McStu's fiction. Neustadt was able to show that the signs of a break-in were a sham and quickly arrested Mary, then a young mother with no husband to stand up for her. Mary was put on trial, early in the new year, 1952, for the murder of her mother. The Crown was able to show a history of conflict and bad feeling that had existed in the house since the father's death. This was exacerbated when Mary found herself pregnant and in due course gave birth to a baby girl. When the older girl, Margaret, moved away, things got worse. Mary was a wild young woman who had friends who were allowed more liberty than the old-fashioned Anastasia allowed her. Neighbours testified to having heard running arguments, as well as the baby's cries, coming through the walls of the house. Counsel for Mary stated that the defendant had taken sleeping pills after the most recent noisy confrontation and that she was asleep when the crime occurred. The Crown, through the testimony of an expert, was successful in proving that the pills could just as well have been taken after the murder had been committed. They had apparently been taken in sufficient quantities to suggest that Mary intended to take her own life.

The trial was short. Although the jury recommended mercy, the judge pronounced the sentence of death. The appeal, which was based on the circumstantial nature of much of the evidence, was rejected, and a few minutes after midnight on Thursday, December 18, 1952, Mary Tatarski walked to the gallows. She was the second-last woman hanged in Canada. It was typical of her bad luck that she couldn't have contrived to be the last, which would at least have put her in the record books. She was only twenty-two.

On the face of it and judging by today's standards, the sentence and the punishment were barbaric. But stranger things happened in the 1950s. Other celebrated cases were reopened and retried, sometimes with a change in the verdict. A few years ago Donald Marshall, a young Micmac Indian from near Sydney, Nova Scotia, was freed after spending eleven years behind bars for a murder he had no part in. Certainly there were always activists, like Duncan Harvey locally, who were interested in rehearing the Tatarski case. Edwin Neustadt called them "pinko subversives" and "bleeding hearts." He fought all their efforts to reopen the investigation. I was beginning to get a fix on the late former deputy chief. He was a charmer, all right. The world was divided into two kinds of people: good guys and bad guys. There was no crossing over, no grey areas, no special cases. I guess, for a policeman, it would simplify things. But what about people like Wise? He has never been convicted of breaking a city by-law. He gives to charity, supports the arts, helps pay for *Tannhauser* whether he can sit through it or not. Lots of business people today operate in grey areas where the law can't touch them. Such people would be shocked if you called them crooks. This was the realm of white-collar crime that someone of Neustadt's frame of mind would have a hard time dealing with. Subtlety and ambiguity are hard to judge on a scale from zero to ten. It's hard to get a fix on the bottom line. I suddenly imagined Neustadt's tombstone with the following epitaph engraved upon it:

Never indicted

I was saved from more speculation by a blast from the telephone. Picking it up, I heard a voice with a rasp in a high register. "Mr Cooperman?" the voice began. It didn't sound familiar. It was a woman, but beyond that, I was stumped.

"That's right. Who is this?"

"I'm calling from the office of the Registrar, Ontario Provincial Police."

"Uh-huh. What can I do for you?"

"I'm looking at a list of recent complaints against you," she said. "You are well aware of the fact that the Registrar takes a dim view of licensees bringing this office into bad repute. If there is a repetition of the complaints we have been getting, we may have to convene the licensing committee."

"This sounds a lot like a threat. My licence isn't due to be renewed for a year. And why are you calling me at home to tell me this? I have an office."

"All licences are subject to review, Mr Cooperman. It's a question of maintaining standards."

I told her to put what she had told me in writing. They hate doing that. I've used the ploy before and it always works like a charm. I would have liked to suggest that she give the name of my client to the active departments of her OPP office, but it seemed both futile and disloyal, so I kept my mouth shut.

I tried to imagine where the complaints were coming from. The names Shaw and York quickly came to mind. I was getting in the way of a profitable scam and they, quite rightly, resented it. There's nothing in the rule book that says that the bad guys can't enlist the help of the law. After all, wasn't I going to be paid off in money earned in all sorts of ways I didn't want to know about?

I was just beginning to think about lunch, when there was a knock on the door. When I got there, I saw two familiar faces. "Are we going for a ride? Have I been summoned?" I said to one of them. "I thought you preferred the early morning, Mickey." I backed away from the door to allow Mickey and Victoria Armstrong to come in. Victoria's eyes ran fingers over all my dusty surfaces.

"I was just checking up on you, Cooperman. You didn't go to your office in the middle of the week, so I wanted to see if you were being cute with me. Phil Green's taking the afternoon off. He has to go to the dentist. So, I'm the guy with the short straw. You met my wife the other night, right?" Victoria and I shook hands and momentarily achieved eye contact.

"I just came along in case there's a chance to do some shopping," she said. "Mickey's schedule makes for a rough marriage, Mr Cooperman. Mr Wise treats us well, but he often forgets that Mickey needs time off."

She was dark and tidy-looking, with large brown eyes and nice skin. Her heavy wool skirt and brown boots told me about the weather outside and the pastels of her blouse and sweater told of the spring we were expecting every hour.

"I was thinking of lunch," I said. "Any takers?" The Armstrongs looked at each other and then Mickey grinned.

"I guess we have to eat somewhere. And you're on expenses."

"Aren't *you*? Or is this bodyguarding included in normal duties?"

We didn't go to the Di, or to the Wellington Court, but to the restaurant downstairs, which was now called *Beit al Din*, a Middle Eastern place with travel posters showing off the beauties of Lebanon: vistas of crusader castles, glimpsed through Gothic arches, the cliffs of the Beirut seafront. I had been keeping an eye on this place ever since the Hungarian restaurant that it displaced closed down. The location had seen half a dozen unsuccessful attempts at exotic cuisine. This was the first to survive for more than a year. A waitress, who echoed what Paulette must have looked like in her bosomy prime, gave us a big smile and seated us near the back. Neither Mickey nor I could make head or tail of the menu, so

Victoria ordered for all of us.

"Are you always called Victoria?" I asked. "It seems such a formal name."

"Believe it or not, I was named after Queen Victoria. My father wanted only the best for me. Before I met Mickey, my friends called me Vicky, but the combination of Mickey and Vicky was too much. And Mickey refuses to go back to Mike or Michael. When I was in high school I envied a girl with the same last name as me. She was called Lally Tate. Isn't that marvellous? Wouldn't you die to be Lally Tate? Are you always called Benny?"

"I hate to admit it, but I can't get anybody to make it just Ben. I can live with anything, even Benjamin, but I'm hoping one day to meet somebody who'll take a shine to just Ben."

"I'll try it on," Victoria said just as the plates began to arrive. First there was a beige-coloured paste called "hummus" which went well with the flat pita bread, then came some vegetable salads with rice and tomatoes, followed by pieces of grilled chicken on skewers. There was some eggplant too. When I asked what that was, she gave me a name that sounded like a sneeze.

"Where did you learn about this stuff?" I asked her. Victoria threw her head back and laughed.

"I may have been born here, Ben, but I have lived all over the place. There's a place in Old Greenwich, north of New York, where I used to live, with the same menu. There are dozens of places like this in Toronto and New York. My first husband was a broker and, because of his clients, he enjoyed all the varieties of Middle and Far Eastern cooking. Do you know the cookbooks by Madhur Jaffrey?"

I told her that I hadn't run across them. Then she started in on traditional Jewish cooking and I found I knew as little about that as I did about the food we were eating. "I eat simply," I said. "Soup, a sandwich. Basic fare. That's me. Were you always interested in food?"

"I can't remember a time when I wasn't. The kitchen is the heart of a home, for me anyway. I've always loved to cook." That seemed to stop further conversation in the food line so we ate in silence for a few minutes.

"How did you two get together?" I asked, wondering what kind of answer I might get. They both answered at the same time.

"Victoria came to cook for—"

"Mickey was working—" We all laughed, attracting the attention of the waitress, who smiled at our pleasure.

"Mr Wise had business in Old Greenwich, and when he heard…" Victoria looked at Mickey for help.

"Victoria's husband was in a boating accident. They never found him."

"I'm sorry," I said inadequately.

"So, I came to Grantham to live," she said, and added, taking Mickey's hand in hers, "and I haven't regretted it." Mickey moved in the direction of a blush, but he strangled it at birth.

"I dug that slug out of the hutch in Mr Wise's office, Benny," Mickey said, biting into a round, brown meatless meatball. "It was a smallish bullet like a .32."

"Is the glass in that room anything special?"

"Antique, like the rest of the house. But, I see what you mean: it wasn't bullet-proof, just ordinary window glass."

"Wise talked to me of two attempts on his life: the shot and then the steering on the Volvo. Were there other attempts that you know about?"

"We watch him pretty well," Mickey said. "Victoria does all the cooking in the house. Next door, the boys manage on their own. Fast food, mostly pizza."

"Give them their due, Mickey. They fry up a storm for breakfast."

"When they're not filling their faces, they're a good team."

"I didn't get a very good look at where exactly the house is in relation to the rest of the nearby houses. Do you have a good view of traffic in and out?"

"That's why Wise picked that place. Dorset Crescent is a dead-end street. No through traffic. There's always a lookout checking who's coming and going."

"Mr Wise is pretty strict about the lookout, Ben," Victoria said. The mail gets delivered next door, where one of the boys sorts it and checks odd-looking parcels."

"There's no way a letter bomb could get through to Mr Wise," Mickey added. "And if anything came to his uptown office, they'd catch it there."

"Tell me about uptown, Mickey."

"The legit operation. Wisechoice Import and Export."

"Gotcha. You were talking about security?"

"He doesn't even use the Volvo all that much. But if he uses any of the cars, that's the one he likes to drive."

"So, whoever it is, it's someone who knows Mr Wise very well," Victoria said, echoing the thought percolating in my head.

Soon the bouncy waitress brought coffee served in little brass ewers. Victoria caught me admiring the bounciness and we both smiled. The coffee inside the ewers was sweet and thick. I liked it. The meal was rounded off with some cake made of puff pastry with green pistachios bathing in honey. I liked that too. Anna would have enjoyed the meal. I promised myself to suggest the *Beit al Din* the next time it was my turn to be inventive.

"Was there a special reason you wanted to see me again, Mickey? So soon after our chat in your car?"

"Mostly I just wanted to get out of the house. He's been hell to live with since that cop's funeral yesterday. He tore my head off six or seven times. I was glad Phil got an abscess."

"What is the link between Wise and Neustadt? That's what I want to know."

"It's just cops and crooks. Nothing strange about that," Mickey said.

"No, there's something more. I'll be damned if I know what it is."

"The deputy chief could never make a charge stick against Mr Wise," Victoria put in. "He says that all the time. But why would that make Mr Wise angry? I see what you mean, Ben."

"It's a puzzlement, all right. Mickey, was Mr Wise upset about Neustadt before his death?"

"Mr Wise hated that cop's guts. He hasn't talked about it lately, but after Neustadt's accident, you couldn't shut him up."

"I can vouch for that," Victoria said.

"If Wise felt that bad about Neustadt, Mickey, he could have done something about it. Would you know about that?"

Mickey took a moment to answer, sipping his coffee. "I'm his regular link with his usual people. But, he has a phone in his office and one by his bed. He knows people who do that sort of work. Beyond that, I can't say."

I couldn't quite get over this sudden *glasnost* in the air between me and Mickey. Maybe his wife had softened him. I guess it made better sense keeping an eye on me from across a table. It beat sitting in a chilly car or trying to keep out of the wind on St Andrew Street. From my point of view, I didn't mind sitting opposite them. It's easier to study faces close up. And Victoria's face, which I hardly had noticed that early Monday morning, was beginning to grow on me. She was attractive in a more subtle way than the waitress, and concealed her age very well. She had a style of dressing all her own. Sort of arts-and-crafts school. I doubted whether Julie had been giving her fashion tips.

When they said goodbye, I thought that it was at last time to go to work.

Chapter Fifteen

At the office, my service passed on the facts that I'd had a call from the Registrar of the Ontario Provincial Police and a message from Har Twize, according to the spelling I was given. I thanked my service for passing on my home number to the OPP and told her never to do it again. When I called Hart Wise, I got an answering machine, which gave me the best idea I'd had all day. I left my number and put my shoes up on my desk. I formed them into a "V" for "Victory" and thought of Joe Tatarski fighting through the war and then coming home to an early grave. It was dirty luck, no matter how you looked at it.

I called Duncan Harvey's office. Apart from being the big authority on the Tatarski case, next to McStu, he was in a partnership with a couple of people I was in high school with. When Pat Voisard's voice came on the line, I could still hear him reading out the athletic announcements to the senior assembly. It was a breathless staccato that made me feel young again. I told Pat who was speaking and with only a moment's delay I was talking to Duncan Harvey. I told him about just finishing McStu's book and that I was wondering whether I could see him.

"An architect has all the time in the world these days,

Mr Cooperman. The economic climate can't be helping you either. Do you want to meet me here at the office, or would you like to meet outside?"

"Your place will be fine," I said. We set a time, just an hour away, and I hung up. I was a little surprised and a little flattered that I didn't have to explain my line of business. If Duncan Harvey was anything to go by, it was common knowledge.

I took a yellow block of foolscap and wrote a few names on the top page:

Margaret Tatarski (sister)
Freddy Tatarski (brother)
Mrs Neustadt
Neustadt's daughter
Dave Rogers
Major Patrick

I put in a call to Dave Rogers and another to the Sally Ann officer who had been such a great pal of Neustadt's. The policeman's family could wait. They had their hands full just managing their grief. I might never have to bother them. Pete Staziak would help me with the whereabouts of the leftover Tatarskis I hoped, if I couldn't get the information from Harvey or McStu. They weren't listed in the local phone directory or in the Buffalo or Hamilton books. I tried Toronto and struck out again after a few wrong numbers.

While I was killing time waiting for people to phone back, I compared the photographs in *Haste to the Gallows* with the list of names. There was Joe, the sergeant in uniform with a big grin and his arms akimbo. It was battle-dress he was wearing, with a short tunic and a wedge cap on the side of his head. From the look of him, the army had been a home away from home for Joe. He looked comfortable, like a foreman getting a bottle from his work gang. Ready for a scramble-net or a three-day pass, he had found his full achievement in a khaki uniform. Since he was murdered in 1946, he only had a few months to adapt to Civvy Street.

Across the page was a blurred picture of Anastasia, his wife. She was a big-boned woman, strong, by the look of her arms and back, and determined, if the line of her jaw was any guide. Her dark hair was mostly covered in a babushka. She had been a handsome woman, but in this photograph, taken according to the cutline just after Joe's murder, she appeared middle-aged, even older. Was this the girl Joe came home to?

On the next page were pictures of the children of this unlikely couple: Margaret, in rimless glasses, wearing a wartime nurse's aide or Red Cross uniform; Freddy, the youngest, a weedy lad in a Boy Scout outfit, holding a large roll of what might have been aluminum foil; and the biggest picture: Mary Tatarski, the second-last woman to be hanged in Canada, looking very much alive and ready to go out dancing. She had her mother's strong features, but with a lightness and vivacity. Her lips, coloured red in real life, but here in the picture looking nearly black, were parted in a smile that showed even teeth and a memorable smile. Was this the face of a killer, I asked myself. Not at first glance, no.

Duncan Harvey's face was a familiar one when I saw it in his bright studio-like office. I'd seen it on King Street and around town over the years. It was a rugged, handsome face, the sort that comes with ski clothes and Alpine peaks. Behind his desk he was dressed more conventionally, but there was a trace of the great outdoors about him and the sun-filled room was as close to that element as could be found away from the *Beacon*'s Travel Section. When I came in, he and Pat Voisard were talking shop. I heard "Abu Dhabi" and "Shiraz," which sounded like nice places to visit, but they broke this up when they saw me, and, after an exchange of greetings with Pat, I was left facing Duncan Harvey, who sat back in a chrome and black-leather chair that inspired confidence. I told him again that I had just finished reading McStu's book about the Tatarski case, which he applauded with a smile.

"McStu's book is an excellent beginning, Mr Cooperman. All the facts are there. He did a first-rate job. The next trick is to get enough publicity so they'll reopen the case."

"But the woman's dead, Mr Harvey. I don't get it. Why are you carrying the banner?"

"Some of my friends would say it's because I'm a damned fool. Others think it's because I'm one of nature's born crusaders. One in every hundred thousand of the population. I don't know, I think it's because you can't let them get away with it. Maybe. I guess I want to show that we have to be careful with human life. Look at the Marshall case. Who gave a damn about what happened to him? Harry Wheaton, the Mountie who dug up the evidence that cleared him, that's who. Some of us have to wave the banner so that there's some direction to the march. I don't know. And, you're right. Mary Tatarski will be just as dead at the end of a retrial as she is right now."

"I'm interested in the part that Ed Neustadt played in the story," I said. "I'm also curious about what happened to the people who survived."

"Yes. Nobody survives a trauma like that intact. Mary's sister..."

"Margaret," I added to be helpful.

"Yes, well, she moved away, as did the others. She

killed herself in Sarnia about four years after Mary was executed. You can't tell me that those deaths aren't related." I shook my head in disbelief.

"You see, Mr Cooperman…"

"Benny, please."

"Well, Benny, a case like this is like a great plane crash. Not only are there out-and-out casualties, but there's all kinds of indirect fallout. Casualties on the ground, lives bent out of shape, careers ended, relationships forever altered. You can see that operating here. Margaret is just the most dramatic case. The young brother, Fred, had to get out of town too. Grew up in foster homes. Only he came back here with a changed name and made a big success of his life. He was a credit to the Children's Aid, if you disregard his alcoholism and occasional violence." Harvey's voice was deep and touched with the echo of an English accent, although I would bet he was native-born. Maybe he'd worked abroad or married into the Old Country.

"I guess that just adds more reasons for staying away from the death penalty."

"We see that now, it's just too bad we didn't see it earlier."

"When did Fred Tatarski die?"

"It was a little over two years ago. Bone cancer."

"How did he make his big success?"

"Ever hear of the Nuts & Bolts garage chain? That's Fred Tatarski. Only he changed his name to Tait."

"Any family?"

"A boy, Charles Edward, who died young. Meningitis or something. And a girl, Drina. She's Mary's daughter. He brought her up as his own as soon as he was settled and working. Joe Tatarski had a brother who used to work at Patterson and Corbin in the shop. Retired now, I guess. He's changed his name too. He's Bill Tarson, lives over on Eastchester. Glengarry Apartments. We did that building back in the seventies. Needs updating, but we can't—"

"Wait a minute! Back up a bit. Who was the father of Mary's kid and what happened to him?"

"Now that's a mystery that leads nowhere. He was a kid who had dropped out of school. Grew up next door. He went out with Mary when she could escape from that house—old Anastasia used to guard the doors like a prison warden—and he had vanished from the scene before she knew she was pregnant. He went to work in a winery in Jordan and then went out to Delhi to the tobacco farms. I found him in Kitchener, working in a hostel for unemployed men. There wasn't a lot he could tell me. It wasn't a case of somebody erasing a bad memory from his mind so it wouldn't torment him; he just couldn't remember Mary very clearly and had never heard about his daughter until I told him."

"Does he have a name?"

"For what it's worth: Thaddeus Nemerov."

"Thaddeus Nemerov," I repeated.

"Now don't tell me you're going to remember that?"

"It might turn up again. You never can tell."

"As Shaw is always saying."

"What! Shaw?" I surprised Harvey with my sudden animation. "What about Gordon Shaw?"

"I don't know a Gordon Shaw; I'm talking about the writer: George Bernard Shaw. Benny, are you feeling unwell?"

"I'm fine, Duncan. Just fine," I said, relaxing my grip on the arm of the chair. "I know it's not in the book, but do you know of any connection between Abram Wise and the Tatarski case?" I was shooting wild and blind, but what the hell?

"Abram Wise? You mean the crime boss? No, I haven't seen any mention of his name. There wasn't any involvement with organized crime in this case. Just incompetent investigation and incomplete disclosure to the defence lawyer. Neustadt was responsible for both."

"What was behind Neustadt's zeal, do you think? Did he know the family?"

"No. After the first blunders, I think he was covering up for himself. He was an ox of stubbornness. Of course, he was the first officer on the scene when the father was killed. That's in the book. So he knew the family. Did you know him, Benny?" I shook my head. "He didn't want me getting together with McStu on this book. He knew it wouldn't do his name or character any good. He was right. He died just in time."

"Not quite. I think he had time to write to the papers denouncing the book."

"What else could he do? If we are right about Mary Tatarski, he was wrong. I don't want to be too hard on Neustadt. He's an easy target: a prisoner of old-fashioned ideas, a certain inflexibility of character."

"Would you include dishonesty?"

"In a manner of speaking. He wouldn't call it that, though. Any shifting of facts in aid of a foregone conclusion was legitimate as far as he was concerned. If a nasty fact got in the way, he'd dispose of it somehow, just as we have to get rid of older buildings when we put up new ones."

"The law's supposed to be different. If the facts don't fit, you're supposed to look for a new theory. That's what makes it scientific."

"Don't tell me about it. I know. And most of the people at Niagara Regional know it. Neustadt was a sport, a throw-back, a walking dinosaur who didn't know he was extinct."

"Who knew him best, would you say?"

"Talk to Major Colin Patrick. They were good friends."

"I've heard that. Would you say that Ed Neustadt had a, shall we say, sadistic side?"

"Is this just curiosity, Benny, or are you working on something? Pat told me that you're an investigator. Am I likely to be called on to give evidence?" Something in my question had put Harvey on his guard. I wanted to know what it was.

"I don't think so. But it's more than curiosity. I think that there was a sadistic side to the prosecution of this case. Had that ever occurred to you?"

"Hell yes! But I couldn't say anything as long as Neustadt was alive. McStu has already been on the phone to his publisher about a new edition of *Haste to the Gallows*. It's a hard world, Benny. But, I must say that I won't be worried about libel any more. Those nightmares are gone forever."

"Whatever happened to Mary Tatarski's daughter? Is she around?"

"She spent a year at Napier McNabb University in Hamilton. That's the last we know about her. She was at her stepfather's funeral, back in 1992, of course. Then she disappeared."

"Disappeared?"

"Perhaps that's a little melodramatic. I mean I think she married and settled down somewhere."

"I guess that's one way to disappear." Harvey laughed at that and asked if I would like a cup of tea. I said "fine," so we had some.

I wanted to tell Harvey that I suspected that my client might have murdered Neustadt, but I bit my tongue.

Bad-mouthing clients is a hell of a way to get ahead. Pat Voisard joined us when the kettle boiled and we talked of general things. Pat told us what it was like growing up in the farming country outside town and going to school way out Pelham Road. Harvey treated us to some photographs taken on a recent skiing vacation. Before I left the architects' office, Harvey asked me to call around again or to call if I had any fresh ideas on the Tatarski case. I told him I would.

Chapter Sixteen

I spent an hour or two trying to put down on paper what I'd discovered that might be of interest to Wise. It amounted to so little that I widened the margins on my typewriter to stretch out the text a little. Leaving a line blank between paragraphs helped too. It looked better that way from a design point of view.

My typing was interrupted twice, once by each of Wise's offspring: Hart, returning my call as though we hadn't already had words, and Julie, probably at her mother's prompting. With Hart I made an appointment to see him at 9:00 p.m. that evening at a pub he goes to up near Secord University. That sounded promising for the prodigal son.

Julie was another matter. She'd telephoned to say that she didn't want to talk to me.

"Why'd you call then? Because your mother asked you to?"

"You got it. I guess you're a good detective, eh?"

"Would your father put up with less than the best?"

"Do you always answer a question with one?"

"Whenever I get a chance. You know that somebody's trying to kill your old man?"

"I've been expecting to hear that he's been murdered since before I had braces on my teeth. I used to have dreams about it. Every time I use an airport parking lot, I think that's where Daddy's going to be found in the trunk of a BMW."

"I like your imagination, Julie."

"Yeah, I'm not even telling you the good stuff. Mummy says that you're a scrumptious bit, is she putting me on?"

"Mummy's putting you on. And 'scrumptious' isn't one of her expressions, is it?"

"I do like your voice. You've got a ballsy kind of voice. Bet you're a Leo. Leo's are unpredictable and sexy."

"I'm pistachio. That's what I always say."

"What month were you born in?"

"Julie, I haven't got time for this. If you want to see me, fine, we'll pick a time. If you don't want to see me it's been nice talking to you."

"How do you get off using my first name, Mr Cooperman? I'm not a child."

"You tell me what to call you, Julie, and I'll write it down somewhere, okay? Have you any idea who wants to see your old man dead?"

"Me, for one."

"It's a start. How come?"

"He's a lousy father. When I was small, I never saw him. When I was a teenager, he wouldn't let me alone."

"Are you talking abuse?"

"I'm talking about his never letting me have any fun. He watched me like a hawk. Nobody was ever good enough for his precious Julie, so I sat home reading *Vogue* and *Elle*."

"Is that why you married young? To get out of the house?"

"To get away from *him!* That's dead on. The poor young *shlump* didn't know I picked him just to drive

Daddy crazy."

"Did it work?"

"No. Daddy had it annulled before he'd figured out how to unhook my bra. I had better luck the second time. Are you still there, Mr Cooperman?"

"Just. Why don't you name a place where you want to eat your dinner and I'll meet you there. I've got an office full of clients and my assistants can overhear everything we say."

"I can't do dinner. That's out the window. Where will you be around one?"

"In the morning? I hope I'll be in bed. What about tomorrow?"

"If you really want to see me, be at the Patriot Volunteer over the river at one. See yuh," she said and hung up.

The Patriot Volunteer had a familiar ring to it. It was a roadhouse on the Lewiston-Youngstown road, a dance-hall and lounge that catered to locals from New York state and to Canadians who wanted to meet at a discreet distance from their own backyard. I had been there a few times years ago, but I had almost forgotten that it still existed.

I went back to my report wondering whether I was giving my client value for his money. I'd met with most of the people who have been important to him, I had uncovered no plot to send him to join his ancestors. If there was a plot, it was cleverer than I was. But I wrote it all down, all of the things I knew for sure and added the things I suspected. Even with wide margins, it didn't fill a lot of paper.

It was some time later in the afternoon. The shadows had moved along the walls. I must have dozed off in my chair as I sometimes do. I blamed it on the lunch, which almost demanded a restorative nap on an oriental divan to get those rose-water flavoured sweets out of the system. I say I had been asleep, but I wasn't asleep when it happened. When it happens in the movies, it makes a bigger bang. All I heard was the sound of a thud in the wall. That was followed immediately by the noise of shattering glass. A mug, left on top of the filing cabinet just over my left shoulder, was suddenly in pieces both there and on the floor. A fine shower of glass from my window covered the papers in front of me. I dropped to the floor as a second shot came through the window. I pulled the phone down with me and called 911. I told the dispatcher that I was being shot at from across the street; the Russell House was the best bet, I said, but I wasn't about to examine the view from the window too closely. I could see two tidy holes in my window now. The second shot had buried itself in the metal filing cabinet with a loud ping. But the big noise must have been across the street. As the target, I wasn't being treated to either sound or light.

Whoever was doing the shooting must have been on the run already. He couldn't be sure he missed me with that second shot, because I hit the floor at almost the same moment it came through the window. He would have to get out of the hotel fast. If this was the same person who took a shot at Wise, he was still not getting close enough to do any damage. No professional hitman could get away with this amateurish approach.

I crawled along the floor in the direction of my door, pulled my coat down and upset the stand as I overbalanced it. The crash to the floor was the loudest noise of the whole encounter. I pulled my coat after me into Dr Bushmill's office next door. Frank was a chiropodist, a scholar and a friend. He'd taken lumps on his head on my behalf more than once. In the waiting room there were two middle-aged women and a young mother with a little boy with a tear-stained face. I rushed in and looked out from the window farthest from my own. The hotel stood where it always had. The shot had come from almost directly across the street, from a second- or third-floor window. I wanted to rush down the stairs and across the street, but the gun could even now be trained on the front door of my building. I raked the second-floor windows with my eyes. One window was open, the rest were closed. The floor above looked deserted. I watched the street door of the hotel. Nobody came out. Nobody on the street had stopped. Nobody was looking up at my windows.

"What! Benny? What brings you here?" It was Frank Bushmill.

"Sorry to intrude, Frank, but I wanted to look out your window." I didn't want to mention shooting or bullets from across the street. I was pretty sure that it wasn't a random shooting nut that had fired at me. That meant that Frank's clients were in no danger. They were sitting with their backs to a safe wall anyway.

"A heavy snow is rare this late in the season," Frank observed. Snow? I hadn't even noticed.

I gathered my coat and carried it to the back of the building, where I climbed down the fire-escape for the first time in over fifteen years. It was snowing all right, whitening everything in sight, and making the rusty stairs treacherous but not a bit quieter.

My office backed on a ravine leading down to a textile mill, so I had a longer way to go down than I realized. At the rear, my office was four floors up. I didn't worry about all the irrelevant garbage going through my head.

It was the voice of shock or panic or something. I just had to listen and keep moving.

I walked up the incline of the alley between my building and the bank next door. I still couldn't hear sirens. And there was a noise behind me.

"Jesus, Mary and Joseph, Benny, what's afoot?" It was Frank. He must have bounded down the fire-escape after me. I don't remember hearing him.

"Frank, somebody in the Russell House just put two bullets through my window." Frank's snow-bedecked eyebrows rose to his hairline.

"No! You've called the garda? The cops, I mean?"

"They're taking a hell of a long time getting here!" Great fat flakes were falling silently between us as we shot at them with steaming breath.

"Thanks for not frightening my pigeons. I'd better get back to them, unless I can help. I left Mrs Sampson with her foot soaking. I'd best pull her out. God bless," he said and was gone down the alley again, slipping and sliding, to Mrs Sampson's bunions.

When I looked again across St Andrew Street, there were two cruisers parked in front of the James Street door of the hotel's pub. One man sat in the front seat of the closest cruiser. Pedestrians seemed unaware of the situation; they came out of stores and crossed the street with the lights and against the lights as usual, their heads tucked in against the weather. After a minute, three men in uniform came out the pub door. A passer-by laughed to her friend at this, and said something that set them both giggling. I was watching them when I also caught a glimpse of the skinheaded hood who sat beside me on my drive to see Wise last Monday morning. It was him all right, tattoos, earrings, the works. I'd know his blue skin anywhere. Was he the shooter? Or was it just his turn to play minder? The three cops conferred with the driver of the cruiser, who pointed across at my office. My minder, the skinhead, melted into the late-shopping crowd along St Andrew Street. The three uniforms crossed through the one-way traffic. I met them at the street door.

"Hello," I said. "My name's Cooperman. The shots came into my office from across the street in the hotel."

"We better have a look," one of them said.

"Sure, the bullets will wait for you. But what about the shooter? Don't you think you should search the hotel?"

"Look, Mr Cooperman. The hotel is semi-closed down. There are repair people all over the place. We found the room where the shot was fired from…" As he said this, another cop waved a clear plastic bag with two long brass casings inside. "A carpenter said that a guy wearing a heavy parka came through the hall carrying a sports bag. He went out of the pub entrance three minutes before we showed up. So what's the percentage running all over town, when we can phone in a description from upstairs while we look at the holes in your wall."

Since there was no chance to catch the sniper on the run, I did the next best thing: I invited the uniforms upstairs. Here they marked the bullet holes with a magic marker for the next batch of cops, and tried to line up the two window holes and the marked circles. We all could see that they ran straight across the street to the partly open window. I could see a shape in the room, which made me alert the cops, but the figure waved back when the three with me waved across the street.

By the time I'd talked to a young officer and told him that the sniper could have been a whole filing case full of former clients and their disaffected spouses, Niagara Regional wiped its hands of me. I was cautioned to be careful. It was suggested that I get out of town for a few days. I thought of having them forward that request to my employer. The forensic team turned out to be one man, who looked like a telephone repairman. He gouged one of the bullets from the wall and showed me where the other had chewed its way through several dozen files in a drawer, doing the sort of damage you might blame on a hungry gerbil.

When the office was clear, I went next door again, where Frank poured me a tumbler full of Irish whiskey with his own name on the bottle. I wanted to ask him about that, but I didn't have the energy. I downed my medicine and took another shot. Both neat. Soon my hands stopped trembling. By then, the calm voice in my head, the one that is so maddeningly serene in emergencies, had gone away to bother another creature in panic. All I wanted to do now was find a place to have the other half of my interrupted nap. Frank helped out here too. "I'll leave you the rest of this, Benny. There's a pillow and a blanket in the cupboard." I don't know what he did with his last patients and I didn't ask. He clicked his office door's spring catch and told me to close it after me when I left. I helped myself to another ounce from the bottle he'd left, then curled up on his couch and fell asleep. I slept covered by my coat until well after dark.

Chapter Seventeen

The road that wound its way up the Escarpment to Secord University was the road I practised on for my driving test many years ago. It was narrow, curving and steep, and, remarkably, totally unchanged in twenty years. There are all sorts of intersections that are carved up regularly by the Department of Public Works, intersections that offer a clear view on all sides. I wasn't complaining. God knows there's little enough of my home town left the way it used to be.

That night, this familiar hill was thick with snow and slush. The evening rush hour hadn't cleared much of a path; it just made the climb slower. No salt or gravel had been scattered to make our way easier. I could see tracks where a car had applied too much brake coming down. The car could just be seen off to the side in a thicket of saplings. To my right, as I came safely to the top, lay Secord University, named after the heroic wife who brought news of a forthcoming battle to the British officer whose headquarters were not much farther down the road. There was a commemorative plaque attached to the ruins of the house containing the ambiguous information that Laura Secord spent three nights under this roof with Lieutenant (later Colonel) Fitzgibbon.

The university was housed in one huge tower sitting

on the edge of the Escarpment, where it beamed the virtues of higher education to the hundreds of thousands of people living on the plain below (to say nothing of those in passing lake boats).

Smart Alex was a watering-hole for undergraduates. The decor and atmosphere, as well as the crowd, spoke loudly of early cynicism and idealistic values twisted around a pretzel. The beer was fairly cheap and available on draught. The circular room was divided into curved areas on two or three levels, with a long bar running along one side for those who were looking for a listener. The space was punctuated with relics from the past: figureheads, anchors, gum machines, penny scales and old-fashioned business signs.

I sat down on a stool and ordered a draught of the local Grindstone lager and waited. It was still about seven minutes to nine. I watched, by way of the mirror behind the bar, three young women with short hair being sandwiched between crew-cut linemen or their look-alikes. They were all having a great time ordering burgers and potato skins. When one of them caught sight of a sign that read "bust developer," the young woman who least needed this sort of therapy began pounding the nearest male on his chest. They all thought it was very funny. Glasses of beer were emptied as the food was consumed and new glasses appeared to replace them.

"Hi! Come to spy out the talent?" It was Hart Wise and he was right on time. Hart was full of surprises. I moved my gaze away from the pretty sophomores to the expensive leather jacket—black, naturally—and blue jeans of Abram Wise's son. The stiff, cold wind that came with the snow had reddened his face, so that it borrowed colour from his hair. Hart was wearing a grey sweater under the jacket, which he had taken off and placed on his stool before sitting down. He stuffed a wool cap into the dangling sleeve of the jacket. Wise ordered a draught beer from another small Ontario brewery and we both settled into putting foam moustaches on our upper lips.

"Where do you stand in your father's will?" I asked when we had placed empty glasses on the deck.

Hart smiled at my forthrightness, I guess, and said: "Go fuck yourself." He said it smiling, so I ignored the suggestion.

"You know there have been attempts on his life?"

"What else is new? That's the sort of life he's led. He's a first-rate candidate for a closed coffin. He always was."

"But you're not trying to put him there?"

"Hey-hey! Let's keep this friendly. I couldn't be on worse terms with my father. We hate one another's guts. There's too much history between us to change that. But I've been trying to find out who's behind this since my Mom told me. Not a word of this to the old man, you understand?" I nodded in some surprise, more to see if I was still hearing correctly than as a promise of anything.

"What have you found out?"

"This latest crop of hired men are the worst set he has ever had. Apart from Mickey, who isn't just one of the boys and has always been above suspicion, I wouldn't trust the rest with delivering handbills."

"Mickey's not above suspicion. That's the first rule. Nobody is above suspicion. It's the only way to operate."

"Okay, okay! I hear what you're saying. But as for the rest of them...!"

"Where did he find them?"

"He picks them up through the jobs they do for him. If they work out, after a while he reels them in a little closer. Finally, they're working for the house. Phil Green's been there longest after Mickey. He's not as dumb as he looks, but not much smarter either. Sidney, he's the driver, has a record of petty crime going back to the seventies. He's great as a driver, but he doesn't know which side of a stamp to lick."

"That leaves one."

"Sylvester Ryan's a punk that fell off a motorcycle and landed where my old man found him, bought him some new clothes and gave him a job. Syl's loyal, as long as he's being paid, and tough, but that's all. Dad thinks he can be pointed against artillery to advantage. He hasn't been tested yet." And then he added, "As far as I know."

"Is that place of your dad's an arsenal? I haven't seen much of it?"

"It could hold off the United States Marines for a few hours. The place is well set up and has an escape tunnel that comes out behind the house."

"I thought I had a headache before I talked to you, now it's worse. Why do you keep up this feud with your old man?"

"Didn't my mother tell you?"

"She told me what she thought. That's not the same as asking you." He was halfway down his third draught and I was just starting in on my second. He paused to think before speaking. A good precaution.

"We've been scrapping since I was a kid. He was the one who sent my mother away. He tried to explain it, but that made things worse. He said she'd always be there for me, but whenever I wanted her, it 'wasn't convenient.' The same thing happened with my dog, Sparky. 'He's still your dog, Hart. He just doesn't live here any more.' Is it any wonder we fought?"

"So you blame him for your rotten life?"

"I didn't ask to be born, Cooperman! I didn't plan on being the son of Abe Wise, the big-shot gangster. Give me a break!"

"Sorry. Just trying to understand. All of the people I've talked to are sure that the threat to Abe's life comes from close to home, not from his business contacts. What do you think?"

"As a crook, he plays it as straight as he can, as straight as anybody. He doesn't talk to the cops, they don't ask him any questions. It's a funny game of cops and robbers. They make the rules up themselves out of I don't know what, but they all stick by them once they're there."

"Isn't it peculiar that he's never been caught?"

"He's clever. He keeps his secrets and pays everybody along the way."

"Does he pay off the cops?"

"Ha! He'd love to hear you say that. They come in too many flavours for that. Besides even the cops are occasionally hit by bouts of moral correctness. It would be a bad investment."

"I've been asking about Deputy Chief Neustadt. You know anything there?"

"Nope. I never had the pleasure. What's he got to do with anything?"

"He may have been murdered for one thing. He probably was, for another. And your old man may have been behind it. He may have been defending himself against Neustadt before the old cop did something to him. There was bad blood. That's known."

"I draw a blank there."

"I was admiring your TR2 the other day."

"I knew you'd get to the car."

"Well?"

"So, I wrote a bad cheque. I'll cover it. I told you."

"You know that Shaw and his lawyer, York, are trying to use you to get some cash from your old man?"

"Lighten up, Cooperman." He finished off the last of the beer in front of him and wiped his mouth before speaking again. "Have you seen my sister yet?"

"Not yet. I may get lucky."

"When you do, give her my love," he said with a sneer. That was the first sign of the Hart I'd seen at his mother's house; and we'd been sitting at the bar in Smart Alex for nearly an hour.

"I'll remember that," I said. He put a bill on the bar and slipped me a grin before grabbing his jacket and heading out past the three sophomores and their football heros to his TR2. I finished my beer, thought about the special burgers with curry fries, and placed an order with a waitress who tried to make me feel that she was having one hell of a time looking after all the empty tables that the snowstorm had created. Over my meal, which was better than I expected, I tried to assess all that I had just heard, and figure out what it told me that I hadn't known when I got up in the morning.

Chapter Eighteen

The tree that Dulcie Osborne had crashed into was still standing beside the sharp curve on the Lewiston-Youngstown highway. Even through the storm, you could still see where she and many other drivers had ploughed into it after misjudging the curve. In her case the steering of her car had been tampered with, so the death was not purely accidental. That had happened years ago, when I was first dealing with a case in Niagara Falls. I hadn't been down this road often enough in the interval to become inured to the sudden appearance of the tree as I came around the curve. There was a guard-rail now. I was safe from the deadly white oak, although I had nearly come a cropper a few times on the terrible roads that night.

The Patriot Volunteer hadn't changed either. You could hear the live band from the parking lot. At five to one, the place was jumping and, if the licence plates in the lot told the truth, most of the jumpers paid Canadian taxes. The hat-check girl fought me for my coat and shook the snow from the collar like it was a vicuna. Most hat-checks have no sense of humour. The maitre d' couldn't find an empty table until I crossed his palm with paper. He led the way to a small table close to the double kitchen doors, where news of the orchestra could be had by e-mail.

Basically, the Patriot Volunteer was got up to look like a frontier fort, with waiters dressed as minutemen and waitresses in hoop-skirts. A collection of muskets, drums, bunting in red, white and blue furnished most of the decor. There were reproductions of scenes from the Revolutionary War: the crossing of the Niagara on the morning of the Battle of Queenston Heights, the shelling of Fort Niagara, the burning of Niagara-on-the-Lake. The New Yorkers tended, just as we did on our side of the river, to confuse the Revolutionary War and the War of 1812. They were both costume pictures with three-cornered hats and clay pipes. The orchestra, a band of seven or eight sidemen, made no attempt at historical accuracy, so they blended better with the clientele. Most of the men were necktied and jacketed; the women wore cocktail dresses, except for a few in long dresses—suggesting that this was still a place to come to put the icing on the evening you had already had.

When the waiter insisted that waiting was something one did while holding a drink, I tried that red stuff that I'd run into at the Wellington Court: Campari and soda. The waiter frowned as though such a drink was quite out of place in colonial America. I thought that it should fit in very well considering that the cocktail was invented just down the road at Lewiston.

Julie came in with an entourage of five people: three men and two women. The three women together couldn't have weighed much more than two hundred pounds. One was blonde, hacked about the head with sheep-shears and wearing a long man's undershirt and making less of an impression in it than I would. Her collarbones were her most prominent frontal appendages. The other model, I took the first apparition to be of that profession too, was a gaminelike presence with red hair sculpted close to her head all the way around. She looked a little more womanly than the first: I could tell right off when she was facing me. She wore a long dress of rumpled earthy colours and never smiled. The three men were wearing dinner jackets, one in pink, one white and one in a floral pastel print. They all surrounded Julie, who seemed to be eating it up like chocolate, if she allowed herself to eat chocolate. I recognized her from her parents: she had her mother's height and sharp features and her father's animation. She wore an amber-coloured dress that clung to her body like it had been put on with shellac. It was a good body, if a little undernourished. Her smile, under a set of big brown eyes, was nothing less than terrific.

They marched through a gap between the tables, followed by a platoon of minutemen, busboys and the maitre d', forming squares around my tiny table, then moved off in good order to a big table with a Reserved sign and flowers on it. I was dragged along as a hostage. If we were any closer to the orchestra, we would have had to join the union. I carried my Campari and a minuteman brought my soda. How Julie recognized me, I'll never know. Champagne came to the table in a magnum, with pink foil on top. There were also cans of Diet Coke and Pepsi for the working girls as well as bottled bubbly water.

"I'm Julie Long," said Julie, whose last name had been the chief mystery I'd run into so far. "My Mom told me what you looked like. If that hadn't worked, I was going to test voices. It would have been fun." The pastel-jacketed guy in the blue aviator glasses was introduced to me as Didier Santerre, the publisher of *Mode Magazine*. The gamine was Morna McGuire, the local modelling success story, and I didn't catch the full names of the others. The blonde was Christa. One of the men was a make-up artist called Pierre, and the other was Felix, a designer of rainwear from New York, who apparently was paying.

"How are we going to talk with this floor show in our laps?" I inquired. Julie just rolled her eyes.

"You have to forgive us, we've been on an all-day shoot on the *Maid of the Mist*. You can't believe how cold it was. We nearly sank the boat with our electric generator. We needed so much light!"

"Couldn't wait for spring?"

"Can you believe this weather? It's—"

"One has to fight the weather in this crazy business," said Santerre. "When it's cold, one shoots for summer. When it's hot, naturally, one shoots with artificial snow and ice. But otherwise, we would have to anticipate the season by an impossible margin. The lead-time is bad enough already." We exchanged names and handshakes.

"We had to get them to put the boat in the water early. Imagine what that cost?" the blonde interjected.

"What's your place in all this?" I asked Julie.

"Julie has flair, style, éclat," the boyfriend answered again for her. I was beginning to regret the bridge toll I'd paid to get here and the one I was going to have to pay on the way back. Julie tried on a shy smile at Santerre's praise. It didn't suit her.

The designer, Felix, whose pink "smoking" appeared to have lost its lapels, was pouring out the champagne into far more glasses than there were people. The models were covering the glasses nearest them with their hands. One said she never drank champagne, the other said she ingested nothing after six. I liked "ingested." She added that it was an inflexible rule.

"Who's trying to kill your father?" I asked over giggles, and Julie's turned head as she spoke with Santerre in French. When she turned back to me, with a little flip of her head and a smile, she said that her mother had robbed her of a night's sleep with the news.

"Can't imagine my life without Daddy," she said, biting down on a slim piece of carrot. "He has always encouraged my interest in fashion and design."

"I was guessing you got this from your mother."

"True. Mommy adores clothes. She loves Sonia Rykiel better than the truth. But Daddy actually puts his money where his mouth is."

"I thought you two didn't get along?"

"Heavens no! He loves it now that I've found myself. Now that Didier and I have found one another."

"That was written in the stars, *chérie*," Santerre added. From it I guessed that *Mode Magazine* was in need of a backer with the financial clout Abram Wise could give it. As long as Wise was putting up part of the money, Julie could think herself into any social butterfly net she liked and Daddy would keep on paying. But, after all, that was what Abe Wise did best.

"Are you two planning to make this permanent?" I asked, trying on a wide ingenuous smile.

"Just as soon as we can make it legal," Julie said, patting Santerre's left hand with hers. There was a white mark on the third finger of one of the hands. It was Didier's. "I'm still legally married to my old John Long but not for long," Julie said making Didier and Morna laugh. The others were involved, thank God, in a conversation of their own. "But my divorce will be final in three months. I've already got my decree nisi. So, I'm going to do the bride thing again. Getting to be a habit with me, as the song goes, but this time, I think Didier's going to make an honest woman of me."

"My compliments to the bride and congratulations to

the groom or vice versa." Both beamed at me and then at one another, exchanging hugs and kisses.

"Benny," Julie said, leaning into me in a friendly but unnecessary way, "would you be an angel and get a white paper bag from the front seat of our car?" She said it in such an intimate way that I thought she had fallen under the magic spell of my charm. In fact, the reverse, for the moment, was true. "I've got a perishing headache and there are some Tylenol there." She took car keys from her bag and told me the car to look for. I took them from her and made my way out into the dark and the snow which was still coming down.

I found the dark red Le Baron under a white shroud and the paper bag with the bottle of pills inside. On leaving, I noticed that one of the headlights had been damaged. Expensive repairs. The night was cold on the back of me, and my fingers tingled from handling the car door. I rushed away from the unpleasant truth about the drive home into the noise and light of the Patriot Volunteer.

"You're an angel, Benny!" Julie said, as she took two pills with a swallow from her champagne glass.

"It's a terrible night out there!" I said, hugging myself and trying to get warm.

"Let's leave it out," drawled Christa, who was holding a sipping straw, and trying to focus on my eyes. Felix and Pierre had straws in front of them too, although they were drinking champagne. Didier was twisting one around in his fingers and got rid of it under the table. Julie lent me an arm to restore my circulation. Santerre applied stimulants of a more conventional kind than they had just treated themselves to. I moved in closer to Julie and tried to keep my mind on my job.

"Tell me, Julie, has your father ever mentioned his

feud with Ed Neustadt to you?"

"Is that the one who just died?" I nodded. "I think he once said that he was the only man who ever questioned him in a police station. Imagine! With all he's done! It's incredible!"

"But, your father has no record. That means, Neustadt didn't follow through. He was still 'assisting the authorities,' they call it, and then they let him walk. In law, a miss is as good as a mile. Why do you think he hated Neustadt?"

"Ask him. He never told me. Maybe he hates to be beholden to anyone. I can understand that." She reached over to get another glass of champagne and toasted me over the rim. She was in great spirits and I was rapidly going downhill. Everybody who knows Abe Wise says just about the same thing about him. If there was a conspiracy, at least it had a good leader. I was yawning into my wine glass. It was time to go home. Our little group was being closely watched by other people in the room. When the designer got up to dance with Christa, the blonde ragamuffin in the underwear shirt, the waiters stared. Didier got up and pulled Julie after him. He must be French after all, I thought. I couldn't think of anyone I knew leading the way to the dance floor.

"You're a detective?" Morna asked. I smiled a sad admittance.

"I've got an office on St Andrew Street," I said, wondering what I could say to this exotic creature.

"My grandfather worked with Pinkerton's for thirty-five years. He used to tell us stories about his cases. He should have been a writer."

"They're a big outfit. Go back to the Civil War."

"I knew that. What's-his-face, the writer, used to be a Pinkerton."

"Hammett," I said. "Dashiell Hammett." She had lovely deep green eyes under her red hair.

"Do you want to dance?" she said with a golden smile.

"Sure," I said. "Why not?"

Chapter Nineteen

Anna was away early: signs of her after-breakfast cleaning around the sink were in evidence. A half-pot of coffee was inviting me to start the day. There was a container of bran for me to pour on top of my Harvest Crunch.

In the shower I thought about all of the characters I had met the night before. It was a peep-hole into another world, a world that my father should know a lot about, if he had ever read a fashion magazine. But he hadn't. His knowledge of women's ready-to-wear came not from *Vogue* or *Women's Wear Daily*, but from his pals the manufacturers along Spadina Avenue in Toronto. Every other Wednesday, he drove to the provincial capital to buy stock and play a few hands of gin rummy with his cronies. After a corned beef sandwich at Shopsowitz's Deli, he would visit the factories and have a shot of schnapps in a showroom before a few more hands of cards. This was the world of fashion as he knew it. To him it was all merchandise. It could have been men's wear or hats as far as he was concerned.

At least Pa knew more about the business than I did, I thought, while I was rinsing the shampoo out of my hair. It had fed us and clothed us for over twenty years. He had sent Sam through university and medical school. He would have anted up for me to go to college too if I'd had the inclination. He made a good living for a high-school drop-out and knew as much about the fashion business as he had to know in order to be a success. In a place like this, that wasn't much. Me, all I knew about the business was how to make coat and suit boxes from the pile of flat cardboard Pa kept under the coat rack. Sam and I both got our first taste of the commercial world making tops and bottoms for a penny each on lazy Sunday afternoons while Pa was going over his accounts or drawing up an ad for the *Beacon*.

I was no reader of *Vogue* either. Anna was and she had told me that Morna McGuire was not just a model, but a supermodel, which meant that she could make good her boast that she wouldn't get out of bed for less than ten thousand dollars.

After cleaning my teeth a second time to get the bran out, I walked to the office. My service had messages from Dave Rogers and Major Colin Patrick for me. Both of them would talk to me, one at eleven and the other at noon. I put in time working on my interim report for Wise.

Once again I was sitting face to face with Dave Rogers. Only this time we were perched on bales of rusted eighth-inch wire in his yard off North Street. The sign outside read "C. Rogers & Sons: Steel Fabricators." Earlier, we had been walking up and down the aisles or paths that led through the canyons of metal heaps. It was filled with every sort of metal imaginable, except maybe lead for toy soldiers. But who knows? Along the right-hand side of the path through the rusty forest were bales of wire: bright red copper, green, older copper, oxidized steel hoops looking like great balls of knitting wool gone off a little in the rain. On Dave's side were stacked shoulder-high piles of H-beams. In and out of the pile three or four feral cats wove their way looking for vermin. Dave picked a place to perch. He lit up a cigarette and I found a final Halls at the end of a package.

"I told Wise I'd talk to you once. I didn't say I'd have you for lunch and dinner too. Are you going to phone up every time you run into a problem? What kind of detective are you?"

"We're talking about your childhood friend's life here, Mr Rogers."

"Call me Dave for Christ's sake and let's get through with this."

"Tell me about Neustadt." He wasn't in a hurry to give me a pat answer. I could afford to wait.

"He wouldn't tell you?" I shook my head.

"He told me a few little things," I said, "but nothing important. Why was Abe so glad to see the last of that cop? Why did he practically dance on his grave at the funeral?"

"You saw that? I can believe it; I can believe it."

"Good for you. Now, let me have the truth."

"Abe, you know, is a self-made man. Nobody gave him a handout. Nobody handed him a family legacy. Abe's proud of that. But that cop, Neustadt, gave him a break when he was still a kid. Neustadt gave him a second chance when he was pinched with a pillowcase full of silver knives and forks. They had him dead to rights, but Neustadt turned him loose. Anybody else and Neustadt would be remembered with honour and thanks. Ha! Not Abe Wise! Wise hated that. He thought the bum was soft. He couldn't find a good thing to say about him. Can you beat that?"

"It still doesn't explain the intensity, Dave. All that happened back just after the war. How much baggage are you still carrying around from the fifties? Not much,

I'll bet."

"Oh, I always thought that Neustadt had him on the carpet for a while, gave him a bad time, scared the shit out of him, then let him go."

"I guess. I guess. Still…"

"Who is it you're going to hate if you're Abe Wise? Somebody who shafted you or somebody who gave you a break?"

"He ever talk about it?"

"He hit that dud note a lot at the time, but after that he never mentioned it again. It was Abe on the ropes, Abe down for the count. He wanted the earth to open up and swallow that cop. It embarrassed him."

"But is it believable that he'd hate the man who let him go?"

"Not you, not me, but Abe? What good is a self-made man if he had help?"

"He could have had one of his boys put him in his place."

"I'll bet he thought about it. Boy, I'll bet he did." Dave put his butt out on the top of an I-beam and we both got up. There was a rusty stain on the back of his coat and, I noticed later, on the seat of my trousers. We walked in silence, thinking.

"We better turn here. There's nothing up that way but railroad tracks my old man bought when they got rid of the streetcars. Could never sell 'em; too much cement attached."

"You hear how Neustadt died?"

"Yeah, it was an accident in his driveway."

"His car settled from a hydraulic jack onto his chest."

"Jesus! That's tough."

"How does a hydraulic jack come down on you, Dave? Neustadt would have had to have ten-foot arms to turn that trick on himself. And they don't release on their own."

"Jesus!"

"Would Abe have done that, Dave? Just to be free of him?" Dave thought about that while we came down the aisle towards the yard hut. At last he shook his head:

"Naw. You couldn't get me to believe that. Abe's not the type. Look, he's been in the rackets for nearly fifty years. He's made his bundle over and over again. He's been into every crooked kind of business you can think of. But, and I say 'but,' not once in all that time did he even a personal score. He had a lot of guys sore at him and Abe as mad at them. But not once did he ever turn it into a hit. It's not his way."

"Maybe one of the boys thought he was doing Abe a favour. Especially if Abe still sounded off at Neustadt. Ever see that movie *Becket*? Richard Burton, Peter O'Toole? O'Toole's the king, you see, and Burton's a bishop. And Burton's handing O'Toole a lot of grief because he doesn't want church law to give way to civil law. Finally, when the king's had it up to here, he shouts out: 'Will no one rid me of this meddlesome priest?' Now he later claims that he didn't mean it, that he was just shooting his mouth off, but four knights heard him say it and they rode out of town and did the job expecting a handsome reward. They didn't get it."

"Mickey wouldn't go off half-cocked like that. And he'd never let any of the boys under him get out of hand. No, I think you're barking up the wrong tree there, Cooperman. You want some coffee? I think there's some fresh-made in the pot."

We entered the shed and Dave Rogers poured coffee from a cracked Silex into a pair of blue enamel cups.

"You know," Dave said, "when you think of us, Abe

and me, it takes a lot of explaining. I've always played it straight down the line and Abe, well, Abe never did see the line, if you know what I mean. Take the case of Julie and Bernie."

"Who?"

"Abe's daughter and my middle son, Bernie. Bernie was Julie's second husband. After she left that painter she married to get away from Abe. I thought that Julie and Bernie would get along fine. He had everything the painter lacked...but that wasn't enough. She wanted more, and this fellow Long she married next, he couldn't give it to her either. Now she's playing with a French magazine publisher, who needs Abe's money. Funny, eh?"

"I don't think I follow you, Dave. How do Julie's bad marriages figure in this?"

"Normally, you'd think there'd have been some friction. Pressure on me, pressure on Bernie. But no. Abe didn't get involved. Our friendship was just as solid after the divorce as it was before Julie and Bernie stood under the *khupe* together. Isn't that a remarkable thing?"

"I guess so," I said.

"It's like Abe's got everything organized into separate boxes. And the Julie and Bernie box doesn't get confused with the old Dave Rottman box, which is one of his older boxes. Funny."

"I see what you mean."

"Like his criminal activities don't get in the way of his going to the opera ball. He even goes to the Policemen's Ball! How do you like that?"

Together we sipped coffee while looking out the window at school kids coming down North Street. It must have been noon hour and I had an appointment again for lunch. I told Dave I had to go, and he lifted his huge bulk from the grip of a swivel armchair and walked me to the car. He was almost friendly.

The Sally Ann worked out of several offices and a church in Grantham. There were listings under Family Services, Correctional and Justice, and Hostel at locations on Church, Lake and Niagara streets. When I began my search for the Sally Ann officer who had recited Neustadt's eulogy, I took a stab at the top number and was quickly shifted about until I was talking to Major Colin Patrick. I'd agreed to pick him up at the Corps, which turned out to be a church with a tin roof not far from Shaw's antique-car lot on Niagara. As he waited for me on the front steps of the church, talking to another officer, I remembered his ruddy face from the funeral. In their navy blue uniforms with red tabs at the collar, the men looked striking against the wooden door of the church. I kept the motor running and watched the puffs of conversation across the street. After three minutes by the car clock, they shook hands and parted. No salutes. Patrick, who had seen me at the curb, came right over and got in the front seat. We shook hands and he buckled up.

"I haven't got more than forty or fifty minutes, Mr Cooperman. There's a place down the street where we can go, if you don't mind sandwiches." He gave me directions and I found a parking space behind Paul's Open Kitchen. Inside, Paul and two assistants were handling the noon-hour traffic. The major ordered a bowl of soup and a tuna sandwich on brown. I joined him in the soup and ordered my usual chopped egg on white with a glass of milk. The milk came in a carton.

"Now, I'm not clear what this is all about, Mr Cooperman. Perhaps, to save time, you can tell me what it is you want." I told him, without mentioning my client, that I was looking into the Tatarski case, which didn't seem to surprise him. I told him that I was aware of Deputy Chief Neustadt's letter to the *Beacon* and that I was examining all aspects of the case.

"I hope you know that McKenzie Stewart, the mystery writer, has just written a book on the case."

"I've read it. What did you think?"

"Ed Neustadt didn't come off very well. I think Stewart was looking for villains. It's only natural. Terrible thing like that. If you can find a villain, then we all feel better, don't we?"

"A kind of lightning rod for our bad feelings?"

"Exactly! Now, I knew Ed as well as anybody. I just buried him yesterday. He died a bitter, unhappy man. I tried to get him to see a psychologist that I know, but he wouldn't. Poor Ed saw most of the things he'd loved and fought for disappear. He wasn't one of these modern moral relativists. He wanted hard outlines, black and white. The grey areas drove him near crazy, sometimes."

"He angered a few people over the years, I hear. Major Patrick, what was he like as a friend?"

"Ed? Well, let me see..." He took a bite of his sandwich, as though that was a thought-aiding process and began to chew like a thoughtful Holstein. "He liked camping. Liked doing the same thing year after year. He got terribly upset if our regular trailer park was full or our normal spot was taken. He'd grumble about that. He liked habits. Habits made him comfortable. Every fall he put on his storm windows and every spring he'd take them down again and stack them in his garage. Do you know anybody who still does that, Mr Cooperman? He took a lot of pride in his cars over the years. Did a lot of the servicing of them himself. Rotated the tires, put in antifreeze, changed the oil. It was a mark of pride with him. But also habit. Take the accident. Ed must have been the only man in town under a car last Sunday. I remember the day: sunny, but cold. First Sunday in March. 'Steal a march on spring,' he used to say. Freddy Tait and I used to kid him about that, as much as you could ever kid Ed Neustadt. Freddy never made a dime off him, you know. He did all his own servicing. His only hobby, really."

"Do you know anyone who hated him enough to kill him?"

"Well, the Tatarski family for a start. And there were other people in other cases where Ed marched right through the evidence to where he wanted to go. Most of the Tatarskis have gone, you know. Margaret took her own life down around Sarnia. Her brother, Freddy, was raised in foster homes after Margaret died. He came back here, though. By this time he called himself Fred Tait. Made a success of himself."

"You mean the Nuts & Bolts car repair garages? What was he like, Freddy Tatarski?" The major suspended his soup spoon in mid-air in front of his face, while he considered what to say. I'd eaten my sandwich first too.

"Outwardly, he was a great success, like I said. Chamber of Commerce, Businessman of the Year, school trustee. But I got to know him through his drinking. Freddy was an alcoholic. I got him to join AA. Freddy was all torn up inside. Well, who wouldn't be after losing both parents that way and after that his sisters? Then he came to me about something else. He had his drinking stopped by then. It was his daughter, Drina, he came about. He caught himself touching her and he wanted help. He had taken a strap to her. Couple of times. Said if he didn't hurt her, he might do something worse. Wouldn't see a doctor about it. I did what I could. But the girl moved away. That was a problem that solved itself."

"This Drina, she wasn't his real daughter, right?"

"That's how he'd brought her up, no different from his own."

"Was he a religious man?"

"At heart he was, but if we waited on people getting religion, we'd sit idle with our arms folded. That would never do. When the Almighty comes around, you want Him to find you busy. That's why Salvationists are always on the move, up and doing."

"So Fred Tait was a drunk and then a child abuser? And he came to you for help when it got too much for him. I wonder why?"

"That doesn't surprise an old Salvationist like me, Mr Cooperman. We're an army family. Third generation. Freddy wasn't the first and he won't be the last. At the Sally Ann we take life as it comes. We've seen it at its best and worst. Poor Freddy was neither of those: just a poor blighter who started going through the sausage machine before he was fairly weaned."

"Where was Drina during all this?"

"She was very close to her stepfather. Used to run around his repair shop like a regular grease monkey when she was in her teens. Drina was a bright girl, did well in high school and went out of town to university. But she quit. Don't know why. She was in Toronto and New York for a couple of years. She married down in the States. Freddy never told me the details, or I forgot. Her husband, let me see, I think he died young, and she came back to try university again. She was nearly finished her first year when Freddy got his bad news. Cancer. That's what took him. Big man like that. He weighed less than a hundred pounds when I buried him two years ago."

"What happened to the girl after that?"

"She nursed him for a year. Tried to cheer him up. She was a good practical nurse. After that, she went away again. Somewhere in the States, but I might be wrong there. Heard she'd remarried. She might have gone out west. No, that was somebody else. Drina was a strange girl. Very strange."

"How do you mean?"

"Oh, I don't think I can describe her. It was just a feeling I had about her. She reminded me a lot of her mother."

"Freddy's wife? Her stepmother?"

"No, Mr Cooperman. Mary. Mary Tatarski. The one they hanged."

Chapter Twenty

Once reinstalled behind my desk, I examined the report I was writing for Wise. It was going well. I added information I had learned recently and worked away at it for another half-hour. A final detail was an invoice for services rendered up to and including Friday, March 11. That done, I walked across the street to the Print Shop to make copies. Back in the office, I took the top copy and put it in an envelope. Then, thinking of its confidential nature, I opened a bottom drawer and brought out a stick of red sealing wax with a wick running through it like a candle. I lit the wick and dribbled a pool of wax on the back of the envelope where the flap was stuck. It was very satisfying to watch the wax puddle and cool. I felt for a moment caught up in a profession as old as the pyramids, full of echoes of ancient Rome, Charles Dickens and Erle Stanley Gardner, all of which induced a welcome feeling of stability and well-being. After it had cooled a little, I impressed my signet ring into the red mass and, on trying to remove it, lost the bloodstone with its engraved "B." I got it out with a paper-clip and blew out the sealing wax. Removing the ring from my finger, I parked the birthstone under the paper-clips in the top drawer.

When my handiwork was all ready to go, I returned

to St Andrew Street looking around for a sign of Mickey Armstrong or one of his merry men. The streets were hoodless, not a heavy in sight. I walked up St Andrew Street a block, hoping to spot Phil or Sidney staring into windows of lingerie stores or babywear shoppes about three or four stores behind me. No luck. I was going to have to invest in a stamp and mail my report if I couldn't find one of Wise's happy runners.

Turning around, I walked west on the main street until I came to the Bernstein Travel Bureau. Inside, I found my old friend Laura behind the counter talking to customers bound for an early spring visit to Galway, Ireland. I hadn't been in the store long before Phil Green came in behind me. He busied himself looking at the rack of brochures while I listened to Laura talk about the beauties of the West Country. Before she had me in her sights, while the ink was drying on her customers' cheque on the counter, I turned to Phil and handed him the sealed envelope with instructions to take it directly to his boss without stopping to pass "Go." Phil blinked at me, crunched a Lifesaver, and backed out the door, not quite understanding what had happened to him. As for Laura, we had a short chat, then I wandered across to the Di for a cup of coffee.

Sitting in my regular golden-stained booth and sipping deeply of the stuff that makes the world go around, I couldn't keep from thinking of the report: small omissions, connections, suspicions. All in all, it was a peculiar case. Abe Wise was the spider in the middle of his web. All of the other people were ranged about him in some way. Whatever they did outside of their association with Wise was irrelevant to my inquiry. I'd talked to a lot of people. In fact this case was almost all talk. Questions and answers. Q and A. Then on to the next. Although I'd

talked to lots of people about Wise, Wise wasn't coming
to life in a different way for me because of what I'd
learned. Wise was the same guy to everybody. There
wasn't anything devious about him, which is a peculiar
thing to say about a master crook. He had the system
beat. He hadn't changed much over the years. The Wise
that Rogers had described to me was the Wise that
Paulette used to wait on back in the 1950s, at this very
table maybe.

I walked back to the office. The first stage of the case
was over. I would get a call from Wise, or from Mickey,
telling me that there was a cheque coming one of these
days: payment to date for services described in the
report, or maybe offering to let me live untroubled for a
few years in lieu of payment. This was reaction time.
Time for Wise to read and think of what to do next. Time
for me to tidy my desk, remove the hair and fuzz from
the mass of paper-clips, get my ring fixed, try to think of
what I was going to do next to earn the second instal-
ment of Abe Wise's bounty. I thought of the coming
weekend with Anna listening to paper after paper up at
Secord at a conference. I thought of Hart and Julie, or
Mickey and Vicky, Paulette and Lily, of Neustadt and
Mary Tatarski. It was a rich cast, but they weren't up to
anything very interesting. Well, Neustadt had entered
upon eternity and someone had seen to it that it looked
like an accident. Staziak was going to phone me one of
these days and tell me that person or persons unknown
had turned the valve on the jack that was supporting
Neustadt's Buick. That made it murder. A murder, he'll
tell me without clues or witnesses, a murder without a
future as far as he was concerned.

But what kind of murder was it? A murder that is committed without a weapon? Was it premeditated? How

could it be? The victim was lying under his car, not in conflict with his killer. The killer could have come and seized
the opportunity. This was a strange killing from any way
you looked at it. I tried to imagine the picture. The killer
came up the driveway where Neustadt was under his car
with his tools around him. It was a quiet spot, a neighbourhood of houses. If the season had been summer, it
could have been a set for "Leave It to Beaver." The old
man and his car. Small-town values. Do it yourself.

Neustadt didn't talk to his killer, or if he did, he did it
from under the car. If he sensed any danger, he would
have run himself out on the creeper board he was lying
on. It had casters in my picture and it would only have
taken a moment to get out from under. No, this seemed
to be a crime without conversation. The killer came up
the walk, turned the valve and walked away without
attracting any attention from the house or along the
street.

And how did the murderer know about Neustadt's
practice of servicing his own car? Did he know that he
changed his own oil? Must have. The major said he was
a man of established habits. Then, it becomes clear,
unless I've lost my way in this thing, the murder of Ed
Neustadt was a well-plotted and well-researched act. The
murderer knew where Neustadt lived, and that he would
be under his car changing his oil on the first Sunday in
March. He also knew that his jack was hydraulic.

And who was this murderer? One of the many people
he sent away to Kingston for a nice long term?
Somebody who felt that Neustadt's zeal as a law officer
was exaggerated? Someone with a long-standing
grudge? This was not your usual murderer. Such a crime
might have been hanging in the air for a long time waiting for all of the circumstances to be right. He had to be

alone. There could not be any witnesses. It had to be the day of the oil change. Neustadt was a man of regular habits. Even on that chilly Sunday.

When the phone interrupted my reverie it was Whitey York, the lawyer who had been dunning Hart Wise. "Mr Cooperman, I said I would be in touch with you."

"That was a few days ago. But thanks for remembering. What's the verdict?"

"I have talked to my client and he has decided not to deal. We intend to carry the matter through normal procedures and let the courts decide."

"You're going to really stick it to him?"

"That calls for interpretation, Mr Cooperman. I just called to let you know."

"Damn! When did you last speak with your client?"

"Early last evening. We discussed it thoroughly. I—"

"You haven't talked to him today?"

"I left a message at his office just after nine-thirty, but—"

That's where I hung up the phone and left the office in a hurry. In less than ten minutes I was parked down the street from Brighton Motors on Niagara Street. Inside, the salesmen, who were flying a paper airplane, told me that Gordon Shaw hadn't been in since early morning. He had had a call and then left the office abruptly without leaving word where he might be reached.

Standing outside, I tried to imagine where he had gone. For him to have taken on Abe Wise in this direct way was foolish beyond belief. It would have been like me telling him to shove his proposition to me last Monday up the nearest city councillor's drainpipe.

Yesterday's overnight snow was already fading away. In spite of the cold, the snow couldn't manage under the bright sun. The cars in Shaw's lot, at the back where the old jail used to be, were still covered, blanketed for the most part, in white, but patches had melted or slipped off, heavy with moisture. One of the cars had lost more snow than the others. It was a stunning red Alfa Romeo. I went over to have a look. Through a line of big zeros written on the windshield, slumped in the driver's seat, I saw Gordon Sawchuck, who did business under the name Shaw. Without opening the door, I could tell that he was dead, an opinion supported by the handle of a knife I could see a few inches away from that dirty old school tie he liked to wear. In the snow by the passenger side, I stepped on a piece of dark metal in the shape of an Indian's head. I moved away from the car to do some private dry retching.

Chapter Twenty-One

As a good citizen normally, I would have let the salesmen in on what I had found in the lot out back, and then I would have telephoned 911 to inform the authorities. But I did neither one. I didn't know how long I could keep my client's name out of an investigation. Technically, I wasn't being a good Boy Scout, but any investigation that didn't trip over Abe Wise's name in the first half-hour wasn't going anywhere with or without me. I knew that I would tell Pete Staziak as soon as I ethically could, but there is an unwritten law about snitching on your employer. Even when he's the biggest crook in the country. Especially when he has just received your invoice.

I got back to my car without walking by the show windows. To anyone keeping track of my movements, and who knows, it could happen, I must have looked as guilty as hell as I crossed and recrossed Niagara Street.

In the Olds, I began rehearsing a speech to be addressed to Abe Wise. It reviewed the circumstances of my coming to work for him and went on to ask how he hoped to get away first with the murder of Ed Neustadt and then with the stabbing of Gordon Shaw. He would deny it, of course, and I would...what? Resign? Hello, Cooperman! Resigning isn't an option. Remember?

"We're not talking 'ifs' here," he said that night.

So, what was I going to do? Sit tight? Keep on looking for people who wanted to see Abe's blood on the floor? It seemed a little distant and abstract for me. I needed to talk to somebody. Where was Anna when I needed her? Off hobnobbing with her fellow historians for the whole damned weekend. This was leading nowhere. Cooperman, don't whine! Gordon Shaw is dead, not you. You don't even come into this. Not directly. You went to see Shaw earlier this week and again today. The *post mortem* examination will show that he was dead some time before your second visit to the showroom. Again I could see Shaw's eyes. They already had the dead look. He could have been killed a short time after he left his office. A call comes in: "Will you show me that Alfa Romeo in your yard? Give me a personal demonstration?"

I parked the Olds behind the Murray Hotel and went in for a haircut. It wouldn't hurt being seen downtown and nowhere near Niagara Street. There were two men waiting for Bill Hall's chair. I picked up a magazine and waited.

On Chestnut Street there is a phone booth that can hardly be seen from St Andrew. It was from there that I called 911 and told the dispatcher where to look for Shaw. I didn't hang around to chat, but even slinking guiltily back to my office, I felt better than I had been feeling. And to hell with Wise! I wasn't snitching on him, just telling the cops where to find the cold meat. When the phone began to ring as soon as I got behind my desk, I wondered how they had traced me so fast. But it wasn't a call-back from 911, it was Victoria Armstrong saying that Mickey was on his way over to pick me up. I tried to ask her what was up, but she said she didn't know.

Mickey was waiting for me in the Volvo this time. It was parked in front of the Russell House or the Sniper's Roost, as I liked to call it. I asked Mickey the same question I asked his wife. "Mr Wise doesn't send out press releases. He just told me to fetch you." I liked the word 'fetch'; it implied a return to where he picked me up. But I wasn't thinking too clearly. We drove in silence out of the city and over the route I'd first travelled last Monday morning. It was prettier with the sun shining on the farms. Once or twice, I caught a glimpse of the old canal. The snow was in retreat.

Victoria was waiting at the door when we arrived. She took my coat and shrugged when I asked with a look if she knew any more about what was going on. She was wearing one of her dark peasanty woollen skirts. When I was ushered into Wise's august presence it was into the same room where our first interview had taken place. The pine hutch, the big partners desk, the arrow-backed chairs and the little terracotta figures that pre-dated Columbus.

Wise was sitting when I came in, but quickly got up and came towards me with a wide smile and an out-stretched hand. "Thank you for coming at such short notice, Mr Cooperman." We shook hands and he kept walking past me to the liquor cabinet. "Will you take a drink at this time of day?" he made a Scotch and water for himself and a rye and ginger ale for me. I wondered where he found that out. "I've read your report, Mr Cooperman. A very impressive piece of work, given the short time I've given you."

"It's just an interim report. It doesn't include the fact, for instance, that Gordon Shaw was murdered this morning sometime. He was the car dealer who was pressing charges against your son. You remember that Hart bought a Triumph sports car from Shaw." I could hear the mounting anger in my voice, so I was glad when Wise broke in.

"A Triumph! You think this is about a Triumph, Mr Cooperman? How naïve you are. But you are right to tell me. Of course, you think I'm behind it. Well, maybe I am and maybe I'm not. But we both know that Hart is involved in this and I don't want to see any harm come to that boy!"

"That boy is nearly forty. The sooner you understand that, the sooner you'll begin getting through to Hart."

"I warned you last time about your free advice for troubled families. Let's hear no more of it. I insist!"

"Why didn't you wait until I was asleep before calling this meeting?"

"Cooperman, I've no time for your hurt feelings. Now shut up and listen to what I have to say." I sat down in a chair near the liquor cabinet next to a particularly ugly Central American mask. My sitting reminded Wise that he had been left standing in the middle of the room. He pulled a chair towards me, leaving tracks in the broadloom.

"I want you to continue on this assignment. I need my head examined for this decision, but you're the best available. Keep at it. I also want to know what you can discover about Julie's new suitor, Santerre. I understand that you met him last night. How did he strike you?"

"That whole crowd is out of my league, Mr Wise. I don't understand the gaudy talk. I don't know what they are on about to be honest. They have enough cocaine when they need it. You may know where they got it."

"Was Julie...? Was she...?" We both got to our feet.

"I didn't see her, Mr Wise. But you know, better than

most of us, the stuff is around for people who know who to ask." Wise rubbed his forehead with a white handkerchief, thinking. I don't know how long I stood there waiting for him to look up. When he did: "Phil Green will drive you back to town, Mr Cooperman. I have a job for Mickey to do this afternoon. I hope that I needn't remind you that it would be in your interest not to involve me in the investigation into this terrible murder of Mr Shaw."

"Then why remind me?"

There was a knock at the door, and I heard Victoria's voice informing Wise that the car was just coming around to the back door. He repeated the message to me, while I was thinking of all the things I would like to put to my client before he again slipped out of reach.

"Good-afternoon, Mr Cooperman," he said. I didn't see him say it, since it was addressed to my back as I was being hurried through the door in the rear. I was a back-door kind of fellow, I thought. I had the feeling that I was being frog-marched away from the facts, being returned to a life in black and white after a delicious flirtation with Technicolor.

Back home again, I soaked in a tub for half an hour, hoping that the phone would ring with some good news. It didn't. My only consolation for the whole day was the contents of the envelope that Phil Green handed me as I got out of the car. It contained a fat cheque.

Friday-night dinner at my parents' went off as usual. I ate an over-broiled steak that had been cooked fifteen minutes per side because Ma puts them into the broiler frozen solid. I treated myself to a movie afterwards. I was still anxious, both about the murder and about my meeting with Wise. I base this on the fact that I ate two Kit Kat chocolate bars before the feature was well started.

The Saturday paper brought the news of the discovery

of Gordon Shaw's body behind his sports car showroom on Niagara Street. Pete Staziak was in charge of the investigation and he said that he had several leads which he was following up and when there were developments he would keep the public informed. The story mentioned details of Shaw's education, marital status, and a few of the cups and trophies he had won in races and rallies in the Niagara district during the last ten years or so.

Other news in the papers looked peculiar and irrelevant, like news from a distant country. European events were on the front page of the *Beacon* while *The Globe*'s dealt with domestic matters that formerly stayed in the closet. I went through both papers without skipping, eating up everything from the ads to the editorials. I needed all this as a spring tonic to get me up and moving again. I was spread out with the papers on the rug when the phone rang. I felt a stitch in my hip as I got up to answer it. I was feeling my years.

"Hello?"

"Benny? Pete. What are you doing?"

"I'm goofing off while Anna is spending the weekend with visiting historians up at Secord. And I've been reading in the papers all about my friend Pete Staziak and his latest investigation."

"Tell you a little secret, Benny. I get help from the public. You couldn't guess how many anonymous tips cross my desk."

"You got a description from the salesmen?"

"Why can't you play by the rules?"

"Sometimes, Pete, you stumble across things and you can't wait, or get involved right then. It's a nasty part of my business."

"Until you lose your damned licence, Benny!"

"Sorry, Pete. Would you rather I just tiptoed away?"

"Isn't that what you did?" he said, letting his anger show in his voice. Before I could respond, he had caught his breath and came back at me on a totally new tack. "How are you anyway, Benny?"

"I feel pretty good, considering."

"Considering. Oh, you've heard, then?"

"What? I was hoping that my client, Abram Wise, might call me to answer some of the questions he keeps sidestepping whenever I see him."

"He's not going to phone, Benny."

"You always were a pessimist, Pete."

"Benny, he's not going to call, he's not going to write and he's not going to fax anybody any more. The spring will come at last, Benny, but not for Abe Wise. He's finished buttoning and unbuttoning forever. Do you get my meaning, Benny?"

"I don't like this, Pete. I haven't even cashed his cheque yet. Will the bank honour it, or is everything on hold?"

"Slow down. You aren't denying that you were working for Abe Wise?"

"I'm not ashamed of work, Pete. I didn't like the threats he gave me to take the job, but once he had my attention, he treated me fair enough. What is it you are telling me?"

"What you've already guessed. Your client is, even as we speak, being moved downtown where he is going to a new address in a refrigerator drawer. Wise is booked to have a *post mortem* first thing Monday morning. Any other questions?"

"When did all this happen? I was over there yesterday! Friday. He didn't just sicken and die, right?"

"Right. He took a nine-millimetre slug between the eyes. That is if the piece that was on the floor did the shooting, which is the handiest possibility."

"How did you learn about me?"

"Not from you, damn it! You might have mentioned the fact when I was talking to you on Tuesday. The housekeeper, Victoria Armstrong, gave me a list of the people in and out for the last couple of days. Not informing the authorities is getting to be a habit with you, Benny. Watch it!"

"Are you in charge of the case?"

"Until I hear I ain't, I am. You think we should have a little talk?"

"I was just going to suggest it. Pete, does this mean we're in the middle of a gang war?"

"If you're lumping in the Shaw murder, you could have a point. Shaw's not too clean when you take a close look. This we don't need, Benny. Remember when that guy got it in the tower overlooking Niagara Falls? That was a real bloodbath. Emptied a lot of files around here. But this time, I don't know. We got the smoking gun, but there are no prints on it."

"When do you want to see me?"

"Gimme an hour, hour and a half, to go through some stuff. Then you better come up here to the house. You been here, right, so you can find your way. See you, Benny." He hung up and I held onto the stinging receiver for another ten seconds or so before I put it down. Damn it! I thought, what next?

I made a single wrong turn on my way to the Wise house, but it was enough to make me later than I'd intended. There were three cop cars parked in front and Pete's own car around back. Inside, Victoria took my coat, just like old times. Her eyes were red. She looked like she'd been through a Cuisinart, the way her hair was all over the place. I saw uniforms and lab-coated forensic people going about their business. Pete stood by the big partners desk surrounded by yellow plastic tape inviting me to stay clear of the Crime Scene. Pete was talking to Mickey and one of the uniforms. He gave me a short grin of recognition when he saw me standing beyond the tape. After a few minutes he climbed over the plastic and came towards me, passed me and went on, past a view of a big, well-equipped kitchen, to a large TV room I hadn't seen before. It too was a show-off location for little brown clay figures, paintings and wall-hangings. Victoria was there with Phil and Sidney. Syl had been taken downtown, I was told later, for questioning about an unrelated matter. Victoria slipped me a smile, but there was worry written in her brown eyes.

"You know everybody?" Pete asked, waving his hand in the direction of those sitting down and not excluding Mickey and the uniform who had followed us into the room. "Remember Corporal Kyle, Benny? He ran you in once on a B and E."

"Thanks for the memory, Sergeant," I said through my teeth. "Hello, Corporal. Good to see you."

Pete asked a few questions of each of the people in the room and then fired some at me. They had to do with times and dates. He was still trying to get the background, who was where, and who could observe whom and when. I found out that Wise slept in a room above the familiar office and that Mickey and Victoria shared a room on the third floor at the back. There were several spare rooms reserved for special guests as well as rooms for both Hart and Julie on the second floor. It was early days in the investigation. Just the same, Pete looked like he had been up all night.

"Let's get out of here for a few minutes," Pete said to me after about twenty minutes of this. "I'm out of cigarettes."

"Great! That's one thing the suburbs do well. Hundreds of places wherever you look." He took another three minutes whispering to Kyle in the kitchen before we finally headed out the door.

"Okay, we'll take my car." We got in and even after driving around for ten minutes, we hadn't seen anything that looked like it might sell tobacco. After another five minutes of turning and twisting, Staziak spotted a 7 Eleven store not far from the Forks Road.

"Abe Wise died before his work was finished," I said, as Pete fumbled with the car door.

"How do you mean?"

"Well, there's a lot of room for improvement in the location of tobacco outlets around here. Wasn't tobacco one of his rackets?"

"See what you mean. I don't think it was a major interest of his for at least a year. I'll be right back." I watched him move away from the car and into the store with its bright red-and-blue plastic soft-drink signs outside. The trees brushed naked branches against the dusty galvanized roof. A girl coming out of the store with a silvery bag of potato chips pulled up her collar as she walked to a car stuffed with kids.

When Pete Staziak got back and had lighted his first smoke in a long while—by the look of him—I knew that he was ready with questions for me. I filled him in on how I had won the opportunity to work for Abram Wise in the first place and then told him how I'd seen him last on Friday. He was interested in my telling him the reason why I was hired and I told Pete I'd send a free sample of my report writing to his office.

"Well?" he asked when I wound down.

"Well what?"

"What direction does your report point?"

"Read it yourself, Pete. I can't see any illumination in it. In fact, a lot of it is padding, just to fill up some paper. If you're asking if I know who killed Wise, I don't. I don't have any idea. It could have come from a number of directions. My favourite theory is one that has both Wise and your Ed Neustadt murdered by the same person."

"What! Come on, Benny! What are you talking about? Neustadt was not much more popular than Wise in official circles, but give me a break!"

"You're asking and I'm telling, Pete. That's the way I see it. If you're talking proof here, I'm not your man."

"Benny, Abram Wise was one of the kingpins of organized crime. You can compare him to Tony Pritchett of the English mob and not get much change back."

"Yeah, I guess so. And since it's a crook lying on the carpet—"

"I told you, he's been taken to get our *post mortem* blue-plate special. Only the best."

"—you aren't too concerned about who iced him. Right?"

"That's as cynical a statement as I've ever heard, Benny."

"It was a question. If you think the killer is also a crook, don't you think you've got your work cut out for you?"

"We treat all serious crimes seriously, Benny. We'll give it our best shot just as we always do." I'm not one hundred per cent sure why I sniped at Pete in that way. Maybe I hoped it would get him to share his findings with me, just to show that the boys in blue were on the job.

"One thing I forgot to tell you: the Registrar at the OPP has been after me in answer to some complaints that have been laid at my doorstep since Wise grabbed me from a warm bed."

"So what? We all have problems. And I'm trying to run a murder investigation. Two murder investigations, damn it!"

"See if you can find out who sicced the OPP on me. It might lead into your investigation. Might not. Just an idea."

"A rare commodity in a case like this, Benny."

"Remember, somebody took a shot at me on Wednesday. He could have been practising, Pete."

Staziak had been driving north along the newest part of the Welland Canal. The prospect was grey. Nothing was moving except for a few canvasback ducks rising from the still moving channel. The shipping season had opened officially, but there was no visible sign of it. Everybody was waiting for the hold of winter to snap.

"A very rare commodity," Pete repeated, forgetting that at least a minute had gone by. "I better get back to the house, my friend." So saying, he moved his Toyota back in the direction of the home of the late Abram Wise.

Back inside Wise's TV room, now empty of the household staff, I learned from one of the uniforms that Sylvester Ryan was involved in some outstanding warrants related to smuggling and hijacking. He was in town being questioned, while Sergeant Staziak picked up the threads of his murder investigation. Once I came into the house with Pete, I was allowed to cross the plastic barrier into the murder room. As far as I could see, there was no secondary crime suggested by the evidence. No drawers were open, no sign of looting. The windows were shut. Just as you find in a mob hit, the gun was left on the scene.

"Where were Wise's stooges when the shooting started?" I asked Pete, who had shoved his hat high up on his head instead of removing it altogether.

"According to Victoria, everybody was eating break-fast in the house next door when she found him lying on the floor behind his desk. Right here," he added in case I couldn't see the blood or the traces of a chalk line.

"Nobody heard a shot?"

"No-body!"

"Who saw him last?"

"Julie, Wise's daughter, who looks like she might be in a lot of trouble. The only thing saving her right now is the fact that Victoria only 'thinks' the front and back doors were locked. They were 'usually' locked but she can't swear they were this morning. There had been a heavy run of traffic in and out of the big room. Mickey says he was still breathing at eight-thirty this morning. That's what Mrs Long, the daughter, Julie, says too, but she has a highly peculiar sense of time among other things. So, say it's eight-thirty this morning. That'll prob-ably be closer than we can get from the body in the fridge downtown, Benny. He was alive at eight-thirty, he was dead at nine-fifteen, nine-thirty. She, this Victoria, isn't too clear about the time she found him. She called us on that phone and hers were the only prints we've got so far."

"What about noise? A shot in here must have made a commotion."

"If I fired off a piece in here, would it normally be heard next door? We tried it just before you got here. You can still smell cordite. Yes, an ordinary gun can be heard above the din of corn flakes, Rice Krispies and frying left-over pizza. Next question?"

"Did you find the silencer? If he wasn't killed with a sound-muted weapon, he's still walking around."

"We've done one search and will do another in a few

minutes. You still connect this to Ed Neustadt?"

"I don't know. Both deaths are bizarre and one at least is premeditated. Did Mickey recognize the gun?"

"It was Wise's, usually in the top right-hand drawer of his desk. He had a permit to keep it. Like everything else around here, it's an antique."

"Which doesn't usually come with a silencer, right? Thing like that could have been flushed or popped down a drain."

"In the movies, Benny. In the movies. In real life, a silencer is not something you can slip into your pocket. The silencers I've seen have all been handmade. Fancy tool or gun-making equipment. Works like the muffler on your car."

"Not my car, or the shot would have been heard."

"We're looking for a cylinder about eighteen inches long and about two and a half inches in diameter. Seen anything like that?" He gave me a grim smile that told me that this was among the more trivial problems he had to deal with. "Just the kind of mess the boys love most. At least we won't have to dig up the whole backyard."

"Why?"

"Christ, Benny, leave us some joy!"

Chapter Twenty-Two

I took the rest of the weekend off. I read a couple of
books, mysteries, some old ones by McStu that I'd
read before, but which hadn't even a nodding
acquaintance with real people, not the ones I know,
anyway. *Haste to the Gallows*, his book on the Tatarski case,
lay where I put it. I didn't want to revisit it at this time.
What I needed was a complete rest. I'd called my mother,
invited myself to dinner, but Ma said that she and Pa
were going out. I don't know where they were going; she
didn't say. She wouldn't have just given me an excuse.

I did my laundry, if you really want to know about it. I
carried it to the place on King Street run by Billy
Watson's sister. Instead of leaving it in her care, I ran it
all through the works myself. Why not? Did I have anything better to do?

The chicken soup at the Di was good, but it wasn't like
Ma's. The chopped-egg sandwiches were a little off their
best and the milk was warm. But even while I was noting
these sensations, I knew that it was me and not the food.
The Di was as dependable as the steady one-way traffic
moving along St Andrew Street from west to east. Much
as I would like to, I couldn't blame my mood on the Di.

Sunday was worse. I took a long drive in the country
to see if I could shake off the depression. I did this after

finding out how all of my friends were leading complete and busy lives that would brook no unscheduled visits. I took a ramble on the deserted golf course at Niagara-on-the-Lake, where a cold wind off the lake raked through my coat even in the lee of the old fort, with the familiar skin disease mottling its brick. I used to know the word for that. Another failure. Another thing to kick myself for. I ate at a seafood restaurant. The place was chilly. The fillet I ordered still retained the shape of the box it had been quick frozen in some months or years ago.

Then, first thing on Monday morning, as soon as I unlocked the office, it happened. Dave Rogers, may the gods be good to him, phoned and asked me to stay on the case.

"What?"

"You heard me! I want you to stick with it. You hear me, Cooperman?"

"I hear you, Dave, but I can't be hearing you right. The cops are still investigating Abe's death. They may not have arrested anybody, but give them time. It's early days," I said, borrowing Pete Staziak's phrase.

"I know all that. But six months from now, they still won't have a clue about who killed Abe Wise. I know the cops in this town: they're good and they're honest and they're too damned busy to spend much time on Abe."

"I think you're wrong."

"Well, that's your problem. My problem is that the kid I used to play hookey from school with has been killed. I can't just sit here with my arms folded. I gotta do something. So, you're it, Benny! Go get 'em!"

"You must have walked into an I-beam, Dave. This is crazy talk."

"Maybe. Maybe not. Anyway, it's none of your business. Are you so well fixed you don't need the business?

I'll call that Howard Dover guy. He gives value. Look, Benny, I was on the phone half the night talking to Paulette. You remember Paulette?"

"Sure. His first wife."

"Well, we both think that I gotta do what I can or I won't be able to live with myself. It's something I gotta do, you understand what I'm saying?"

"You're trying to buy peace of mind, Dave. I'm not selling that. I'm out of stock. Why don't you see a good doctor?"

"Don't give me that bullshit! I want you! I'll drop by some money later on this morning. I got a transport to load and my boy's off sick with the flu. You'll take a cheque, Benny?"

"Okay, I give in. It doesn't even have to be certified."

"You'll be hearing from me." He hung up and I was back in the saddle again. I gave him my best anti-sales pitch and he overrode my apparent reluctance. Trying to cool out new customers was part of my standard operating procedure. It set me up for a cue later on when I could say, "Hey, I told you *that* when you hired me!" Having said that, and still feeling good about the case, I had to recognize that I was no longer just a private investigator, I was a futile token gesture as well. As I hung up the phone on my end, I thought, I can live with that.

The cheque came by messenger and I took it, along with Wise's cheque, to the bank. Both went in without a fuss and I bought myself a good lunch at that Wellington Street place where I had met Lily, Wise's second wife. On the same trip, I dropped off a copy of my report at Niagara Regional for Pete to have a look at.

That night, Anna and I went to see an Irish play in Buffalo. It was directed by Frank Bushmill's niece, who was over from Ireland with a lively professional company.

It was very good and had us laughing most of the way home again.

Tuesday, the Ides of March, dawned gloriously. The sun poured into the apartment from an angle that seemed to be higher than it should be for the time of year. It whitened the grey carpet and crawled up the wall to where Anna was making coffee. I watched her with the grinder, pot and cups.

It looked to me like this was going to be the sort of day when there is always milk in the fridge. Anna gulped her coffee, worked on a piece of many-grained brown-bread toast and came over to the bed. "Are you getting up?"

"Sure! Doesn't it look like it?"

"Not from here. You look pretty inert."

I moved a foot out of the covers. "How's that?"

"It's a start. But I can't stay to watch it develop. I've got classes."

"Lucky classes." Anna walked around tidying and finishing up the last crumbs of her toast and sip of coffee in almost the same gesture. She was a ballet of concise movement. And then she grabbed her coat and ran out the door, leaving my face tingling from a parting kiss.

At the office, I put in a call to Pete and got Chris Savas, just back from his holiday. He promised to tell me all about his time drinking local wine in the mountains at the first opportunity. Meanwhile, he'd pass on the news to Pete that I had called.

I tried both Hart and Julie and got nowhere. Even the answering machines were in mourning. I talked to Paulette, who sounded both heart-broken and relieved at the same time.

"I've been expecting this for forty years, Benny! The second shoe had to drop sometime. And now it has."

"Are you okay?"

"Oh, I can take anything. I'm durable. Made of iron. That's me. It's Hart I'm worried about."

"I tried to call him. His answering machine's disconnected."

"He's staying with me, Benny. He has been very affectionate and is so...broken up about Abe. He says that he was just starting to know his father."

"Tell him I want to talk to him, will you, Paulette?"

"Give him time, Benny. He needs time."

"Sure. All he needs. Tell him I'm sorry for his trouble."

I left word with Lily that I wanted to speak to Julie when she surfaced too. Lily wasn't covered in sackcloth and ashes by the sound of her. But her bright talk betrayed the fact that she had been drinking. Lily wasn't one of nature's drinkers. She was like me. It took a lot to make it happen.

This was the Ides of March. Have I mentioned that? Julius Caesar and Little Caesar both could have been butchered in fine style while I waited for the phone to ring. The Ides were come but not gone. I tried to remember our high-school production of the Shakespeare play. I played Cinna the Poet. It was a part that allowed me to watch a lot of the rehearsals from the empty seats of the auditorium. I think at one point I could have recited the whole script. Now the Ides, such bad news to Caesar, had become good news for me. It was just a week ago that I had been indelicately hauled from my warm bed to attend Abe Wise in his lair. I rehearsed all of last week again in my mind. It seemed like three months ago.

I reread my report, hoping that the killer's name would jump out at me like a piece of toast from a badly adjusted toaster. It didn't.

There must be some way to match my sudden good luck with action. Reading my own prose didn't exactly ring with clanging claymores. I wasn't storming the barricades. I could see who was answering the phone at Wise's secret number, but I thought better of it. The last thing in the world I wanted was to step on the heels of Pete's investigation. I'd have to give Mickey and the boys a wide berth for a day or two. Just in case Pete was nearby.

One thing I knew I'd have to get was some idea of the timetable. Who saw Wise and when? Pete had it, or had been working on it, but I couldn't pester him. I was involved enough in the story, so that I knew Pete would get back to me before too long. But I also knew that I was nowhere near the scene of the crime during the likely hours.

He'd told me that Julie had seen him last. It had been a busy morning. Hart, Julie and others had come over to talk to him. The last one had brought one of Wise's old guns with a silencer attached. The gun was recovered at the scene. Pete said there were no prints. There hardly ever are on the grips of handguns. It was the silencer that intrigued me. The killer had carried it away. Why? Silencers aren't items you can buy over the counter. They have to be made. Maybe the workmanship could be traced. That was an idea. I could easily see the reason for the silencer: it gave the murderer the chance to get away undetected.

The Three Stooges, with Mickey Armstrong thrown in, were excellent bodyguards. Their security was pretty good. At least that's what Wise thought. In practice, they were less good than advertised. Once a pizza was introduced among them, they became side-tracked like errant Ninja turtles. They took their breakfast seriously too. Mickey told me they were a good team except when they were eating. The clear message was that the boys weren't on the job and that the murderer was counting on this.

This review was interrupted by the phone ringing away at the ends of the earth. I didn't catch it until the third ring, even though I was sitting within easy reach. I'd been far away in my thoughts. It was Hart. He was excited and hard to understand. I tried to calm him down, expressed my sympathy and heard from the horse's mouth some of the hearsay I'd got from Paulette. Paulette was a good witness. After a few minutes of rambling through reports of his last few meetings with his father, he got on to the very last one, which was what I wanted to hear.

"It was early, you see. He was always at his best then. I gave him a cheque for the car. At first he wouldn't take it."

"You mean the sports car that you bought from Shaw?"

"Yeah. The Triumph. He covered my bad cheque and now that I had the money, I wanted to pay him back."

"May I ask where you got the money?"

"I unloaded a few things I didn't need any more. And I moved. I was paying too much where I was living. The sublet gave me some cash in hand."

"And Paulette?"

"Sure. She helped. Anyway, in the end he accepted the money and we got to talking about my future. For the first time ever, he was listening instead of telling me what he wanted me to do. It was okay. Then, he had to go because there were other people waiting. We started to shake hands and then he brought up Shaw and Whitey York and how they were trying to shake him down. I got mad and he became the monster he had always been again. That was my last view of him."

"He had a thing about control."

"Yeah. He governed by moral terror when I lived at ome."

"I still don't like the way this bounces," I said, shak-ng my head at the window opposite me. "Shaw and 'ork are trying to get at your father through your bum heque, right?"

"If you say so."

"So why was Shaw killed?"

"Yeah, I read about that! I guess he was not a team ind of guy. What do you want me to say, Cooperman?"

"One thing is sure: he wasn't killed over a debt as mall as the one you're talking about. Your dad could ave bought ten Triumphs if he wanted to and put it lown for petty cash."

"A slight exaggeration. But, I get your point. A guy ike Shaw could have had lots of enemies. Lots of quasi-atisfied customers."

"Okay. Back to the morning your dad was killed. Who lid you see on your way in and on your way out?"

"Nobody special. Victoria was in the kitchen baking a ie. Mickey was cleaning his boots on a newspaper, also n the kitchen. The other fellows were out of sight, in the other house, I guess."

"Did you see any strange cars in front or in back?"

"No. And there were no cars parked anywhere near he house as far as I can remember. Wait a minute! There vas a Chrysler Le Baron, now that I think of it. Parked ust outside the crescent where the house is."

"Colour?"

"Red, I think. Sort of burgundy red."

"Old or new?"

"Newish, although it had one eye bashed in."

"A broken headlight? Remember which side?"

"Right side, I think. Yes it was. Why? Do you know

whose it was?"

I told him that it sounded familiar but that was all then thanked him for his help and told him that I might be getting in touch again fairly soon. I had to cut off the conversation, because he began to go into the whole thing again from the beginning like a television rerun. And I had a job to do for a change: I had to try to place that car.

Chapter Twenty-Three

With Chris Savas back on the job at Niagara Regional, and after a two-week vacation to Cyprus, I suspected that I might find both him and Pete Staziak at the little café run by a cousin of Chris's. It was on Academy Street near the bus terminal, which was becoming an uninterrupted asphalt wilderness with a few old houses standing like brick icebergs in the sea. One of these was the home of the Spitfire. I don't know why Chris's cousin called it that, but that was what it said on the plastic sign, next to the familiar red-and-white Coke symbol.

When I got there, the place was deserted and I felt strange, like I'd walked into the women's john by mistake. The cousin tried to place me but failed. His welcome was cordial but lacking the warmth I had seen on my earlier visits with Savas. I took a small table near the back and ordered a kebab of chicken. I somehow guessed that they wouldn't stock my usual chopped-egg sandwiches. I had taken about three bites of the chicken-filled pita, when Chris and Pete walked in. Not only the cousin but the cousin's wife were all over Chris like a rash inside of ten seconds. The warmth of the greeting spilled over on Pete Staziak. Even in Greek it made him smile. I nibbled my kebab with the bits of salad that had been thrown in with it. Two tables were pushed together and coats were collected. Pete was the first to spot me. He alerted Chris and soon I was included in the bubble of friendliness and moved plate, fork, body and napkin to their table.

At first we quizzed Savas about his holiday. There were no signs of a tan on his big meaty face, but his eyes, usually as cold as steel ball-bearings, danced with the pleasure of recalling it for us. "The island is still divided," he said, draining a glass of something the proprietor-cousin had pressed on Chris. "There aren't as many UN blue berets as when I was there last. My village is still lamenting the loss of its orchards on the other side of the mountain. They say that talks are going on, but that things will never get better." Here Chris laughed. "They've been saying that since the Turks came the first time. When the Venetians came. When the English came." Pete asked a few astute political questions and we all nodded at Chris's answers.

Without our ordering from the menu, the proprietor brought a feast to the table—soft roast potatoes, hummus, and darkly roasted pieces of chicken, lamb and maybe even goat. As our faces became rosy with contentment and grease, Chris continued to tell stories about his trip, his family, and the adventures he'd had along the way. By the time the coffee came in brass ewers like the ones in the Lebanese restaurant below my apartment, Chris was beginning to sound hoarse. I just sat there listening and chewing on a slice of lamb cooked "in the thieves' style," which turns out to be roasted with herbs and potatoes in a sealed container.

It wasn't really until after we left the café that Pete had anything to say that had a special interest for me. I told him that I had been retained by Dave Rogers and that I was thus still interested in Abe Wise's murder.

"Just as long as you stay out of my way, Benny. That's all I ask." He tried to give me a serious look, but the shine of grease on his face torpedoed the effect. I mentioned it and he went to work with his blue-and-white polka-dotted handkerchief. I told him that I intended to stay as far away from his investigation as possible. Then I gave him an example of the kinds of questions I would not be asking him. Sometimes that worked with Pete. This time it didn't.

"I knew it! I knew it!" he yelled, blowing me off the curb into Academy Street.

"Stored information's no use to you, Pete. Information only gets hot when it's in movement. That's when things begin to happen. Like when there's an exchange."

"Benny, you know what you're shovelling? Besides, you don't have anything to trade."

"Easy on him, Pete," Chris said, putting a big hand on his partner's shoulder. "He has to make rent this month. And he never got paid when we put Julian Newby away, remember?"

"Okay, okay. We'll entertain a few questions." Chris rolled his eyes and dropped behind us where he could watch this process of reciprocity advance. I guess he didn't like what he saw because he quickly caught up to us again.

"Hart Wise told me that he'd given his old man some money during their last meeting. Did you find a cheque with his name on it?" Pete looked at me like I was a stranger. He thought a minute, then shook his head.

"Why would the kid lie?" he asked both of us.

Chris shrugged. "Maybe he's invented the story of a reconciliation just for our benefit. Maybe there was no cheque."

"What do you know about Julie Long's boyfriend?"

"Oh, that's a good one. Didier Santerre is another of your fast operators. Only he does it in black tie. His magazine has been losing money steadily for the last three years. Hart Wise isn't the only bad paper hanger in town, Benny. Santerre's face is as well known in local banks as the Queen's."

"Ha!" I said. "I thought so. Didier made a half-hearted attempt to pick up the check at the Patriot Volunteer the other night. And I'd already been tipped they had a sucker to pay. I thought he was trying to impress Julie. A guy with a bankroll doesn't have to impress anybody. It's the poor buggers who have to spend the money."

"Sure, toilet paper's cheaper by the case. But who do you know who buys it that way?"

"It's bad luck to buy it by the case. You might drop dead while you're still on your first roll."

"Listen you two comedians, I didn't come back to this cold climate to hear you bellyache. Besides, your example stinks. It's a bad analogy if I ever heard one. This is my first day back, you guys, give me a break!"

We walked along in silence down the right-hand side of Academy. Ahead of us we could see the scaffolding around the Folk Arts Festival office at the top of the street. The building, the original "academy" for which the street was named, was the oldest secondary school in Ontario. City Council cherished it and kept property developers at bay. They had recently rejected a plan to have the old place sandblasted after discovering that the process would do serious damage. My reflections were interrupted when Pete slipped on a piece of ice. I caught his arm and we both went down. As we brushed one another off, ignoring Chris's laughter, I asked:

"Did you ever hear back anything about Neustadt's

death, Pete?"

"You still trying to tie that to what happened to Wise?"

"I'm keeping an open mind, that's all. Well?"

"There was nothing wrong with the jack, Benny. Somebody had to have turned the valve."

"Maybe Neustadt hadn't tightened it before he got under the car?"

"Nope. If the valve's not turned off, you can't hoist the car in the first place. The jack can't suck and blow at the same time. Only it's not air, it's hydraulics, Benny. How the hell did you get onto this? You a closet engineer?"

"So, you are saying that you are considering his death murder?"

"Considering, Benny, but not flapping the news around. We're keeping quiet until the monkey thinks he's safe."

"I'll keep buttoned up too, Pete. By the way, was he lying on a creeper board with casters on it?"

"Yeah. Why?"

"I've been trying to imagine the scene. It got so real, I had to make sure I wasn't inventing the evidence."

By now we had come along Church Street to the front door of Niagara Regional. We stood for a while together, blowing hot vapour with a garlicky perfume at each other.

"Yeah," said Savas, "I was away for that. Jesus! Not a nice way to go."

"Did you know him well, Chris?" I asked.

"Benny, you don't want to know about Ed Neustadt. You don't want to know."

Chapter Twenty-Four

The last man in the world I expected to see was standing in front of my desk. He looked terrible. His shock of fair hair no longer made his face look fresh and pink. Whitey York was grey and bloodless as he tried to catch his breath after his climb up my twenty-eight steps. His camel-hair coat was unbuttoned and stained along one side. His necktie was askew and his shirt looked dirty. A pong came off him like he'd been taking lessons from Kogan, the former panhandler who was now my landlord. He was in serious condition, so I got up and helped him into a chair.

"You know about Gord?" he said, still out of breath. I nodded my head. When had that happened? It was hard keeping track of the days. It was before that terrible weekend: Friday. Yes, Wise was still among the living on Friday. York looked like he had been in hiding since Friday.

"Could you use a shot," I said. He shook his head and waved his hand in an ambiguous gesture.

"No!" he said. "I don't need any more than I've already had." Good, I thought. I'd have had to ask Frank Bushmill to lend me some of his Irish. My file drawers were empty. "Cooperman, what should I do? I can't go home. I don't want to be murdered."

"Hey, hold on! Hold on! Who do you think is trying to kill you?"

"They got Gord Shaw. I'm next."

"What makes you think that? Wise is dead. You know about that?"

"Do you think that it's over then? His boys might... You know. I'm scared, Cooperman. I don't care who knows it."

"Look, Whitey, Shaw was involved with other people besides you, wasn't he? Why do you think it was Wise?"

I had my own ideas about this, but I wanted to hear it from York himself. "It was a scam," he said. "Biggest thing I've ever been involved in."

"It was about a car, wasn't it? But not that old Triumph. That was just a come-on. Right?" York nodded his head, letting it fall on his chest at the end, as though he'd just run a mile in under three minutes.

"Yeah. Yeah. You got that right. The kid was in on it, of course. The whole scheme turned on the father-son relationship."

"You better tell me about it."

"You ever hear of the 1964 Alfa Romeo Giulia 1600 Canguro?"

"Can't say I have. But you would have guessed that already."

"The Canguro never went into production. There were a couple of prototypes, but that's all. The last of these test models was destroyed in 1970. Except for a few spare parts, the Canguro no longer exists."

"I'm listening. Go on."

"Don't look at me as though I'm the expert. Shaw told me all this. When a car is rare, Mr Cooperman, it fetches a very high price. When it is extinct, you can write your own ticket. This one car is worth a couple of Renoirs, a van Gogh, a Rembrandt. Shaw knew where the only Canguro in the world is under wraps in a garage in Southampton, England. He needed operating money to get it fixed up. The three of us were partners. Hart was the link to the money we needed."

"Which is more than the cost of a TR2, even an antique TR2, right?"

"That's it. We were using the Triumph as bait."

"So, on the surface it looked like you were going to press charges against Hart for the bad cheque, but really the three of you were counting on the old man buying you off."

"I told Shaw not to talk to Wise directly. I told him to let me handle it. But he was that sure…"

"And it cost him his life. Now if you'd been the contact…Well, who knows?"

"Shaw kept saying that when we had the Alfa here, we could pay back our debts. We could make it all right after we had the car."

"Where did you spend the weekend?"

"I have a married sister in Guelph. I didn't think he'd find me there. Then I read about his murder. I don't know where I stand."

"Have you talked to Hart?"

"I tried to, but he hung up on me. What the hell am I going to do, Mr Cooperman?"

"Well, it's my guess that you are in no immediate danger except maybe from Hart. Wise's death has stirred up the mud at the bottom of the pond. It won't clear overnight. You can go home and take a shower. That's my free advice, go home and take a shower."

Whitey York pulled himself out of the chair, gave me a hunted look and left the door wide open. I could hear him clumping on the stairs. I nearly sent him down the fire escape in back, but I don't think I could have done it with a straight face.

I was about to shut the office and call it a day when Frank Bushmill stopped in to greet me.

"Stately, plump Benny Cooperman," he said. "Where have you been keeping yourself? Has anyone else been shooting holes in your walls?" I told him, without going into detail. He nodded sagely, looking stately and plump himself.

"And have you run into any exciting corns or bunions since we last talked?"

"Ah, Benny. You don't know the half of it. The practice of medicine, even below the knee, continues to be rewarding, but my private life is a burden. I don't want to go into that. I feel a little like the philandering surgeon that Oliver St John Gogarty commented on: I made my reputation with my knife and lost it with my fork. I see myself as the arch mender, if you'll excuse the horrible pun." He went on in that vein for a few minutes, with all sorts of references flying high and wide, well beyond my fielding skills. He always had nice things to say about Anna and I appreciated him for those.

Then Chris Savas was there standing in a pool of water from rain dripping from his raincoat and holding an umbrella that had been blown inside out by the wind. He looked awkward standing there until I remembered how seldom he had climbed the stairs to my office. After introductions and a few pleasantries which again required a Dublin scholar to understand them, Frank tried out his Greek on Chris. There must be more kinds of Greek than one because both of them looked bewildered by what the other added to the three or four exchanges, and then they gave up and returned to English, where I tried to join them. As it turned out,

Frank knew the island of Cyprus from some years ago and so I was again excluded from the conversation while unfamiliar place names filled the empty hallway between our offices. In the end, Frank begged off further palaver, said good-night, and went down the stairs and into the chilly night.

"Is Dr Bushmill a good friend, Benny?" Frank asked when the street door closed.

"He's taken a few lumps on the head on my behalf since I've known him. Yes, he's a good friend. He's also trying to become my university."

"Whenever you can find him sober after hours."

"Oh, you know about Frank, do you?"

"I live in this town, Benny, and Frank isn't inconspicuous."

"He's a damn good friend, Chris. I wish he could be less of a pain to himself."

"And St Patrick's Day is coming. He's taking the short road to the cemetery if you ask me."

"What brings you to my consulting rooms?"

"Pete's been filling me in about Wise and Neustadt. I thought that maybe we should talk after all."

He pulled up a chair, one of the leftovers from my father's store, and I pulled my swivel chair around so that the desk didn't come between us. It was my training in amateur theatre that suggested this approach.

"Did you know Wise?" I asked.

"Knew? Who knew Abe Wise? He was always a mystery man. The only time he was arrested was before you were in long pants. My very first partner, dear old Michael Prescott, had the pleasure of bringing him in with a bag of illegal goodies one night on Louisa Street. It was his first collar, Benny. He told me about it one night on Lake Street when he'd been shot up and I was trying to keep him talking until the ambulance arrived. Michael—we never called him Mike—was a lot older than me; he would have been well away into his retirement now if—"

"If he hadn't died in the line of duty?"

"Michael? Dead? Not a chance. He's still running a resort up on Lake Muskoka. Still plays squash every morning like he's forty. Still collects Toby mugs. Still dresses like a kid. No, Benny, Michael quit Niagara Regional when Neustadt got too much for him."

"When was that?"

"Nineteen seventy-nine."

"No, I mean when he arrested Wise."

"That was in nineteen fifty-two."

"The year of the Tatarski case."

"Yeah. This happened about a week into her trial."

"Pete told me that Neustadt turned Wise loose. Is that right?"

"Yeah. And after Michael had worked so hard. He'd been watching the kid, see. Saw him go into the house and was waiting for him when he came out with the loot. He was feeling like a real cop when he brought him into the station. Michael said that Neustadt questioned the kid for half the night. Then he asked Michael to step into the interrogation room with them. Wise was sitting with his head down on the table and Ed came over to Michael saying that he thought that since the stolen goods had been recovered and since the lad—he called him a lad— had been only playing at breaking and entering and since... He went on and on with his 'sinces.' Michael could see what was coming, so he was ready for it. I mean, hell, Ed was a sergeant, for Christ's sake, and Michael was still on probation..."

"So he let Wise walk."

"Yeah. And that was the last time Abe Wise was in a police station."

"He tried to make Michael Prescott believe that he had caught Wise taking his first step on a road of crime and this was the moment to reclaim him. Is that it?"

"That was his version."

"But Prescott didn't buy that?"

"Hell no! That kid had been in and out more windows than Peter Pan, for Christ's sake! That's what Michael said. He had been watching him."

"That fits with what his first wife told me. Do you know why he let Wise walk? Did your friend?"

"I used to drag it out every couple of years, usually when I'd had a run-in with Ed. Never could figure it."

"I think I'm beginning to see some light. It's the only thing that makes it make sense."

"What's that?"

"We know that Wise was working that part of town: Welland Avenue and north of there. Suppose, just suppose for a minute, that Wise also broke into the Tatarski house. Russell Avenue. It's in the same part of town."

"Hey, what are you saying?"

"I'm not *saying* anything, I'm supposing, thinking out loud." I tried to focus again before speaking. "Wise goes into the Tatarski house. Unfortunately, Mary's mother hears him. She comes downstairs, there's a struggle, and she's killed. It's murder while a robbery is in progress. Neustadt isn't the first cop on the scene, but he is called in. Came running, I'll bet, because he had been in that house before."

"So, when Michael Prescott collars young Wise, Neustadt says nothing about what he suspects, or even what he forced Wise to admit. Mary Tatarski's trial is going on." Chris stared out my window with his fingers coming together under his chin. I let him think for a second. "Well, well, well!" he said.

"Yeah. Does he call up the Crown prosecutor and say 'Let the girl go, I've got the real killer,' or does he let the kid walk?"

"Neustadt was the chief Crown witness. He headed the whole investigation. He would have had to admit he'd read all of the evidence wrong. His whole career was riding on this trial and his handling of this case."

Savas blew some air between his teeth. It wasn't quite a whistle. "Well, well," he said.

"What do you think, Chris?"

"Benny, I've been a cop all my working life. If you'd said that about anybody at Niagara Regional except Ed, I'd have hit you so hard you wouldn't be able to stand until Christmas. But Neustadt..."

"But Neustadt..." We didn't speak for a couple of minutes.

"It makes sense, Benny. I never would have thought... You see, Ed was the first man on the scene when the Tatarski house was robbed five years earlier. Did you know that? He let the girl walk that time. Old Ed wasn't going to be played for a sap twice. Two break-ins stretched the plausible."

"He saw the second break-in as a copycat of the first, the real break-in. It made a believable story. It covered the known facts or I've misread McStu's book."

"Neustadt had this tenacious streak in him. He wouldn't let go."

"So, there was an understanding between Wise and Neustadt. A deal had been agreed to, even if they didn't put it into words. Wise would walk and keep his mouth shut. And the trial would move on just the way it was planned."

"You know, Benny, there are no living witnesses. They're all dead: the Tatarski girl, the mother, Ed, and Wise."

"Yeah, we won't be able to prove a thing without digging out your former partner from Lake Muskoka. What you just told me is officially hearsay. But it has the ring of truth."

"I guess it doesn't change diddly."

"You know, Chris, Wise hated Neustadt for that. He was at the funeral, you know. I've never seen such hate. You knew Wise when you came on the force yourself?"

"He made a career of staying away from the bright lights. Except when there was a charity ball or two hundred of our best citizens in tuxedos dressed to the nines for some reason. I saw him a few times, was part of a couple of campaigns to try to nail him for something. Hell, if they could only get Al Capone for tax evasion, I thought we might get Wise for spitting on the sidewalk. But, we never could. The part of his life that we can see is—was—exemplary."

"And Neustadt, Chris. Did he support the schemes to bag Wise?"

"Ed could be a stickler for boxing in a suspect. If there was an escape hatch visible, he would try to cool things down until we really had him in the bag." Chris scratched his belly at the belt-line and considered what he had just heard. "I hadn't thought about it, but you're right: while Ed was gung-ho for all kinds of villains, he kind of soft-pedalled Wise."

"Sure. Know why? Because a tacit blackmail situation had been established."

"What do you mean 'tacit blackmail situation'?"

"After he was allowed to walk, after Mary Tatarski was allowed to hang, Wise had Ed Neustadt in his pocket."

"You mean Ed was paying Wise off all those years?"

"No. As far as I know they never met again. But this secret was lying there between them. If Ed pursued Wise too closely, then Wise could tell what he knew. Wise had Ed Neustadt's career in the palms of his hairy hands. Neither one of them probably noticed it at first. Wise had some growing and maturing in crime to undergo before his threat ripened."

"But Ed Neustadt gave Abe Wise a fresh start. What did he have to complain about?"

"What does a fresh start mean in a community that will take an innocent woman and hang her?"

Chapter Twenty-Five

Invited Chris to join Anna and me for dinner at a place Anna had found near Turner's Corners. It was an old coaching inn that had also been a gas station and a hamburger joint. Now it had been dolled up as its original self, without exaggerating things the way the Patriot Volunteer did over the river. This was authentic without hype, not a movie designer's idea of an old inn, but the inn itself with all of its blemishes showing. The best thing about it was a huge fireplace which had a fire going in it, while a few birds and joints turned on spits above twin andirons. It was the sort of place you felt you had come home to as a familiar haunt, even though it was my first visit.

Chris and I kept clear of the case and Anna made light of a brewing crisis in the university's history department. The focus of the talk turned on Chris, whose recent adventures on the island of his birth held our complete attention. He was a good raconteur. Better than that, he was a good delineator of political and social differences. By the time he had finished, both of his listeners knew more about the present situation on the island and the subtle differences between the professional and other classes in the villages, towns and capital. As for the meal, it was simplicity itself, roasted meat and boiled potatoes served with greens. The dessert was apple pie. It was what the food editor of the *Beacon* would have called a cliché meal, but all of our faces were rosy with contentment as we gathered our coats, and ran through a fine Scotch mist to the car.

The following morning I called Napier McNabb University in Hamilton to try to catch up with the record of Drina Tatarski, or Tait, as she was calling herself. The voice in the office at the other end took a lot of convincing. I heard a prepared speech about giving out confidential information. I explained my business, the woman on the phone explained the rules. I suggested that she should be the judge of what information was confidential and what was for public consumption. She suggested that I drive to Hamilton to see her in her office. I asked whether the rules were different for people on the spot and didn't that tend to prejudice inquiries from, say, Halifax or Vancouver. There was a sigh at the other end, a sign either of frustration or capitulation. I pressed my advantage.

"We have her as Alexandrina Tait, not Tatarski, Mr Cooperman. Tait was her legitimate name. It had been legally changed. She dropped out at the end of her first year. I can't tell you what her grades were, but they were above average for first year."

"You mean she could read and write?"

"What a cynic you are, Mr Cooperman. Miss Tait appears to have been able to do more than that. She was quite accomplished. French Club, Fencing Club, Archery Club."

"Is there a reason given for her dropping out?"

"There's a note about sickness at home in Grantham."

"I see. Is there anyone who knew her? I'm looking for a friend or teacher; someone who can give me a clue to where she might be now."

"You might talk to Professor Hardy. He does first-year English. I think he might remember her." She gave me a telephone number and wished me luck. By the end, we were getting on famously.

I had no luck getting in touch with Professor Hardy. He wasn't at the number so I left a message on his machine. I began to feel the urge to drive to Hamilton to spy out the land for myself, but there was work to do on other fronts. Professor Hardy could wait.

Julie. I decided to focus on Julie. Together with her brother, Julie had the most to gain by her father's death. She also had a ready market for any money she came into: *Mode Magazine*. I called her mother. Julie hadn't been seen. I called Wise's secret number and got Victoria, who said she hadn't seen Julie since the morning of the shooting. I finished the dregs of cold coffee in a styrofoam cup and was sitting back in my chair wondering where to look next, when the phone rang. It was Julie.

"You're lucky I'm a dutiful daughter, Mr Cooperman. I just called my mother. She told me she'd spoken to you a minute ago. What can I do for you?" She sounded a trifle breathless, but it was part of her manner to appear to be in a rush. I shouldn't imagine that she had just raced up three flights of stairs to place the call. I told her that I needed to see her. She mentioned The Snug at the Beaumont Hotel, which was still one of the few places in town where it was not chic to order draught beer, and the only place for miles around where free peanuts were supplied to every table. She gave me a couple of hours to get ready for the meeting, so busy was her schedule. I accounted myself lucky that she didn't want to meet at the top of the CN Tower in Toronto. I spent some of the time back at the library and some of it on the phone with

Duncan Harvey, the architect and crusader for the quiet repose of an innocent Mary Tatarski.

"Sure I remember our talk, Benny. How is your case going?"

"I'm still digging in, Duncan. There's a lot that's been hidden."

"Ah, you begin to see what McStu and I had to go through."

"Mary didn't ever confess to anything, did she? Anything at all?"

"No. She admitted that she and her mother had had words on the night of the crime and that relations between them were not happy. But that's all. Margaret, the older sister, didn't get on that well with her mother either. That's why she was planning to move out. Her 'motive' was at least as good as her sister's. The first story Mary told to Sergeant Neustadt was the one she stuck to: early to bed with sleeping pills after an argument, and didn't hear anything until she was wakened by her sister after the body had been discovered and the police had been sent for."

"Was there any serious attempt at suicide?"

"That was all Neustadt. She took an ordinary dose and was on her feet before the police arrived. If you need an example of 'facts' made out of whole cloth, that's a dilly."

"She never changed any detail in her story?"

"Not as far as I could read in the transcripts of the pre-trial and the trial. Her statement to Neustadt was almost word for word what she said on the witness stand. I talked to the matron at the jail, Mrs Strippe, and she saw her from the first night they brought her in right up to the moment she said goodbye. She said that her story never changed. McStu talked to all of the warders, and, apart from little human stories, there was nothing new.

Unless she unburdened herself to the hangman, she went through the trap with her secret untold."

"Did you or McStu talk to him?"

"When the book was being researched, Mr McCarthy was in the old country, somewhere in the Aran Islands. We tried, but we couldn't reach him. I heard that he had come back to Ontario and was living in a house in Grimsby. I doubt if he would have anything to add to her story. They say he works fast. You can't say a lot in thirty or forty seconds, can you?"

"Is that how long it takes?"

"So I've read, Benny. There are no speeches, you know. The sheriff doesn't read the death warrant. Nothing like that. Strictly business. Why I remember reading in the famous Palmer case—"

I interrupted Duncan's extensive store of gallows lore by telling him that my other line was flashing. I have often wished I had a second line, but the excuse of having to answer the imaginary one works almost as well.

At the appointed hour, I was waiting in The Snug for Julie Long. I hoped that she'd come alone. I didn't think I could cope with the entourage again. And if it ever came time for me to buy a round, I'd be wiped out. Dave Rogers hadn't said a word about expenses.

The waiter brought me one of those Campari things and I sipped it for about twenty minutes, when the waiter returned with a note:

Benny,

Will you please come up to Room 614 when you get this right away. I'm in a lot of trouble.

Julie

I paid for my drink, pocketed the rest of the peanuts against the unknown situation in Room 614 and walked through the darkened lounge to the door connected to the hotel lobby. I pushed the button and waited for the elevator.

The ride up to the sixth floor was in itself uneventful, but it reminded me that there was such a thing as an "elevator feeling." I can't describe it, but it happens all the time. Room 614 was on the side of the narrow corridor facing and looking down on St Andrew Street. Julie opened the door. It was a big room, placed a few floors above the rooms set aside for salesmen showing their lines. The place was a mess with clothes strewn everywhere. I couldn't help thinking that the pantyhose on the chair and the three or four blouses on the bed and hanging on doorknobs was a glimpse into an untidy mind. Then I remembered my own room and swallowed the thought.

"Oh Benny, I'm so glad you could come!" She carefully closed, bolted and chained the door. She was wearing a sheer something-or-other covered by another semi-see-through wrap. They were both the colour of milky coffee. She may have sounded distraught, but her make-up was intact, which is always a good sign. I moved a few peanuts to my mouth, while she turned to clear a space for me to sit down. In the end, I shared a love-seat with an intimate garment, which she hadn't thought enough of to move out of sight. Across the room near the bathroom door was a room-service trolley with the remains of a meal on it. I was thinking that "at least her appetite is healthy," when it hit me that she might have been planning on me for dessert.

"I was sorry to hear about your father," I said, by way of opening. She couldn't pounce on me after that.

"He's to blame for this!" she said. "Daddy, Daddy. It's always been Daddy!"

"Why don't you tell me the whole story from the beginning?"

"Would you like a drink? I can get anything you want from the bar." I accepted a Coke and watched her pour Scotch into a glass and smother it with soda. "There's a whole basket of fruit if you want something to eat, Benny. Cashews the size of kittens."

"No thanks, Julie. What you can do is tell me what this is all about. Is it your father's death?"

"It's Didier!" she said. "He's gone off! Just like that. He checked out of his hotel and left no forwarding number. I can't believe it! Could he have been kidnapped?"

"Anything is possible. When did you see him last? And have you talked with his regular cronies? What about that model, Morna McGuire? He's not likely to go very far from her, is he?"

"Didier and Morna? What are you talking about? Morna's got a boyfriend in Hollywood. The actor Byron Aslin, you know? You didn't think…? No, it's been Didier and me. And now I can't find him!"

"Where does he edit this magazine of his?"

"Why in Paris! What's that got to do with it?"

"Well, how much work can he do on the banks of the Welland Canal? He had to go back to work eventually, hadn't he?"

"But why not tell me? Why just…just…vanish?"

"You said that your father was behind this. How?"

"He didn't like Didier. He never liked any of my friends. He jinxed it. He always does!"

"Did," I corrected, not meaning to hurt, but not wanting to shut out the real world either from this room with its imitation French furniture and luxurious cashews, which I had found and had been working my way through.

Julie, sitting on the edge of the bed, leaned towards me. "Benny, I need to find him." She was crying now, and the make-up around her eyes was being put to the test. Her outer wrap had fallen open and it left a good deal of Julie on display through the diaphanous other thing. Usually, I'm a pushover for a cheap thrill, but there was something about Julie that made me feel detached and reserved. The hand of the stage manager was all but tangible. She was faintly comic and consequently what was bothering her was comic as well. She was an attractive woman; I had to give her that, but it wasn't working on me. It was a note too high for me to hear, or, maybe, too low. Anyway, what I'm saying is that all these see-through layers, the tears and the pleading voice had the emotional appeal of a block of orange Cheddar. Anna would have been proud of me. But this didn't have anything to do with my feelings for Anna. I was totally committed to Anna, but I recognized that my maleness was not totally under my control. I remembered Pia Morley and Helen Blackwood from a few years ago. And I mustn't forget the beautiful Cath Bracken. No, Julie was never in their class.

"Tell me about your last meeting with your father," I said.

"What has that got to do with anything?" She seemed shocked at the change of subject.

"I need to know. How did you get to the house?"

"Didier," she said.

"A red Le Baron with one headlight broken?"

"I did that near Stowe. We were driving back from skiing in Vermont. He was awfully nice about it."

"So, he waited for you in the car?"

"I think so. I guess he could have followed me. The back door was open."

"What happened next?"

"I talked to Daddy and then I left. That's all."

"Not so fast. You came in the door. Who did you see?"

"I remember now. I could smell baking in the kitchen, so I went in to talk to Victoria, who had been making pies. Her husband, that Mickey, was there, but he went out as soon as he had tugged the old forelock. Mickey is always very deferential. Victoria and I don't have a lot to say to one another. I don't think she approves of me. She's very judgmental, I think, although she hardly opens her mouth."

"Did you see your brother?"

"My *half*-brother, you mean. No."

"Okay, go on. You went from the kitchen into the big office to see your father?"

"That's right. Then we talked. He gave me a lecture, not one of his better ones, and then he gave me some money to take away the bad taste and I left the same way I came in."

"See anyone on your way out?"

"No, just Victoria. But Didier wasn't in the car. I had to wait for a few minutes."

"How long? This could be important."

"It wasn't more than five minutes. Maybe longer. I had my fur coat, so I wasn't cold. The car was open, and I just sat and waited."

"What did Didier say when he came back?"

"Nothing. He was in a mood."

"How convenient."

"You have no right to say that! You take a cheap, cynical view of artistic people, Benny. Didier's an exceptionally talented artist. How could you appreciate him?"

"How much money did your father give you?"

"Thirty-five thousand dollars."

"That would take away quite a lot of bad taste. Did he give you cash?"

"No, it was a cheque. He never keeps large amounts of cash in the house. He didn't used to anyway."

"What did you do with it?"

"Is that any of your business?"

"I'm no gossip, Julie. I'm just vacuuming as much information as I can in the hope that some of it might tell me something I don't already know. I think I can make a good guess about the cheque. You endorsed it and gave it to your friend. Right?"

"What if I did?"

"Well, Julie, you might have given him his airfare back to Paris. Ever think of it that way?"

Chapter Twenty-Six

I was sitting in my office trying to sort the files that had taken the bullet meant for me. They were in shreds, partly because of the bullet, that had run around inside the filing drawer and partly because of the forensic man's efforts at finding the bullet amid the confetti they both had created. It was the morning of the following day, St Patrick's Day, and I was feeling virtuous about having extricated myself from Julie's hotel room with my dignity intact. She hadn't seriously intended to seduce me; it was just a reflex. When she calmed down we took a walk to the end of St Andrew Street and back again. I suggested to her that she might invest some of her inheritance in putting some life back into the closed-up stores on both sides of the street. It got her mind off Didier for a few minutes, which was what I was trying to do.

My housekeeping was cut short by a phone call from a Professor Hardy in Hamilton. "Who?" I asked, and he repeated his name: "Lee Hardy, of Napier McNabb University."

"Oh!" I said, suddenly remembering that line of inquiry. "Yes, Professor. Thanks for calling back. I'm trying to track down one of your former first-year English students from a few years ago: Alexandrina Tait.

Ring any bells?"

"The bells have been ringing, Mr Cooperman. You see, I had an earlier call from Mrs Wood at the college, who told me about your inquiry."

"A thorough and responsible woman, Mrs Wood. I remember our conversation well."

"About Drina, though, even with the off-stage prompting, I can't come up with much. She was a disturbed young woman—we aren't allowed to say 'girl' any more, Mr Cooperman; the thought police are at our backs. The new political correctness is the old prudery, if you ask me. But you were asking about Drina, weren't you? I said 'disturbed.' 'Preoccupied' might be another word. I don't mean busy with undergraduate things— from what I remember, Drina was almost a loner. There was something, well, something that makes it easy for me to remember her, while other faces have all drifted out to sea. I guess 'memorable' is the word I've been searching for. Memorable. And there was an oddness about her, a slate in her machinery somewhere, although she was bright enough."

"What became of her?"

"Ah, that's the big question. She wrote to me from New York that she had met and married a businessman of some sort, a man who dealt in trader bonds, whatever they are. That, and a few postcards from Connecticut, represent the latest news I have of her."

"Did you know her apart from your classes with her, Professor?"

"Ah, well, she was part of a group that used to come and drink beer and listen to Bach at my house."

"Is there anything else you can remember?"

"She had a great capacity for concentration when she wanted to focus on a project. She would work things out very methodically. Oh, another thing: she knew everything there was to know about cars and engines of all sorts. She fixed an MG sports car for me that a garage rejected! She was quite a remarkable g—young woman."

I thanked Professor Hardy and jotted down the gist of what he had said.

Over lunch at the Di, which had been decorated with green flags and balloons in honour of the great Irish saint, I talked with Ned Evans about his plans to restage the old chestnut, *Disraeli*. He had once done it with my brother, Sam, playing the prime minister and I think he still got us confused. He drew attention to our table when he acted out the scene where Disraeli threatens the governor of the Bank of England. At the climax of the scene, Ned yelled "I will smash the bank!" at the top of his voice. I tried to pretend I was a set of initials carved into the wood of our booth.

From the pay-phone outside, I called Pete Staziak. "What can I do for you today, Benny? Have you found another case to work on? Or are you still waiting for handouts from me about Wise? I know you have to make a living."

"Pete, when you went over the room—"

"What room?"

"Where Wise was shot, Pete. This is serious. What did you find on the floor besides the body and the gun?"

"Nothing that wasn't supposed to be there. Dust mites, paperclips, Wise's hair, about three cents in change. Canadian. And some traces of flour from Victoria when she used the phone to call us."

"Is that all?"

"Sure. Except for the blood. I forgot the blood."

"Is there some way I can meet you later at the Wise place? Can you fix it up? I'd like to talk to all of your suspects, if you can round them up."

"Benny have you departed from your sanity? Are you still with us or are you playing Ellery Queen again?"

"I'm serious, Pete. I think I can prove who killed Abe Wise and how it happened. And I think I know who killed Ed Neustadt and Shaw too. Can't you ask your suspects and witnesses to assist you at the house? You often get them to come into your office."

"Why don't you whisper the name to me over the phone?" he asked in a doubting voice that tried to sound humorous. I whispered the name over the phone.

"Holy shit!" Pete said. "And you can prove it?"

"I think I can, I think I can, I think I can," I said in imitation of a storybook I once read to Sam's kids in Toronto.

"Where will you be this evening?" he asked.

"I'll be at home waiting for your call."

"I'll call, I'll call!" he said. And he repeated the name.

Chapter Twenty-Seven

From the outside, Abe Wise's two houses at the end of Dorset Crescent looked like they always had, only now they held less terror than the first time I was driven there. Several passenger cars of various sorts were parked along the street nearest the crescent. A couple of police cruisers were parked too, with a large grey police van sheltering around the back next to Pete Staziak's own car. I parked close to the official party to gain status.

The inside of the main house was also unchanged with the exception of the yellow plastic barrier that the police had hung around the scene of the crime: it may have been drooping more, like it had been hanging there a long time. Chairs from the TV room had been moved into the office and some of the people I had met since that early Monday morning awakening were talking in a group with Pete Staziak when I came into the room. Pete hadn't really filled the hall for me. Unless the law has a hold on you, it can't tell you to drive to Dorset Crescent, just like that, even to help them in their investigation. Paulette and Lily hadn't come. Neither had Dave Rogers, Whitey York or Major Patrick. Duncan Harvey was nowhere to be seen, and of the Three Stooges, only Syl Ryan was there, seated beside a uniformed officer. Didier

Santerre, looking sorry for himself, stood apart from the group, near another uniformed officer. It didn't look like the last reel of *The Thin Man*. The rafters were not bulging with suspicious characters. I wasn't going to have to shout to be heard above the din of crosstalk. I should have looked on the bright side. Both of Abe Wise's kids and the Armstrongs were in attendance. And, of course, McStu. I'd invited him myself, since he knew all of the fine print of the Tatarski case.

For a few minutes I stood examining an early American terracotta figure with a broken ear, then Pete called on everybody, all eight of us, to be seated. He reviewed what was already known about the death of Abram Wise—stealing my thunder—and introduced me as a friend of the investigation. He mentioned a couple of my successful cases, not all of them, then pulled me to the front of Wise's old desk.

"The answer to why Abe Wise was killed is obvious," I began. "He was killed because he was hated. 'Hated' is strong language, but when you think about it, it fills the bill."

"Are you going to give a lecture, Benny?" McStu asked, innocently. "Why don't you sit down and join the party?" He gave me a big grin, giving me a fine view of the space between his two front teeth. I found a chair, and we all moved our chairs into a circle, except for the Armstrongs who were sitting on a velvet couch.

"Look, all of you." It was Mickey. "Nobody says Mr Wise was an angel, but, given his...his..."

"Questionable activities," prompted McStu.

"Criminal past and present," suggested Pete.

"Whatever," said Mickey, shaking his head. "Mr Wise was well respected inside the community he worked among. I can't believe that he was killed by another...by somebody he did business with. Because he always played fair. He told me that it was the only way to play when you couldn't write down the rules." Victoria took his hand when he stopped talking.

"Fair enough," I said. "I agree with Mickey. What happened to Mr Wise had nothing to do with his criminal activities. He was killed because of something that happened many years ago."

"I should have brought a sandwich," Syl Ryan whispered to Victoria.

"When Abe Wise was still a young burglar, back in 1952, he was picked up, caught with the goods and arrested one night by probational patrolman Michael Prescott of Niagara Regional. It was a fair cop. Wise had been under surveillance for some time and he was caught with enough evidence to have sent him to Kingston for a few years or at least to a reformatory. But, Ed Neustadt, Prescott's senior officer, let Wise walk. Why? We'll have to subpoena Prescott up in Muskoka. All we know right now is that Wise hated Neustadt. He went to his funeral, he told me, expressly to dance on his grave and to tarnish Neustadt's reputation just by showing up. The only conclusion we can draw from this is that there was something between them: a guilty secret, perhaps. Let's suppose that it was a secret. Something known to the young burglar and the ambitious policeman. What could it have been?

"Nineteen fifty-two was the year of the Tatarski case. I've checked the date of Wise's arrest and the trial date. The trial was in its eighth day. It went to the jury on the following afternoon. For those of you old enough to remember, it was a major story around here and it made national headlines because it was a capital case involving a young unwed mother. Ed Neustadt was in charge of the investigation and I suggest to you that the secret had to do with this case. What could a young punk like Wise know about the Tatarskis? Did he live near them? No. Did he go to school with them? No. Did he know their house because he had gone into it during the commission of a robbery? Possibly, very possibly. Wasn't he caught in the act in that same neighbourhood while the trial was in progress?

"But Mary Tatarski was convicted of killing her mother and then making the scene look like a burglary had been interrupted. Remember that Mary was old enough to remember the break-in five years earlier when her father was killed. A young impressionable girl like Mary, with a grievance against her mother, the Crown argued, wouldn't have forgotten that.

"We know that Ed Neustadt needed the conviction of Mary Tatarski to advance his career. He also may have had some personal reason for proceeding with the case after he had got Wise to admit that he was the burglar who had been interrupted by Anastasia Tatarski that night. I don't think this is the place to probe Neustadt's warped character. We know he was tenacious, unforgiving—"

"He was an avenging son of a bitch!" shouted Sylvester Ryan, the studs and rings in his ears catching the light. "He never gave anyone a break."

"Well, at least some of us agree that Neustadt had a certain zeal in doing the work he was paid to do. But why would he purposely overlook testimony that would clear the Tatarski woman? To my mind there is only one possibility: he was sure that if she hadn't done this crime, she had done the earlier crime. He was sure Mary murdered her father!"

"But she was just a teenager!" McStu protested.

"Even so," I said. "I didn't say she *did* murder her father, I'm saying that Neustadt was sure she did. It was his way of getting himself off the hook for not telling the Crown prosecutor that Mary Tatarski was innocent. She had played him for a sucker when he was a fresh young cop. He had been beguiled by her, McStu. So, now he was going to show her, pay her back, and protect his own, simply by saying nothing."

"I'm beginning to see through this," McStu said, pulling at an earlobe. "His big problem is what is he going to do with young Wise. He has to shut him up."

"Right! He trades liberty for silence."

"Wise walks and the Tatarski case goes to the jury," Pete said, half to himself.

"That's no deal," Hart volunteered. "It's an invitation to blackmail."

"The Abe Wise of 1952 wasn't as canny as the Wise who was just murdered. It would have taken him a while. Don't forget, Neustadt had been browbeating him all night trying to get him to confess to having broken into the Tatarski house as well as all those other houses. And when Wise finally realized what had happened, how he had been used, Mary Tatarski was dead, forgotten, except for Duncan Harvey's efforts to clear her name. Wise grew to hate Neustadt for his big favour: for letting him go on those terms."

"Are you saying that Abe Wise killed Neustadt because of what happened forty years ago? Nobody's going to believe that!"

"Sit down, Mickey. When did I say that Wise did the deed? I know all he had to do was have a quick word with you, or Phil or Syl, but I didn't say he did. Still, you raise a very good point, one we should all remember: why did the murderer take so long to act? Why the delay? Remember that. What I hope I've been able to establish is the connection between Wise and Neustadt running through the Tatarski case."

"Benny, Duncan Harvey's been saying that Mary Tatarski was innocent for years. I just wrote a book about it. She shouldn't have been hanged."

"You're right. Both of you deserve a lot of credit. It's because of you that we know what happened next."

"What did?" asked Julie, her face still puffy and red from the night before. "What happened to her family?"

"First, they left town and changed their names. There was fallout as there always is after an execution. Margaret, the older daughter, committed suicide after failing to re-establish her life on some firm basis in a new town. Freddy, the youngest, on the other hand came back to Grantham when he was still fairly young and started up a business. He made a success of himself. He started up the Nuts & Bolts chain of automobile service centres and made a lot of money."

"Freddy Tait! Are you saying that Freddy Tait was Mary Tatarski's brother? I never heard that!" Hart Wise was suddenly taking more of an interest. "He was a great mechanic."

"But, according to some, he was an unhappy man. He had reason enough to be happy, he had a wife, a son and a lovely, bright stepdaughter, he had a successful business, he had a big house in a nice part of town. Yet it wasn't enough. The past was still alive for him. He drank. He quarrelled with his stepdaughter so much that she left home. She only returned when she heard that he was dying of cancer. She nursed him through that, and during those long days and nights Freddy told her about the death of her real mother. You can imagine the shock to her. A sudden, unsuspected shock that came just as her stepfather was dying. In a manner of speaking, his death put her in touch with her past."

"Are you saying that Drina Tait killed Ed Neustadt and Abe Wise?" asked McStu.

"That's what I'm saying."

"But where is she? Who knows anything about her?"

"We know more than you think, McStu. But before we go into that, let's try to trace the cheque that Hart left with his father. It's a detail that has been bugging me."

"There wasn't any money found on or in the deceased's desk," Pete said. "So, logically, it was carried away by one of the people who saw Wise after Hart left."

"I don't see the mystery," Julie said. "I told both of you that Daddy gave me a cheque for thirty-five thousand dollars."

"And that was the amount of the cheque I gave my father," added Hart.

"Well, Benny? Does that clear up the mystery?" Staziak was looking a little smug.

"Julie, did your father just hand you a cheque that had already been written, or did he write one while you were there?"

"Oh, *merde!* Yes! He wrote it out! Then what happened to Hart's cheque?"

"I think I know the answer to that," I said. I turned to Didier Santerre. "Well, Didier? Julie left you in the Le Baron rent-a-car, the one with the broken headlight. When she got back, you had vanished and didn't get back for a few minutes. Will you tell us where you were?"

"I was peeing in the bushes, Mr Cooperman."

"Oh, you can do better than that. Remember, the cheque went through your bank account. I'm sure it has been traced. In fact, I wouldn't be surprised to learn that

that bum cheque and a few other financial irregularities have kept you on this side of the Atlantic."

"Oh, all right! I went into the house to talk to Mr Wise. We had some business to discuss."

"You didn't tell me that!" said Julie, looking at Santerre, who was looking everywhere but at Julie. "What sort of business?"

"Your father wanted to put some money into *Mode*. It was his idea."

"So, Julie," I said, "your father gave you thirty-five thousand, which you turned over to Didier for the magazine. And then he signed over Hart's cheque and gave that to Didier for the magazine."

"Lucky magazine!" mused McStu out loud.

"Only half-lucky," Hart said loudly enough so that we could all hear. "Dad's cheques were always good. But my cheque was made of India rubber! I intended it to bounce. It was to pay my father off for his goddamned high-handed interference in my life!"

"And that's why Didier's bank is unlikely to forget that cheque."

"Didier!" Julie called, still looking and hoping for a better explanation.

"Shut up, you silly fool!" he said. "Just keep quiet."

Didier pulled her over towards him, and when she protested, he cuffed her in the face. "You little idiot! Be still!" The sensation of the slap, even the echo, continued in our imaginations for some moments. Julie's sobbing brought us back to Dorset Crescent.

"It's good to see that there's justice in small things, even if not in the large. Hart's bum cheque scuttled, or half-scuttled, Santerre's plan to strip Julie Long of her spending money," I said, wishing there was something to drink within reach.

"Some spending money," Syl Ryan observed to Mickey.

"You know, Syl, the spending money for both Julie and Hart has changed dramatically. Abe told me that his whole estate, barring a few bequests, is to go to Julie and Hart in equal shares." Didier Santerre was beginning to look enviously at the woman he had just slapped. I looked over at Hart. "Doesn't that scheme with the Triumph seem silly, Hart, now that you've become a man of substance?"

"I don't understand what you're on about, Cooperman."

"Oh, I think you do. Let's see, this is a case with two bad cheques in it. Both of them for thirty-five thousand and both with your name at the bottom. You told me that you didn't know the cheque was bad, and that you had tried to raise the money by selling your things and borrowing from your mother. I don't know how much she gave you, but you didn't put it in your bank, you gave it to Gordon Shaw to finance your scam to bilk your father out of as much as his love for you was worth. And all this to recover an Alfa Romeo Canguro from a garage in Southampton. You let Shaw talk big money at you. Your bad cheque, the first one, would be like a kidnapping victim. You knew that your father would redeem it at whatever cost. Unfortunately, Shaw jumped the gun. The numbers he was asking put Wise on guard. They were too big for a little Triumph. Then he took steps to remove the threat. But more about that later."

"Benny, this is all very well," said McStu, "but it's moved a little off topic. Aren't we looking for Drina Tait?"

"I haven't lost sight of that. I'm just trying to wade through this mess as tidily as I can. Now, Didier, how did you get into the house? You weren't seen by anyone."

"I used the door by the garage. The one Mickey calls a tunnel. It's just a back door as far as I know. This isn't *Fantômas*, you know."

"Who did you see on your way to and from your meeting with Wise?"

"I saw this young woman." He indicated Victoria. "She was holding, what do you call it, a rolling-pin."

"Great detective work, Benny! We already know that she was making pies!"

"Easy, McStu. I'll try to put everything in its place. Just the way you did in your book. You did your homework. I hope I'm doing mine. Look in your book McStu. Page 39. You're describing Mary Tatarski's family. Let me read it for you:

> Although this was an immigrant family, with aspirations not unlike those of other newcomers, Anastasia Tatarski tried to imbue her children with as much of the culture of her adopted country as she could...

Do you remember writing that?"

"Sure. The mother really loved the Brits. She used to read to them out of an old public-school history textbook."

"And she named some of her kids after English sovereigns: Freddy was Alfred in his obituary, named after Alfred the Great."

"I hope this bedtime story is leading somewhere," Julie asked, looking a little more composed than when I last noticed her. "I suppose Margaret was named after that mad queen who runs through all of those history plays of Shakespeare? Or was it Princess Margaret with her pretty doll house? And what about Mary? Wasn't

Queen Mary the consort of George the Sixth?"

"Fifth," said McStu, who had had a good education.

"Right. It's all in your book. Margaret, Mary and Alfred, or Freddy. Freddy's son was Charles Edward, after Bonny Prince Charlie, and Drina, the daughter of Mary, was named after the dear queen herself: Alexandrina Victoria."

"Victoria?" Mickey Armstrong was on his feet. "What are you talking about?"

"Why don't you ask your wife, Mickey?"

All eyes turned of course to the woman sitting quietly next to Mickey with her hands in her lap. She was smiling slightly.

"Well, Mrs Armstrong?" prompted Staziak gently.

"What Mr Cooperman says is absurd," she said. "Oh, I admit to being Drina Tait. But that was never a great secret. I think I even told you once over lunch, Ben. I hope you still want me to call you Ben. I was brought up in a family on the run. I didn't know it at the time, but I sensed something. We weren't like other people. Even in Bracebridge, where I spent my early life. Even though my girlfriends were the daughters of lawyers and judges. We weren't the same and I never knew why until I came home to be with my father—you call him my stepfather, and that is of course legally correct, but he was the only father I ever knew. That was in the spring of 1991. He told me the story. Congratulations for discovering what many people in this city could have told you.

"As to the question of killing Chief Neustadt and Mr Wise, don't be silly. I didn't know the one, and Mr Wise has always been very kind and generous to Mickey and me."

A few heads nodded at the good sense of what they had just heard. Victoria smiled across at me. Mickey tried to comfort her, but she kept her eyes on me.

"Your crime, Victoria, wasn't like most crimes. It wasn't motivated by greed or frustration, but by revenge. Neustadt and Wise between them had destroyed your family. You are the only one left. It was up to you. It had nothing to do with like or dislike. It was a pure crime, if you like. You didn't come into it at all, not as Drina Tait or as Victoria Armstrong. You were simply the instrument of retribution, a settling of accounts, an evening of scores.

"You studied your quarry from afar. It wasn't hard to learn that Neustadt was an amateur mechanic, who used to tinker with his car in the driveway. You knew about cars yourself. You grew up around cars and grease pits and tools. It was no trick for you to turn the valve on Neustadt's hydraulic jack. It took someone like you to tamper with the steering on Wise's Volvo.

"But Wise was a harder nut to crack than Neustadt. He had built a wall around himself. To cross over, you sought him out through your connections in Old Greenwich, Connecticut. You knew enough about cooking to get into the house. You hadn't planned on Mickey. But it worked out very well. Better than you'd hoped, maybe. Once inside the citadel you found all the weapons you needed ten times over, but how could you kill him with the boys always hovering near? That posed a problem, but you solved it masterfully. You used a silencer. That covered the sound so that the boys could finish their breakfast never dreaming that it was the last of them that Wise would pay for. You left the gun at the scene—over there," I pointed to the bloodstain still visible on the carpet.

"And what did I do with this silencer you've invented?" Victoria asked, her eyes now flashing anger at me. "You searched the house, Sergeant. Did you find this silencer he's talking about?"

"She's got you there, Benny. We went through the house several times room by room."

"I have to admit, you nearly had me there, Victoria. But let me show you how I discovered your secret. Hart, you told me that when you came in to see your father for the last time, Victoria and Mickey were in the kitchen."

"That's right. She was baking."

"And Julie, when you got there some time later?"

"I could smell cinnamon and apple in the kitchen. She was baking pies."

"Good," I said. "And Pete, you say you found flour near the body. Isn't that right?"

"Yes. But since it was Victoria who discovered the body, I don't see how—"

"Pete, Julie says that she *smelled* the pies. They were in the oven by the time she got there. How was it that Victoria was still wearing a floury apron after the murder had been committed?"

"I wasn't wearing an apron. I took it off after I'd tidied the kitchen. I told you that, Sergeant." Victoria Armstrong said this as though it had figured importantly in her statement. Mickey looked like he was going to lash out at me all the same.

"You better have a good reason for putting us through this, Cooperman," he said, which came off less effectively than it might have with the women removed from the room. Mickey watched his tongue with women about.

Suddenly everybody was looking at me. I hoped that what I was going to say was made out of the right words. "So, the flour didn't come from the apron, and yet it was in the room. Could it have come from her shoes, Pete?"

"Not according to the forensic people. It wasn't connected to a footprint. There were no footprints. The flour—and we're talking about slight traces, you understand—was evenly distributed in the area where the murder took place."

"I see. Pete, will you come into the kitchen with me for a minute?" Pete got up and assured the others that we would be right back.

When we returned, Pete was wearing a puzzled expression. "You were baking pies, Mrs Armstrong, but we don't seem to be able to find your rolling pin. Can you help us?"

"What has baking pies to do with anything?" asked Hart.

"More than you think," I said. "Didier told us that Victoria was holding a rolling pin some time *after* Julie sniffed pies cooking in the oven. What was Victoria doing with the rolling pin after all of the pastry had been rolled out? And the latest of the mysteries: what has happened to the rolling pin?"

"Who gives a damn?" said Syl Ryan, looking at Hart for support.

"Pete, you told me that an effective silencer for a gun like the gun that killed Abe Wise would be a cylinder about eighteen inches long and around two and a half inches in diameter. You didn't say it, but you might have: a silencer for Wise's gun would be about the size and shape of a rolling pin without the handles. Drina, we know, was familiar with car motors and the tools in the shop of Freddy Tait's garage. She would be capable of making such an object, together with the rod and clamp she'd need to install it."

"Rod and clamp, Benny? I don't follow you."

"You need the one to align the exit hole of the silencer

with the barrel of the gun, McStu. The clamp holds the silencer firmly on the barrel. Dudley Dickens would have known that."

"Well! That's quite a yarn. It's not proof, of course, but it's a good story. I may use that silencer idea. I think it might work in fiction, but Benny, this is real life, for Gawd sake!"

"Yes," said Hart. "Lots of people had access to the kitchen, just as they had to the guns."

"And what about that shot through the window at Wise?" asked Pete. "And the one at you," he added as an afterthought.

"You already know about the tunnel, Pete. A shot from near the garage into this room could have the shooter back inside the house within a minute at the outside."

"Cooperman, I'm going to get you for what you said here tonight!" It was Mickey's red face that was glowering at me.

"I'm just doing my job, Mickey. And if I were you I wouldn't stray away from your wife right now. It could be—" Just then we heard a sudden cry. Victoria had jumped over the arm of the couch and come down on Julie's foot. Before Julie had recovered, Victoria was in the kitchen. Pete was the first off the mark. He moved after her with astonishing speed. By the time I got past the preparation table in the middle of the kitchen, they were both gone.

"The tunnel!" Syl Ryal shouted, and started in after her. To the hounds a quarry is a quarry, it doesn't matter whether it's a fox or a hare.

The tunnel didn't do justice to its name. There was nothing mysterious about it: just another back way out that happened to run down a set of stairs and come out near the garage. From a distance away, we could hear raised voices, sounds of a struggle. "Let me through!" shouted Mickey, shoving both Pete and a uniformed man aside. But before he could get to the stairs, Syl Ryan came up, followed by two men in uniform carrying a struggling Victoria Armstrong between them.

Chapter Twenty-Eight

The next few days are a bit hazy. I don't remember much. I cleaned my office, got rid of a lot of old files, emptied the drawers of ancient apricot stones and Kogan's empty bottles. I didn't sleep much, and I wasn't much fun for Anna to be with. But I hadn't been much fun to be with when I was working either.

I got a call from her father. He was prompting me to name a date and time for me to make an honest woman of his daughter. I told him that I didn't know a more honest woman than Anna and that if she had lost the family honour by staying with me on occasion, then there was something rickety about the family honour. I'm not usually so outspoken with Jonah, who could buy and sell me a million times over, but there was something about the limbo state I was suspended in that gave me courage.

I didn't see Pete Staziak or Chris Savas for a week. I got a letter from Dave Rogers with a cheque in it. I hadn't even billed him yet. When I opened the letter, it was just a blank page so that the cheque couldn't be seen when held up to the light. I wouldn't have minded hearing a word or two from Dave. I thought we always got along well.

It was one of the biggest funerals in years. In death, Abe Wise had it all over Ed Neustadt. There were limousines with licence plates from all over eastern North America. The floral tributes were a little more tasteful than those in Capone's day, but there were easily enough to satisfy the world of crime that they had given one of its own a proper send-off.

Hart and Julie were standing side by side near their mothers, a sight Abe himself may not have seen in the last twenty years. Mickey was there by himself, although he had been in for questioning almost every day during the week. Phil Green and Sidney were there, but Syl Ryan had been detained downtown. Although he had left no fingerprints on the knife he used to kill Gord Shaw, a big handprint on the roof of the Alfa Romeo was plainly his. A little something extra to go with that Indian-head buckle I found in the snow.

I didn't know the rabbi who led the service, he was from out of town. He didn't appear to be enjoying himself the way Major Patrick had at Neustadt's funeral. But then Abe hadn't been committed to the earth as fast as Jewish traditions require. The casket was massive, of course, made of bronze judging by the shine on it. There was an engraving on the top: it was a copy of the ugly terracotta mask in his office. He must have left very explicit instructions.

By the time I left the grave-side, the others had gone on ahead. I knew there was going to be a traffic tie-up, so I killed some time with my former client. I hadn't kept him alive, but I never said I could. I never believed in security. It always makes headaches for the innocent and presents no problem to the dedicated villain. All of the cars but mine were gone from the verge of the road through the cemetery. The weather felt warmer. It wasn't spring or anything dramatic, but the hold of winter was broken. Slabs of ice were breaking off and running down the creek as I drove over the high-level bridge. I stopped to have some won-ton soup and fried rice at the Chinese place where I had first met Dave Rogers after the service. The place was empty.

One night, just after I locked up the office, Pete came by. He honked his horn and I slid into the front seat of his car. "You eaten yet?" he asked. I shook my head. "Me neither, and the wife has some women friends in to play cards tonight." Usually I would chide him for using such terms as "the wife," but that night I didn't have the energy. I was washed out.

"We've got the Shaw case in good order, Benny. Next to the Wise case, it's simplicity itself. Thanks for putting us on to Ryan."

"Yeah, I saw that Indian-head buckle in the snow. You found it?"

"Sure, but what could we make of it? You had a head start on us with that bunch."

"Don't remind me. Syl Ryan used to be a biker and bikers are all crazy about the famous old Indian bikes. Syl was the only biker connected to Wise and his gang."

"Of course, we had the handprint on the car."

"Sure."

"Your friend Mickey's going to be away for a long time, Benny. We got him on weapons, hijacking and smuggling. He and his pals were using boats to run booze and cartons of drugs across the Niagara River. That's small stuff, but enough to put him down for a few years. By the time we get an understanding of the whole operation, we'll both be getting our pension."

"Did he put up a big fight?"

"Bigger than I expected. I thought we had him at a weak moment, what with his wife...you know. But, it took three good men to hold him and make the collar."

"He have a good lawyer?"

"Yeah, that fellow who used to be such a drunk around town."

"Rupe McLay. Good for Rupe!"

"Hell, Benny, you sound like you want Mickey to walk."

"Half and half. I feel like hell about Victoria, Pete."

"What you made sound like a crime without greed or personal advantage comes out looking premeditated and cold-blooded, Benny."

"What's been happening this week? I've been out of circulation."

"Hart's moving into one of his father's houses. Julie and Didier have broken up all over again. You know anything about that, Benny?"

"A little. Santerre was only interested in refinancing his magazine. Julie was his road to Wise. Wise was willing to pay off Santerre if he would leave Julie alone. Santerre tried to have it both ways. But Hart's cheque bounced."

"That's where we were called in. The bank gets weary of rubber cheques with Hart Wise's name on them."

"Those two kids have a long way to go. Look at the Tatarskis. You never know where it will work itself out."

"What put your nose into the wind on this case, Benny?"

"I was robbed of a night's sleep."

"Yeah, but after that."

"First time I talked to Dave Rogers he said that some old woman had got herself killed by a burglar over on Russell Avenue. Nobody else knew that. It had to have come from Abe Wise himself. Next question?"

"Where do you want to eat?"

"I don't know. Where do *you* want to eat?"

Chapter Twenty-Nine

The Queen Elizabeth Way was built to commemorate the visit in 1939 of King George VI and Queen Elizabeth. It was at that time the finest divided highway in North America. It was still the fastest way to get from Grantham to Toronto, Hamilton or, as in this case, Grimsby. I pushed the Olds along at a good clip, keeping the lake to my right and the beetling escarpment to my left. Also on my left ran miles and miles of vineyards and orchards. There was pink blush about the naked twigs. Buds? I couldn't tell. Once I turned off the familiar highway, I was in strange country. I didn't know these quiet roads or streets. I tried to keep to the directions Mr McCarthy had given me on the phone a day or so ago when I first talked to him. Pete had got the number for me and it took me the better part of a week to get the nerve to call it.

The house was small, with a muddy driveway leading up to a tin garage with a door hanging halfway open or closed, whichever way you wanted to look at it. I parked the Olds in the driveway behind a beat-up blue Pontiac. It looked about the same age as the other cars parked in driveways and along the treeless street. There was mud on my shoes when I mounted the porch of the sun-blasted, artificial-brick-sided bungalow. The mat looked too new for the shoe-cleaning I had in mind, so I did what I could on the edge of the top step, leaving the mat for a final polish. I rang the bell, and heard the ring resounding through what appeared from the outside to be an empty house. On the second try, I could hear footsteps coming up from the basement. A dark form came between me and the light coming through a long hall from a back window and dusty lace curtains.

"Yes?" said the man who opened the door about as wide as it would go. The man I was looking at was eighty. I'd figured out his present age from an article on his retirement in a Toronto paper. In the flesh, he looked older. He was a tall, rangy man, with lines on his face that were closer to furrows than wrinkles. There was a worried bloodhound expression on his features as he took in what he saw standing in front of him. Was he sizing up my height and estimating my weight, I wondered.

"I'm Cooperman. Remember? I phoned."

"Cooperman? I don't..." He rubbed a grizzled grey beard with the back of his hand while he tried to recall the conversation.

"You *are* Mr McCarthy, aren't you?"

"That's right, but my memory is starting to go. They told me it would and now I guess I'll have to believe them. Will you come in, Mr Cooperman?" He moved away from the door and I followed him into the front room of the tiny house, which was decorated with brownish prints of sailing ships and sea captains in nor'westers. Next to the front window was a table with a fringed cloth on it. A bowl of nuts was its only decoration. A velvet wall-hanging of a stag at bay dominated the space above an upright piano with its lid closed.

"Make yourself at home, Mr Cooperman, and try to

give me an idea of why you are calling on a gaffer like me on a nice day like this. You're not a reporter, are you? I don't talk to reporters, you know." I tried to remind him of our conversation and he nodded from time to time as though what I was saying was striking chords in his head.

"Mary Tatarski!" he said with some surprise. "Yes, I remember her very well. It's the recent things I have trouble with. Mary Tatarski was back in December of 1952. That was a crowded week. I'd just come back from Toronto, where I'd hanged two bank robbers who shot a policeman. No! I did them *after* I did Mary Tatarski. It was a Thursday and then the next Tuesday, if I remember right. What do you want to know about her? I've signed the Official Secrets Act, you know. I'm no gossip."

"Did she make any confession at the end? Did she say anything that gave any indication as to guilt or innocence?" McCarthy looked up at the ceiling with its smooth cool plaster sheen, as though the memory could be found there.

"You understand, there's not much talk," he said in a low confidential voice. I wondered about how much he could expect me to understand about his work. What was the given here? How much did he think was common knowledge? Maybe I should have asked him.

"Yes, I know. I just thought that—"

"A lot of them tell you they didn't do it. They think I won't hang 'em if they protest their innocence. I remember one time, in Calgary, I think it was—. But I'm sworn to uphold the law and I have my duty to perform. Guilty or innocent: it's all the same to me. Let them tell the lawyers and the judges about that. It's too late when they send for me. Although I've had a few false alarms in my day. They pay me half, when I don't have to go through with it. It makes no nevermind to me. And I'm just as glad they made me put away my little bag of tricks. I'm like most people in this country, I don't believe in it any more. The times have changed. You can't go against that."

"What about Mary Tatarski?"

"She went to the drop as bravely as I've ever seen a man go. Not swaggering. I don't mean that. But steady, if you know what I mean. I remember now!" he said, leaning towards me as though he had just been given an electric shock. "She made me do something I try to avoid. It's been one of my rules. Makes it easier afterwards. I try not to let them catch my eyes. You don't want to have bad dreams, you know; bad enough as it is, but you don't want the eye contact. It'll give you the blue devils, I'll tell you. Well, I broke my rule. She looked me in the eye, while Wilkes was strapping her legs together and I was about to cover her face, and she said, calm as ever you please, and with a sort of quiet smile, 'I had no hand in the death of my mother.' She didn't say it swearing to God, like some of them do, but just flat out and looking me in the eye, 'I had no hand in the death of my mother.' I gave her a nod so as to show I understood and would remember what she said. Then she shook her head a little and opened her eyes wide and whispered, 'It was different with Papa. He kept me from seeing Thaddeus.' That's all. She smiled to show she was finished talking. And then I did the necessary and that was the end of it." The necessary! All trades have their jargon. The necessary! Is that how he remembers it from that December night forty-two years ago? Are the mental pictures from that night among the lost or discarded memories of this old man? I hoped they were, but I wouldn't have bet on it. It was more likely he'd already forgotten my name than the events of that night.

"And was it the truth? With all your experience, what did you think at the time?" He looked me straight in the eye. I couldn't help thinking of Mary Tatarski looking into the eyes of her executioner.

"I was sure I was hanging an innocent woman that night. I still think so. And I've faced more murderers on the point of death than any man living. But that last bit always bothered me. Never could figure that out." We both sat in silence for a few moments. If he was going to add anything, he didn't need me to cue him.

"Did you know the former deputy chief of police, Ed Neustadt?"

"I knew him," he said without emphasis. That in itself was a give-away.

"Was he there?"

"Neustadt was always there. In Ontario, anyway. He once turned up in Montreal. He had no business... But I guess he had connections."

"What did you make of him?"

"None of my affair to make anything of him. And now he's dead..." He let the idea trail off. I could tell that Mr McCarthy didn't like Neustadt. He and everybody else I'd met.

"Did he get in the way?"

"He had no business there at all. I spoke to the jail people, but they couldn't stop him. These things are best when kept simple. There shouldn't be anyone there who's not part of it. It's not a show. But you can't keep some of them away. Neustadt was the biggest pest of all. He wanted to speak to the prisoner, but I wouldn't let him. I told him to stand aside. I was sharp with him. I didn't care if he was the prime minister. He had no business there that night."

"Thank you, Mr McCarthy. You've told me what I couldn't find out from any other source."

"Glad to help. Always glad. Most people want to know whether the people I've hanged suffered. Hell, I know my craft! I wouldn't keep them waiting any longer than I needed to. There are tricks to the whole thing, you see. Nothing you can learn in five minutes. It took me years to get it just right. And hanging a woman's no picnic, I'll tell you. Givers of life and all that. The fellow before me was a real bungler, but you had to sympathize. He didn't have much to go on. There's only been ten women hanged since Confederation. That makes a hell of a poor pool of experience, I'll tell you. No records, no facts to pass on for those who came after. No way to get a handle on it. No wonder he was a bungler. I tried to do better. I studied it, like. Talked to that fellow who kept a pub at Hoole, in England. *The Rose and Crown*. Used to keep one called *Help the Poor Struggler*, but he sold that. Small wonder. He retired before they abolished hanging. Had enough of it." I could see that Mr McCarthy was a mine of information, Official Secrets or not.

"Old Pierrepoint, that was his name. He told me of one time when a client he was just about to top looked him in the eye and said: 'The sentence is just, but the evidence was wrong.' How do you like that for a summing up, Mr Cooperman?"

I nodded; it did sum things up. In general and for me. While the hangman spoke, my memory had been reaching back through these past chilly March days. It came to rest at the name Duncan Harvey thought I wouldn't remember: Thaddeus Nemerov, the boy next door.

I began making movements to show that I was finished. I thanked him again for his help.

"Would you drink a glass of beer with me?" He asked

so tentatively that I couldn't say no. Not everybody's idea of good company, the last official hangman. He went into the back of the house and came out with two bottles and glasses on a tray. He told me that he was keeping house for himself since the death of his wife some years ago. He opened the first of the bottles and shared out the beer into the glasses. We nodded at one another and drank. I needed the drink more than I would have guessed. The inquiry I was concluding had made this visit and my questions necessary, just as McCarthy's job made the hanging of Mary Tatarski necessary. "The necessary," in fact. I had been looking for a murderer and he had punished one. Or had he? Had she been able at that terrible moment to look into the eyes of the hangman and lie? That was the question I pondered while the hangman poured out the second bottle of beer.